The Governess Tales

Sweeping romances with fairy-tale endings!

Meet Joanna Radcliff, Rachel Talbot,
Isabel Morton and Grace Bertram.

These four friends grew up together in
Madame Dubois's school for young ladies,
where they indulged in midnight feasts, broke
the rules and shared their innermost secrets!

But now they are thrust into the real world,
and each must adapt to her new life
as a governess.

One will rise, one will travel,
one will run and one will find her real home...

And each will meet her soulmate,
who'll give her the happy-ever-after
she's always dreamed of!

Read Joanna's story in
The Cinderella Governess
Available now

And look for:

Rachel's story in
Governess to the Sheikh

Isabel's story in
The Runaway Governess

And Grace's story in
The Governess's Secret Baby

Coming soon!

Author Note

The Cinderella Governess was a treat for me to write and a unique experience. It was the first time I'd worked with so many talented people to craft a story and characters. It was a pleasure and an honour to collaborate with the other authors, to learn from them and to exchange ideas on character traits, locations and history. Together we developed the physical world of Madame Dubois's school, deciding where it would be located and what it would look like. In the end we based it on the Mompesson House in Salisbury. Co-ordinating other locations throughout England between the four stories was also fun, and a good reason to do some interesting research—especially on the little-known beach resort of Sandhills.

In regards to the characters, the creation of Madame Dubois's backstory was the most surprising part of the process for me. Her story was inspired by a line in the prologue that I'd added for a touch of humour. It caught people's interest and was developed by the authors into a subplot which weaves its way throughout the four novels. This type of discovery arises from working with such creative authors and editors, and it's what made writing *The Cinderella Governess* an exciting process that I will never forget.

THE CINDERELLA GOVERNESS

Georgie Lee

First published in Great Britain 2016
By Mills & Boon, an imprint of HarperCollins*Publishers*
1 London Bridge Street, London, SE1 9GF

Large Print edition 2017

© 2016 Harlequin Books S.A.

ISBN: 978-0-263-06744-6

Special thanks and acknowledgement are given to Georgie Lee
for her contribution to The Governess Tales series.

Our policy is to use papers that are natural, renewable and
recyclable products and made from wood grown in sustainable
forests. The logging and manufacturing processes conform to
the legal environmental regulations of the country of origin.

Printed and bound in Great Britain
by CPI Antony Rowe, Chippenham, Wiltshire

A lifelong history buff, **Georgie Lee** hasn't given up hope that she will one day inherit a title and a manor house. Until then she fulfils her dreams of lords, ladies and a Season in London through her stories. When not writing, she can be found reading non-fiction history or watching any film with a costume and an accent. Please visit georgie-lee.com to learn more about Georgie and her books.

Visit the Author Profile page at
millsandboon.co.uk.

To the authors of The Governess Tales
for all your creativity, collaboration
and hard work.

Prologue

August 1811

'Joanna, what are you doing in the library?' Rachel gasped from the doorway.

'I'm wondering if Madame Dubois would notice if I took this book with me.' Joanna Radcliff clutched the thin volume of fairy tales between her hands and threw her friend a mischievous smile. 'In case I have to thump the son of my soon-to-be employer should he make any untoward advances at me.'

Rachel rolled her brown eyes. 'Sir Rodger's sons are still boys and away at school. You won't even be teaching them.'

'Then I'll use it to make his daughters behave.' She laughed and Rachel joined in.

Joanna's cheer faded as she slid the book in the

gap on the shelf. This had been her favourite one as a child. It was as difficult to leave behind as her friends, but she couldn't steal it. It would be a poor way to thank Madame Dubois for all her years of kindness.

'Come on, the carriage will be here soon.' Rachel took her by the hand and pulled her to the door. 'We don't have much time.'

They hurried out of the dark library and into the brightly lit entrance hall. Madame Dubois's School for Young Ladies was a stately house on Cathedral Close facing Salisbury Cathedral. At one time it had been the home of a squire. Echoes of its history remained in the classical cornices above the doorways and the endless lengths of chair rails. The furnishings were less regal, but sturdy to accommodate the many young ladies who'd passed through its rooms over the years. The old rumour whispered to the new students stated it was one of Madame Dubois's lovers who'd deeded her the house. To see the woman in her stern black, her dark hair shot with silver and pulled into a bun as severe as her stance, no one could believe she'd ever been swept away by a passion worthy of property.

At the far end of the entrance hall stood a wide staircase. Rachel pulled Joanna towards it and past a sitting room filled with little girls sitting on benches.

'*La plume de ma tante est sur la table,*' Madame La Roche said, pacing in front of her pupils.

'*La plume de ma tante est sur la table,*' the girls repeated in high voices.

It wasn't so very long ago when Joanna, Rachel, Isabel and Grace had sat in the same room repeating those phrases. Their time as students was over. They were at last taking up positions as governesses. Today, Joanna would be the first to leave.

'Hurry.' Rachel rushed up the stairs.

'Any faster and I'll fly.' It wasn't possible, not with the many memories weighing Joanna down. Madame Dubois's school was the only home she'd ever known. She wasn't ready to leave it, but she must. This was what she'd been trained for by Madame Dubois and the other teachers who'd raised her. It was a parting, but also an opportunity. Perhaps as the governess to the Huntfords, she might finally experience what it was like to be part of a real family.

At the top, Isabel came around the corner, stopping so fast the hem of her skirt fluttered out before falling back over her ankles.

'What's taking so long? I'll die if we can't give Joanna a proper farewell before we're all sent into exile.' Isabel pressed the back of her hand to her head with all the flair of the actress they'd seen performing in the seaside resort of Sandhills last year.

Rachel crossed her arms, not amused. 'It isn't so bad.'

'Says the lady going to the country of Huria and not Hertfordshire.' She waved one hand at Joanna, then pointed at herself. 'Or Sussex. Although I don't intend to stay there for long.'

'What are you plotting, Isabel?' Joanna focused suspicious eyes on her friend.

'Nothing. It doesn't matter. Come along, Grace is waiting.' Isabel tugged Joanna down the hall and Rachel followed.

'You'll be sure to write me when your nothing turns into something,' Joanna insisted, knowing her friend too well to be put off so fast. 'I'd hate to find out about it in the papers.'

'I told you, there's nothing,' Isabel insisted, adjusting a pin in her copper-coloured hair.

'Too bad, I might need some savoury story to enliven my days in the country.'

'Me, too.' Isabel nudged Joanna in the ribs and they laughed together before Rachel placed her hands on their shoulders and pushed them forward.

'Keep going, before we run out of time.'

They hurried to the last room at the end of the hall and stopped at the door to the bedroom they'd shared since they were all nine years old.

'Close your eyes,' Rachel insisted.

'Why?' Joanna didn't like surprises.

'You'll see. Now do it.' Isabel raised Joanna's hands to her eyes.

The two girls giggled as they led Joanna inside. The faint dank of the chilly room warmed by the morning sun combined with the lavender used to freshen the sheets, the sweet smell of Rachel's favourite biscuits, and Grace's Lily of the Valley perfume to surround Joanna. It reminded her of the coming winter, their Christmas together last year and how far away from one another they'd be this December. Sadness dulled the thrill of the surprise.

'All right, open your eyes,' Isabel instructed.

Joanna lowered her hands. Isabel, Rachel and Grace stood around a little table draped with linen. Rachel had baked Joanna's favourite lemon cake and it sat on a small stand surrounded by three wrapped presents.

'Congratulations!' the girls chorused.

'Oh, my goodness,' Joanna exclaimed, amazed at what they'd done and their having kept it a secret. There wasn't much they'd been able to keep from each other over the last nine years.

'Since you're the first to take up your new post, we couldn't let you go with only a goodbye,' Grace insisted with the seriousness which still haunted her after her unfortunate incident. 'We don't know when we'll see each other again.'

Joanna threw her arms around Grace. 'Stop, or you'll make me cry.'

'Don't be silly, you never cry.' Grace hugged her tightly, then released her. 'Let's have our cake.'

They ate their treat while Joanna unwrapped the pen from Rachel, the stationery from Isabel and the ink from Grace.

'It's so you can write to us,' Rachel explained through a mouthful of cake.

'Thank you all, so much.' She clutched the items to her chest, deeply grateful. These three women had been the closest she'd ever had to sisters. She didn't want to lose touch with them, or the deep bonds they'd forged.

Their happy celebration was interrupted by a knock.

Everyone froze as Miss Fanworth stepped inside and closed the door behind her. The short, brown-haired teacher with the soft plumpness of a mother hen tapped her foot in admonition. 'What's this? Food in your bedroom. Madame will have a fit if she finds out.'

'You won't tell her, will you?' Isabel pleaded with more drama than earnestness.

A smile spread across Miss Fanworth's full lips. 'Of course not. Now cut me a slice.'

This wasn't the only secret their favourite teacher had kept for the girls. The other would see Grace ruined and all Madame Dubois's faith in her best teacher and her favourite pupils destroyed.

'I have a present for you, too.' Miss Fanworth

exchanged her gift for the slice of cake Joanna held out to her.

Joanna unwrapped it to reveal a small leather pouch half-full of coins.

'It's for the postage, so you can pay for the letters we send you,' Miss Fanworth explained as she tasted her cake. 'I expect to receive a few in return.'

'Of course, how could I not write to everyone?'

Miss Fanworth set aside her plate, then rose. She laid her hands on Joanna's shoulders. Tears made her round eyes glisten. 'You were just a little babe when we first found you on the doorstep with nothing but a blanket and a torn slip of paper with your name on it. Now look at you, all grown up and ready to leave us.'

'I hope I can do you, Madame Dubois and the school proud.'

'As long as you remember everything we've taught you, you will.' She laid one full arm across Joanna's shoulders and turned them both to face the others. 'In fact, you must all remember your lessons, especially those I told you of the gentlemen you might meet. Don't be taken in by their kind words, it never ends well—why, look at poor Madame.'

She tutted in sympathy as she shook her head, making her brown curls dance at the sides of her face.

'What do you mean?' Isabel asked. All of them leaned in, eager for more. This wasn't the first time Joanna or the other girls had heard Miss Fanworth allude to something in Madame's past. Perhaps, with them leaving, Miss Fanworth would at last reveal the headmistress's secret which had teased them since their first day at the school.

Miss Fanworth's full cheeks turned a strange shade of red. She was as horrified by her slip as their interest. Then the clop of horses and the call of the coachman drifted up to them from the street below. Miss Fanworth blew out a long breath, as relieved by the distraction as she was saddened by what it meant. 'Joanna, it's time for you to go. Are you ready?'

No. Joanna laced her hands in front of her, determined to be brave. She'd stay here as a teacher if they'd let her, but Madame Dubois had insisted she seek a position. She hadn't argued. She never did, but always went along, no matter what she wanted. 'I am.'

'I wish I was going with you.' Rachel huffed as she took Joanna's one arm.

Isabel took the other. 'Me, too.'

'I wish we could all go together,' Grace echoed from behind them, at Miss Fanworth's side as they left the room.

'We wouldn't get a stroke of work done if we were in the same house together.' Joanna laughed through the tightness in her throat.

They walked much slower down the stairs than when they'd ascended, all but Joanna sniffling back tears between jokes and shared memories.

Madame Dubois waited beside the front door, watching the girls reach the bottom. Her black bombazine dress without one wrinkle fell regally from her shoulders. The woman was formidable and more than one small girl had burst into tears at the first sight of her, but they soon learned how deeply she regarded each of her charges. She wouldn't hug or cry over them like Miss Fanworth, but it didn't mean she didn't care.

Though she didn't care enough to keep me here. Joanna banished the thought as soon as it reared its head. The school was full of little girls who'd been sent away by their families. She shouldn't expect to be treated any differently by Madame Dubois just because Madame Dubois had helped raise her.

In a flurry of hugs and promises to write, the girls said their goodbyes.

Reluctantly, Joanna left them to approach the headmistress while the others remained with Miss Fanworth. She stood straight and erect before the Frenchwoman. Outside, the coach driver tossed her small trunk containing all she owned up on to the top of the vehicle.

'This is a proud and exciting day for you, Miss Radcliff. You're leaving us at last to become a governess.' Madame Dubois held her arms at angles in front of her, hands crossed, but the softness in her voice and the slight sparkle of moisture at the corners of her grey eyes betrayed her.

She doesn't want to let me go. Joanna swallowed hard, the request to stay sitting like a marble in her throat. She swallowed it down. There was no point asking for something she wouldn't receive. Madame wouldn't give in to her wants any more than she would allow Joanna to give in to hers.

'Yes, Madame.' Joanna wished she could wrap her arms around Madame and hug her like the other girls did their mothers when they bid them goodbye on their first day, but she couldn't. Madame might be as saddened by the parting as Joanna, but there would be no hugging or tears. It wasn't her way.

'You're a bright, intelligent, accomplished young lady who'll aptly represent the quality of pupils at our school in your first position.'

'I will, Madame. You've prepared me well.'

Chapter One

One month later

Madame Dubois didn't prepare me for this!

Joanna clutched the book to her chest as she stood in the dark corner of the Huntford Place library. Frances, the eldest Huntford daughter, and Lieutenant Foreman had burst into the room aware of nothing but each other. Lieutenant Foreman pressed Frances up against the wall and pawed at her breasts and hips through her dress. Instead of fighting off his advances, Frances embraced the lanky Lieutenant, raising one slender and stocking-clad leg to rest against his hip.

Joanna glanced at the door. The sighs and moans of the couple filled the room as she debated how best to slip away without being noticed.

No, I can't. I'm the governess. She couldn't

allow Frances to ruin herself, but she didn't have the faintest idea how to separate them. Beyond what Grace had told her, lovemaking was outside her range of experience. Despite understanding the more technical aspects of the act, it was the desire part she failed to grasp, the one which had led to Grace's predicament and was about to ruin Frances, too.

She'd learn more about the physical particulars if she didn't stop this. Lieutenant Foreman's hand was already beneath Frances's dress.

'Ahem...' Joanna cleared her throat, her urgency increasing with their passion when it failed to interrupt the amorous pair. 'Ahem!'

Lieutenant Foreman whirled around to face Joanna while Frances straightened the bodice of her expensive yellow-silk dress behind him. He adjusted his red coat, his sword not the only prominent weapon near his belt. Joanna tried not to notice, but it was difficult for his white breeches obscured very little.

'Excuse me, Miss Radcliff.' He bowed to Joanna, then bolted out of the room, leaving Frances to face her fate alone.

Joanna opened and closed her sweaty fingers

over the cover of the book. She hoped this taught
Frances something about the man and made her
realise her mistake. She was about to say so when
Frances, cheeks red with anger instead of shame,
fixed on Joanna.

'How dare you barge in on me?'

'I didn't barge, I was already in the room when
you and Lieutenant Foreman—'

'Don't you dare speak of it, not to me or anyone, do you understand?' She flew upon Joanna
and slapped the book out of her hands. It landed
with a thud on the floor between them.

'No, of course not,' Joanna stammered, startled
by the command. She was supposed to be the one
in charge. She remained silent, afraid to point out
this fact and make things worse.

'Good, because if you do, I'll see to it you're dismissed without a reference.' Frances threw back
her head of light blonde curls and strode from the
room as if it was she and not her father, Sir Rodger, who owned the house. Like all four Huntford
girls, Frances was spoiled by her parents. All of
them had treated Joanna with nothing but contempt since her arrival.

Joanna found the arm of the chair behind her

and gripped it tightly as she sank into the dusty cushions. This wasn't how being a governess was supposed to be. The girls were supposed to look to her for education and guidance, and keeping Frances's secret should've brought her and Frances closer, like it had with her, Rachel, Isabel and Grace. It shouldn't have garnered spite from a young lady clearly in the wrong. She should tell Sir Rodger and Lady Huntford about their daughter's compromising behaviour, but if she did, they might blame her.

I wish Rachel were here. She had a gift for dealing with the young children and even some of the older girls at the school. She'd know what to do, but she wasn't here, none of her friends or Madame Dubois or Miss Fanworth could help her. She was on her own, just as she'd been until she was nine and Grace, Rachel and Isabel had first arrived at the school. She wished she had a copy of the drawing of the four of them Grace had done last Christmas. It would lessen her loneliness to remember how happy they'd been together and make them seem closer instead of hundreds of miles away.

She stood and plucked the book from the floor,

refusing to wallow in self-pity. Her friends weren't here and, despite Frances's threats, it was Joanna's duty to guide and chaperon the young lady. She'd have to find a more subtle way to go about it. There was little else she could do.

Luke strode up the steps of the Mayfair town house. The must and damp of the ship which had brought him back from France permeated the wool of his red coat. He rubbed his hand over the stubble on his chin. He should have stopped at the Army Service Club to bathe and shave, but the moment he'd landed in Greenwich, all he'd wanted to do was see Diana Tomalin, his fiancée.

He'd been brought home with instructions to marry and produce an heir for the family. The faster he made things final with Diana, the sooner he might achieve this goal and return to his regiment in Spain. It had hurt like hell to sell his commission four months after he'd risked his life to earn it and he'd be damned if he let it go for good.

Collins, the Tomalin family's butler, pulled open the front door. His small eyes in his soft face widened at the sight of Luke. 'Major Preston.'

'Morning, Collins. Is Miss Tomalin here?' Luke

removed his shako and handed it to the man as he strode into the Tomalin family entrance hall.

'She is, sir, but—' He fumbled the army head-dress, making the feather in the front waver like his voice.

'Collins, who is it?' Diana called from the sitting room.

'It's me.' Luke strode into the sunlit room and jerked to a halt. His excitement drifted out of him like smoke out of a cannon.

Diana stood in the middle of the rug, her eyes not meeting his as she ran her hand over her round belly. The gold band on her ring finger clicked over the small buttons along the front of her voluminous morning dress. 'Welcome home, Major Preston.'

The pendulum on the clock beside him swung back and forth with an irritatingly precise click.

'When did you intend to tell me we were no longer engaged?' Luke demanded. 'Or were you hoping Napoleon would solve the matter for you?'

She twisted the wedding band, the large stone set in the gold too big for her delicate fingers. 'Mother said I shouldn't trouble you, not when you had so many other things to worry about.

She also said I shouldn't wait any longer for you, that five years was enough, and you might die in battle and then my youth and all my chances to marry would be lost.'

'Yes, your mother was always very practical in the matter of our betrothal.' It's why he'd agreed to keep their engagement a secret until he could return from Spain with a fuller purse and a higher rank. Heaven forbid Mrs Tomalin endure the horror of a lowly lieutenant, an earl's mere second son, for a son-in-law. 'Who's the lucky gentleman?'

'Lord Follett,' she whispered, more ashamed than enamoured by her choice of mate.

'I see.' Like nearly all the women he'd encountered before he'd enlisted, and whenever he'd come home on leave, she'd run after a man with more title and land than him. He watched the pendulum swing back and forth in the clock case, wanting to knock the grand thing over and silence it. 'So it's Lady Follett now. Where is your distinguished husband? In Bath, taking the waters for his rheumatism?'

'With Father's mounting bills and you possibly never coming back, I didn't have a choice but to accept him,' she cried out against his sarcasm. 'So much has changed in England since you've been gone. The cold winters have taken their toll and, with crops failing year after year, Father began to fall into debt like so many others.'

No doubt his gambling habit helped increase it, Luke bit back, holding more sympathy for her than he should have. Her family wasn't the only one facing ruin and struggling to hide it. His father and grandfather had spent years rebuilding Pensum Manor after his feckless great-grandfather had nearly gambled it away. The continued crop failures were threatening to send it spiralling back into insolvency. Like Diana, Luke needed to marry and well. He hated to be so mercenary in his choice of bride, but it was a reality he couldn't ignore. However, it didn't mean he had to wed the first merchant's daughter with five thousand a year who threw herself at him in an effort to be the mother of the next Earl of Ingham. 'Surely you could've chosen someone better suited to you than that old man.'

'My first duty is to my father and my family, not to you, not to even myself.' She settled back into her chair, her brown eyes at last meeting his and filled with a silent plea for understanding. He couldn't withhold it. He'd abandoned his men and his military career to come home and do his duty for his family. He couldn't blame her for doing the same.

'It seems we're both obliged to make sacrifices. You with Lord Follett, me as the heir.'

'But your brother and his wife?'

'After ten years, there's been no child. If things stay as they are—'

'You'll inherit.' She pressed her palm to her forehead, realising what she'd given up by following her parents' demands. However, Luke knew the way of the world. A possible title at some future date was not the same as an old, wealthy baron on a woman's doorstep with a special licence.

Not wanting to torture her further with his presence or his ire, he took the shako from Collins and tucked it under his arm. 'I wish you all the best and future happiness. Good day.'

He left the house and climbed into the hack waiting at the kerb. He knocked Captain Reginald Crowther's feet off the seat where he'd rested them to nap.

His friend jerked upright and tilted his shako

off his eyes. He was about to crack a joke when a warning glare from Luke turned him slightly more serious. 'I take it all didn't go well with your fair damsel?'

Luke rapped on the roof to set the vehicle in motion. As it lumbered out of Mayfair towards the Bull in Bishops Street, he told him what had happened inside the Tomalins'. 'This isn't how I imaged this would go.'

'And I can see you're utterly heartbroken over losing her. More like inconvenienced.' Captain Crowther threw his arms up over the back of the squabs. 'You thought you'd marry a tidy little sum, produce an heir with the least amount of bother and be back in Spain with the regiment inside of two years.'

Luke fingered the regimental badge of a curved bugle horn hung from a ribbon affixed to the front of his shako, unsettled by Captain Crowther's frank assessment of his plans and secretly relieved. If he and Diana had entered into marriage negotiations, the Inghams' debts would have been revealed. Diana's family would probably have made her cry off and all England might have learned of his family's financial straits. His rapture for her had faded too much during their time apart for him to go through so much on her behalf. 'Her refusing to marry me before I left and insisting we keep the engagement a secret always did rankle.'

'Now you must give up the hell of battle for the hell of the marriage mart.' His friend chuckled. 'Wish I could be here to see you dancing like some London dandy.'

'When I agreed to come home, I didn't think I'd have to face it.' Or the ugliness he'd glimpsed in Diana's situation. He set the shako on the seat beside him. Worse waited for him in the country. With the future of the earldom hovering over him, all the tittering darlings and their mamas who'd ignored him as a youth because he wouldn't inherit would rush Pensum Manor faster than Napoleon's troops did a battlefield.

'You don't have to do this. Write and tell your brother to pay more attention to his wife and come back to Spain,' Captain Crowther urged.

'I'm sure their lack of a child isn't from a lack of trying and it isn't only an heir they need, but money.' Luke stared out the hackney window at the crowd crossing London Bridge in the distance.

He couldn't have refused the request to come home even if he'd wanted to. His father had called on his old friend, Lieutenant Colonel Lord Henry Beckwith, using the connection he'd employed to begin Luke's Army career to end it. Luke might have ignored one or two orders in battle, achieving both victory and forgiveness for his transgressions, but he couldn't dismiss a direct command from Lord Beckwith to return home.

The carriage lumbered to a stop in front of the arch of the bustling Bull Inn. Luke tucked the shako under his arm and stepped out, as did his friend. Behind them the driver unloaded Luke's things while Captain Crowther's stayed fixed on top. After he visited his sister, Reginald was going back to Spain, his mission of delivering dispatches complete.

Luke flicked the dull edge of the bugle-horn badge with his fingernail. He would catch a coach to Pensum Manor, his family's estate in Hertfordshire and take up the position of second in line to the earldom and groom-to-be to some willing, and as of yet unnamed, wife. 'I wish you'd accepted my offer to buy my commission.'

'You know I don't want it, or the debt to secure

it. Don't look so glum.' Reginald cuffed Luke on the arm. 'We aren't all meant to be leaders like you. Your intelligence, wit and daring will be missed.'

'But they'll have your ability to charm the locals, especially the gambling men.'

Reginald grinned with self-satisfaction. 'I do have a flair with language.'

Luke snapped off the Forty-Third Regiment of Foot bugle-horn badge affixed to the front of the shako and handed the now-unneeded headpiece to his friend. 'Stay safe.'

Reginald ran his thumb over the bare felt front, a rare seriousness crossing over his face before it passed. 'You're the one who needs to watch yourself. I hear those unmarried ladies can be dangerous.' He tossed the thing inside the coach then took Luke's hand. 'Go on to Hertfordshire, find a wife and give your family their much sought-after heir.'

Reginald climbed back into the carriage and then hung one elbow out the door window.

'Give Napoleon hell,' Luke encouraged, the edge of the badge biting into his palm where he clasped it tight.

'I intend to.' With a rakish salute, Reginald tucked inside as the hack rolled off down the crowded street.

With each turn of the wheels, the most accomplished and contented ten years of Luke's life faded into the past. He opened his palm, the tin against his skin tarnished with Spanish mud and rain. What waited for him in Hertfordshire was everything he'd joined the Army to escape: the oppressive weight of previous generations which hung over Pensum Manor, and his own insignificance to the line as magnified by his brother's importance.

He slipped the badge into his pocket and strode into the inn to arrange for a seat in the next coach to Hertfordshire. He'd do his duty to his family, as fast and efficiently as he could, then he'd return to the Army and a real sense of accomplishment.

Chapter Two

Joanna had never been to a ball before. The Pensum Manor ballroom was decorated with autumn leaves, straw bales, scarecrows and bunches of wheat tied with orange-and-yellow ribbons. The same musicians who played in the church on Sundays now performed on an equally festive stage at the far end. In front of them, young ladies and gentlemen danced in time to the lively music. Everyone in attendance seemed happy and carefree, except Joanna, and, it appeared, Major Preston.

Joanna glanced at the guest of honour again, admiring the dignified arch of his brows, the subtle wave in his dark brown hair where it curled over both ears before touching the smooth skin above his collar. It wasn't only his commanding stature which drew her to him, but the discontent deepening the rich coffee colour of his eyes. He stood beside his brother, Lord Pensum, near the door, nodding tersely at each passing guest while his brother greeted them with a gracious smile and a few words. More than once Joanna saw Major Preston's sturdy chest rise and fall with a weary sigh and she sympathised with him. Like her, he was clearly ill at ease in the midst of all this merriment.

'Watch where you're going,' Frances snapped as she stopped to examine the dancers, forcing Joanna to come up short to keep from bumping into her tiring charge. Then Frances set off again on another circle of the room, no doubt searching for Lieutenant Foreman. Thankfully, they hadn't seen him, but it didn't stop Frances from looking. The girl was stubborn in her desire to ruin herself.

Joanna followed wearily behind her, tugging at the pale-blue secondhand dress Frances had tossed at her last night after Lady Huntford had announced Joanna would attend as Frances's chaperon. It spared the mother the bother of hovering around her headstrong daughter. Joanna played with the small bit of lace along the thankfully modest bodice. It fit her in length, since she and Frances were nearly matched in height, but

Joanna had been forced to stay up late to take in the chest. The lack of sleep, combined with Lady Huntford having instructed Joanna to try and manoeuvre Frances to Major Preston, added to her disquiet. The young lady was as co-operative as a donkey. With Frances relentlessly circling the room and refusing to dance, Joanna had been denied the company of the other governesses sitting along the wall and chatting together. She needed some hopefully polite conversation with someone, anyone. She rarely received it at Huntford Place.

To Joanna's luck, Frances's hurried steps brought them closer to Major Preston and Joanna hazarded another glance at him. This time, his eyes met hers and the entire ballroom faded away until only the two of them and the soft melody of the violin remained. There were no wayward charges, laughing country squires or gallant young men to concern her. His gaze slid along the length of her, pausing at her chest which increased with her drawn-in breath.

Instead of stopping him with a chiding glance, she stood up straighter, offering him a better view of her in the prettiest dress she'd ever worn. His silent appraisal of her continued down to her feet and then up again. It kindled the strange fire burning near her centre which spread out to engulf her skin. She touched the curls at the back of her head, returning his attention to her face. With a slow, refined movement she lowered her hand, linking it with the other in front of her, each fingertip aching to trace the angle of his jaw to where it met his stiff cravat. She envied the linen encasing his throat and whatever woman he chose here tonight for his bride. She would experience the thrill of his body against hers, the heat of his wide hands upon her bare skin, the luxury of his height draping her like a heavy coat on a windy day.

'Stop gawking at everything,' Frances hissed, snapping Joanna out of her licentious daydream. 'You're embarrassing me.'

Considering the lady's encounter with Lieutenant Foreman, Frances possessed a strange idea of what might embarrass her. Joanna held her tongue, eager to avoid cultivating any more of Frances's ire.

'Might we not go speak with Major Preston?' Joanna slid a sideways glance at Major Preston. He continued to watch her with an allure which almost made her rush to him, but she didn't move.

Instead, she tugged at the back of the dress, wondering what had come over her. She was here to chaperon Frances, not lose her head over a man so far above her the only relationship they could enjoy would risk her livelihood and go against everything Madame Dubois and Miss Fanworth had invested in her. They'd trained her to teach young ladies, not to become a kept tart.

'Why would I want to talk to him?' Frances shifted back and forth on her toes to look over the guests' heads.

'To save your slippers for the delight of dancing,' Joanna joked. Her attempt at humour withered as Frances narrowed her eyes at Joanna. 'And because I've noticed him admiring you.'

It was a lie, but an effective one.

'He has?' Frances's attention whipped around to Major Preston so fast, the blonde curls at the back of her head flew out before they settled back against her neck. Frances thrust out her ample chest and cast Major Preston a none-too-subtle smile.

Frances's interest in him ended his interest in them. He offered Frances a polite nod, then turned to speak to a gentleman Joanna vaguely recognised as someone of local importance. On the dance floor, one dance ended and couples began to form up for the next. Mr Winborn, the son of another local baronet who Catherine, Frances's younger sister, had teased Frances about during their last visit to the village approached them.

'Miss Huntford, may I have this dance?' The lithe gentleman with a head of wild red hair held out his freckled hand to Frances.

'Yes, I suppose I must be seen dancing with someone or people will talk.' Frances placed her hand limply in his.

'We can't have that, now, can we?' Mr Winborn concurred, not offended by her blunt acceptance and just as blasé about taking her to the dance floor as his partner.

Joanna sagged a little in relief. Frances couldn't get into trouble while she danced. Joanna turned, excited to at last be able to join the other chaperons when a mountain of a man stepped between her and them. A badge of a bugle horn hung by a tin ribbon met her before she peered up to the peak to find Major Preston standing over her.

The scent of cedar surrounding him enveloped her and she pressed her heels into the floor to keep from wavering under the pressure of it. His dark coat ran tight along the horizontal plane of his shoulders. Brass buttons with crossed sabres held the wool closed at his navel and emphasised his narrow waist. The dark material stood in stark contrast to the white breeches covering his legs. She didn't dare check to see what kind of buttons held those closed.

'May I have this dance?' He held out his hand to her. His palm was wide, with a faint scar starting at the first finger and crossing down to his wrist. Light red circles of old blisters further marred the plane of it. Here was no soft London gentleman, but one who knew something of hard work and danger. His nearness didn't overwhelm her like the ones of the other titled men and women filling the room. Instead, she admired his confidence and wanted to emulate it.

She raised her hand to accept his, then jerked it back to her side, remembering herself. 'When it comes to reels, I appear more like a horse trotting around a millstone than a lady of poise. It's best for me to avoid them.'

He grinned at her, amused instead of insulted by her refusal. 'Dancing doesn't bring out my natural agility either. Despite lessons, I never developed the talent for it. I mastered riding instead.'

'If only you could do both the way they do with the horses from Vienna I once read about.' She froze, waiting for him to chastise her as Frances had for speaking out of turn. Instead, he rewarded her with a smile as captivating as his height. He was a good head taller than her.

'Not my horse. He's more mule than Lipizzaner and would throw me if I tried to make a dancer out of him.'

'But you'd both be majestic for the moment you stayed in the saddle.'

'It would be a very brief moment.' He smothered a laugh behind his hand, the delight it brought to his eyes as captivating as the pensiveness which had called to her from across the room. 'Do you ride?'

'As poorly as I dance.' Horsemanship was wasted on a governess.

'I imagine you'd be quite elegant in the saddle if you tried.'

'I'm sure I would be, for the brief moment before I was tossed out of it.'

He leaned in, the intensity of his woodsy scent

strengthening with his closeness. She noticed a slight scar running along the hairline of his temple, the skin a touch whiter than that of his face. 'I would catch you.'

Joanna stiffened, panic as much as excitement making her heart race. As a governess, she shouldn't be speaking with him. She should draw this conversation to a close, remember his place and hers, but she couldn't. She hadn't been this at ease since the last time she'd been with her friends. She offered him an impish look from beneath her dark lashes, emboldened by his relaxed manner. 'I'd do the same for you.'

He straightened, his laugh uncontained this time. Thankfully, the music reached a high crescendo, keeping all but those closest to them from hearing him.

'Your catching me would make me a spectacle, more so than I already am.' His laughter died away and his shoulders rose and fell with another weary sigh. 'What I wouldn't give to be riding instead of here.'

'What I wouldn't give to be in a quiet corner reading instead of here.'

'Yet here we are.' He opened his hands to the

room as Frances whirled by with her red-headed partner. Mr Winborn said something to her and she rewarded him with a rare and genuine laugh. 'It must be difficult being in Miss Huntford's shadow. You're by far the prettier of the two.'

Joanna studied the square head of a nail in the floor beneath her feet, as stunned as she was flattered by his compliment. Miss Fanworth's warning about young gentlemen came to her and she pinned him with her best disciplining governess look. It worked about as well with him as it did with Frances, which was to say it didn't. 'Thank you, but you really shouldn't.'

'I can't help it. I've been among plain-speaking men for so long it's difficult to not be open and honest with everyone. Imagine if we were all like this with one another.'

'Society would crumble once everyone realised what people really thought of them.'

'They already know but pretend they don't.'

'What about you? Do you pretend?' It was none of her business, but she couldn't help herself.

'Every day.' Sorrow darkened his eyes like clouds over water on a stormy day. 'I pretend to be happy I came home, I pretend to be glad I gave up my Army career for this.'

Luke pressed back his shoulders and clasped his hands behind him, waiting for her to brush away his complaints as his brother Edward, his father and every other young lady he'd spoken with to-night had done. They all expected him to forget his time in the Army, to dismiss it as one might a past Season in London. He couldn't any more than he could forget the faces of all the men he'd lost or the intuition for danger which still kept his senses sharp whenever he rode alone in the woods. All the instincts which had kept him alive in Spain refused to be dulled, but they were use-less to him here.

'It can be difficult after so long in one situation to leave it, especially when it means saying good-bye to friends.' She studied him with eyes blue enough to make the Mediterranean jealous, their colour as stunning as her response. They capti-vated him as much now as when he'd followed her progress around the room as she'd trailed after Miss Huntford. Seeing the sisters together had re-minded him of following Edward at school until he'd railed at him for embarrassing him. Luke had caught similar exchanges between the two sisters tonight. The last time he'd seen the Huntford girls had been at a picnic nearly fifteen years ago and they'd proved as vapid as their mother. Whichever Huntford sister this was, and he could only assume she was the second eldest, she'd matured into a beautiful, wise and witty young lady.

'Eventually, you'll settle in again,' she assured him, the light auburn hair framing her round face emphasising her subtle beauty.

'Settling is exactly what I'm worried about. As the second son, there isn't much else for me to do. The estate isn't mine and it may never be.' From an early age, the house, their legacy and their duty to it had been drilled into Luke and his older brother. It had meant something to Edward, the heir. To Luke, it had been nothing but a heavy reminder of his lesser status, the one his family hadn't failed to reinforce. After reluctantly paying to educate Luke alongside Edward, Luke's father had spent as few pounds as possible to purchase Luke's paltry lieutenant's commission. It had been left to Luke to claw his way up the ranks, borrowing from friends to purchase every next higher rank until the day he'd won for himself, through his own daring, the rank of major. Only now, when Luke had become useful to the line, had his father decided to waste an unnecessary fortune to trot Luke out to look over the local eligible ladies. It irritated him as much as having left so much hard work behind in the dirt of Spain. 'I have no desire to inherit, or become lord of the manor.'

Her shock at his honest declaration was obvious in the horrified surprise which widened her stunning eyes as she stared out across the ballroom. The dance had ended and the couples were bowing to one another and making their way back to their chaperons. She seemed to watch them closely, shifting on her feet as if she couldn't wait to flee from him and the heresy of not coveting an earldom. 'It can't be.'

'I assure you, it is.'

'Please excuse me, Major Preston, but I must, uh, see to something, uh, Miss Hartford, very important, at once.' She bolted from him like a horse whose rider had been shot off its back.

His spirits, buoyed by their conversation, sank like a rock. He'd thought her different from the many other ladies he'd met tonight, deeper and more understanding. He was wrong. She was as shallow and covetous as the rest of her family.

'You look as though you need this more than Edward.' Alma, his sister-in-law, offered him one of the two glasses of champagne she carried. She was tall for a woman but willowy with dark hair, light brown eyes and a playful smile Luke hadn't seen much of since coming home.

Luke took the drink and downed a sobering gulp. 'It seems my worth is once again based on the luck of birth and death.'

'I sympathise with you. Providing an heir is the one thing expected of a woman of my rank and I've failed at it.' She focused on the bubbles rising in a steady stream off the bottom of her champagne flute.

'I'm sorry, I didn't mean to add to your distress. I'm being as thoughtless as Edward.'

'Don't be so hard on him. He's struggling to accept our failure and, like you, the changes it means to the family and the line.'

All of their roles and places in life which had once been so secure were being thrown off kilter like a wagon caught in a rut.

'I've seen miracles on the field of battle, men narrowly missed by cannonballs, or those who walked away from explosions with only minor scratches. It isn't too much to hope for another. Don't despair, Alma. I haven't.' He tapped his glass against hers, making the crystal ring. 'You may become a mother yet.'

'We'll see.' Disbelief hung heavy in her response.

He raised his glass to finish it, then paused. Across the room, a man who shouldn't be here slipped out of the opposite door and into the adjoining hallway. 'What the devil is he doing here?'

'Who?' Alma asked, following the line of his look.

'Lieutenant Foreman.' He'd last seen the scoundrel eight years ago riding north from their training grounds in Monmouthshire with his tail between his legs, transferred to another unit at Luke's insistence for compromising a local vicar's daughter.

'There weren't any officers on the guest list.' Alma tipped her flute at the blue-eyed beauty weaving through the guests. 'I believe your conversation partner is following him.'

The young lady paused at the door, taking advantage of Lady Huntford's lack of interest in her to slip into the hallway where Lieutenant Foreman had just disappeared. Apparently, she favoured lower-ranking men more than Luke had realised.

Luke handed his glass to Alma. 'I won't have a misguided woman ruining herself under our roof, especially not with a man like him. Tell no one about this.'

'I won't say a word.' Thankfully, she understood the need for discretion in this matter.

Luke followed them out of the ballroom, as curious as he was determined to protect his wayward guest.

She travelled the length of the ever-darkening hallway with the agitation of a spy down an alley. Whatever she was doing was wrong and she knew it. Still, she continued on in search of Lieutenant Foreman. Luke was careful not to follow too close. He wanted to make sure he caught them together, but not too much together. Then he'd see to it Lieutenant Foreman never set foot in this part of Hertfordshire again. He detested the man and his lack of honour. He should have done right by the vicar's daughter. At least he hadn't got the young lady with child. Luke would've marched him up the church aisle at bayonet point if he had. He hoped he didn't have to perform the same service for Miss Huntford.

The young lady slipped down another hall, this one poorly lit to disguise the threadbare rug and tired furnishings. The best of the furniture had been moved to the front of the house and the ballroom to keep up the appearance of wealth. No guests were supposed to be in this far-flung and cold wing of the classical-style house.

He stopped at the turn to the hallway and peered around the corner, doing his best to remain undetected. The young lady paused at the door near the far end and took hold of the knob. She turned to survey the emptiness around her. Luke jerked back out of sight and prayed he hadn't been seen. The squeak of the brass and the protest of the old hinges as the door opened told him she hadn't noticed him.

He marched down the hall after her, determined to make his interruption as stunning as possible in order to teach the lady a lesson. He grabbed the knob and threw open the door. 'What are you doing in here?'

He jerked to a halt to keep from colliding with the young lady. She scooted aside as, across the room, Lieutenant Foreman let go of the elder Miss Huntford so fast, she almost fell to the floor.

'Enjoying the pleasures of the country, as you can see,' Lieutenant Foreman sneered, his pointed chin framed by the red coat of his uniform 'And there's nothing you can do about it, *Mr Preston.*'

Luke rushed up on him so fast, he shuffled back into the bookcase behind him. 'I may not have my commission, but I still have my connections, especially with Lieutenant Colonel Lord Beckwith. I won't hesitate to appeal to him to have you drummed out of the ranks for this.'

'No, you can't,' Miss Huntford protested.

He fixed her with a hard look. 'You'd do well to remember your reputation is in grave danger of being compromised.'

Miss Huntford shrunk back, biting her lip like a reprimanded child.

Luke turned to his former comrade, wanting to thrash him for being a scoundrel, but he kept control. His family couldn't afford any broken furniture. 'As for you, Lieutenant Foreman, you'd better think long and hard on your future in the Army because if I ever see you two together again, un-married, or hear one whiff of scandal regard-ing you and Miss Huntford, I'll see to it you're shipped to a remote and disease-ridden post. Do I make myself clear?'

Lieutenant Foreman's beady eyes widened. 'Yes.'

'Sir.'

'Yes, sir.' He raised a shaking hand to his fore-head in salute.

'Now, get out.'

Lieutenant Foreman slid out from between Luke and the wall, offering not one word of goodbye to his lover as he rushed from the room.

Miss Huntford's embarrassment didn't last long past the exit of her paramour. She fixed hard eyes on her sister, reprimanding her as if Luke wasn't there.

'You brought Major Preston here,' she screeched. 'You're trying to ruin me on purpose. How dare you. I'll see you pay for this.'

She advanced on the poor young lady, who shrank into the corner as if doing her best to be-come one with the panelling. Luke stepped between the sisters, shielding the lady from Miss Huntford's wrath.

'Your sister didn't bring me here. I followed her. Unlike you, I'm concerned about her reputation and yours.'

'Sister,' Miss Huntford snorted, 'she isn't my sister. She's the governess.'

Luke stepped out from between the ladies and glanced back and forth at them. So much about their previous conversation suddenly became clear, especially her refusal to dance, her insight and her desire to get away. The governess lowered her stunning blue eyes to the carpet, her head bowed like an inferior. It made his blood boil to see her humbled by Miss Huntford, as it did when he used to see unqualified commanders berate junior officers for daring to display initiative.

Luke turned back to Miss Huntford. With her deep-red dress pressing her generous breasts up against the top of the bodice, she was as well done up as a courtesan searching for a client at the theatre. Her mother shouldn't have allowed her daughter to wear so questionable a dress. Then again, if her mother had shown much interest in her, she might not have been here with Lieutenant

Foreman. 'Your governess has more sense than you do.'

Miss Huntford let out a startled squeak at being disciplined for what Luke imagined might be the first time in her life.

'If I hear any word of Miss—what's your name?' he asked the governess.

'Radcliff.' She twisted her hands together in front of her. The vibrant, humorous woman he'd enjoyed in the ballroom was gone, driven away by her spoiled hoyden of a charge.

'If I learn Miss Radcliff has been reprimanded or dismissed for her attempt to aid you, Miss Huntford, I'll ask for an interview with your father and tell him not only what I witnessed, but something of Lieutenant Foreman's background. He won't like it and neither will you. Do I have your word you won't seek revenge against Miss Radcliff?'

Miss Huntford screwed up her full lips in a pout to make a two-year-old proud. He recognised the delay. It was the same reaction he used to receive from soldiers not wanting to answer a direct question. They would hem and shuffle, working to come up with some false reason to justify their poor behaviour. Like his soldiers, Miss Huntford could think of nothing. Her pout eased into a frown and the red drained out of her face. She was beaten and she knew it. 'Yes, you have my word.'

'Good. I'll escort you back to the ballroom and we'll say nothing of this to anyone.' He offered her his elbow.

She wrinkled her nose at it, stubborn as before, but, seeing no choice except to comply, she slapped her hand down over his coat. She flicked Miss Radcliff a fierce look as they all walked into the hallway.

Miss Radcliff followed a few steps behind them as they made for the ballroom. It was she he was worried about, not the lady on his arm. He might have threatened Miss Huntford, but he doubted her ability to honour her word. If she struck at Miss Radcliff, there was nothing he could do to help or protect the poor governess. He couldn't correspond with Miss Radcliff, or visit her at Huntford Place. Despite the pleasure of her presence and conversation, she was one of the few ladies in attendance not available as a potential bride.

The realisation ground on him like a pebble

stuck in a boot. The woman behind him possessed more dignity, poise and sense of duty than
the daughter of a baronet marching beside him,
yet he was forced to overlook her because she
wasn't of his class. The indignity of it distracted
him so much, he failed to stop on the threshold
to the ballroom and allow the ladies to continue
in without him. The moment he and Miss Huntford entered the ballroom, all eyes fell upon them
and then on her hand on his arm. A few people
noted Miss Radcliff behind them, her presence
as a chaperon restraining the whispers, but it was
clear the pretty baronet's daughter and the potential earl had been outside the room together.

The attention didn't escape Miss Huntford, who
snatched her hand off his arm and made for her
mother. Miss Radcliff stepped out from behind
him to follow her charge.

'Miss Radcliff,' he called to her, not sure why.
There was nothing more for them to say. He hoped
she'd be all right and wished there was some way
he could ensure it, but there wasn't. Meeting his
hesitation, she spoke first, aware of those around
them watching this strange conversation.

'Thank you for your assistance, Major Preston.'

She dipped a proper curtsy, then set off after Miss Huntford, proving she was level-headed in a difficult situation.

It was another reason to admire her and he regretted letting her go, unable to stop watching her until she passed by Alma. His sister-in-law cocked her head in curiosity at Luke, having guessed which lady truly interested him.

He jerked his attention away from them both and strode to a nearby circle of gentlemen discussing pheasant hunting. The topic failed to take his mind off Miss Radcliff's enchanting eyes, or the peace and delight he'd experienced in her presence. She, more than anyone, had understood his frustration at being here and she was the one young lady he was unable to court.

'I bet you're glad to be away from all the nasty business in Spain?' Lord Chilton joked in an attempt to engage Luke. He was one of the many men here with an eligible daughter and money.

'Not when my men are still there dying so we can enjoy balls without Napoleon's boot on our throats.' Luke didn't feel like being pleasant. He hated being forced to parade before all the tittering country women while his men suffered in Spain.

'Yes, bad business, most grateful for their service,' Lord Chilton muttered.

The other gentlemen added a few agreeing harrumphs.

'What will you do with yourself now you're home?' Lord Selton asked. 'I can't imagine country life can hold much charm for a man of your experience.'

No, it didn't. He'd found meaning for his life in the Army, a sense of accomplishment and merit which he'd never had before and now it was gone. 'It does lack excitement, but at least no one is shooting at me.'

It was almost the only benefit to being here.

'I suppose there is that,' Lord Selton agreed before Sir Peter Bell turned their attention back to hunting.

Luke slipped his hand into the inside pocket of his coat and traced the curving line of the buglehorn badge. He glanced to where Lady Huntford stood beneath the chandelier with her daughter. Miss Radcliff stood behind them, as forgotten as the numerous other chaperons scattered around the edges of the room. Feeling him watching her, she offered him a small, encouraging smile. Then, some sharp remark from Lady Huntford pulled her attention away.

He let go of the badge. There had to be something of merit for him to achieve here besides growing fat while he waited for some inheritance which might never come. He must find it and soon. He wouldn't allow himself to be made to feel as useless as he had as a child. He would find purpose, new things to achieve and accomplish, a reason beyond his ability to sire a child to make himself and his family proud.

Chapter Three

'Luke and Frances Huntford. I wouldn't have guessed it considering the way you used to talk about her when you were young.' Charles Preston, Earl of Ingham laughed across the breakfast table at his younger son before rising to help himself to more eggs from the sideboard. 'Can't say I fancy being related to that brood, but if one of them gives me a grandson, I guess I won't mind. The mother is quite capable of producing children. It bodes well for the daughters.'

Alma paled at the mention of Lady Huntford's fecundity.

'Charles, watch what you say,' Lady Elizabeth Ingham chided as she motioned for the footman to pour her more coffee. 'Especially since we might end up related to them.'

She winked at Luke, then lifted her coffee to her lips, hiding her teasing smile behind the steam.

'I'm not interested in Miss Huntford.' Luke sliced his ham into pieces.

'You'd do well to have an interest in her. Her dowry could offset our losses from last year's weak crop,' Edward added from across the table.

'I wouldn't get your hopes up,' Luke countered. 'Sir Rodger won't spend so much as a farthing to repair the roof over his head. I doubt he'll give it away with his daughters. But since I'm not interested in her, it is a moot point.'

After the ball, Luke had done everything he could to forget his brief time with Miss Radcliff, but it hadn't worked. Despite a vigorous ride this morning and a round of sparring with the groom, neither her vivid blue eyes, nor her kindness, had faded from his memory. To her, he hadn't been the catch of the year, but simply Major Preston. He wanted to be Major Preston with her again, but he couldn't. Courting a governess was as fanciful as hoping Napoleon would walk away from war.

'If you weren't interested in Miss Huntford, you should've let her return by herself instead of allowing the whole countryside to speculate about the two of you.' His mother sipped her coffee with a sigh of relief, the late night telling in the dark circles beneath her eyes. 'It could prove troublesome, especially while we're guests for their house party.'

Luke and Edward groaned in unison.

'Sir Rodger has the worst staff, especially the butler,' Edward complained. 'He has no grasp of how things are done. He's surly, too.'

'It's because Sir Rodger doesn't pay him enough.' Luke imaged the pittance Miss Radcliff must be earning.

'If the old miser is spending the money on a party, he must be desperate to get rid of Miss Huntford,' Edward addressed Luke in a rare moment of fraternal solidarity.

After what Luke had witnessed last night, it wouldn't surprise him.

'The only reason we're going is so Luke can look over the other young ladies. Otherwise, we wouldn't bother,' their father offered with uninspiring assurance.

'I haven't said I'll go, but speaking of bother...' Luke sat back from the table and pushed his plate away, determined to discuss the other subject which had kept him up most of the night '...I intend to call on Lord Helmsworth while I'm home. I'd like to arrange for another survey of the disputed boundary land, and, if it's determined to be his, then to arrange a lease of it or the rights to the river. I think it's time we end our feud with him.'

The silence which answered his announcement echoed through the room. Everyone stared down the table at him as if he'd suggested they catch the plague.

Edward's glare was especially sharp. 'You think you'll stroll into Helmsworth Manor and after twenty years he'll deed us the land with the river simply because you asked him to?'

'It's worth a try.' Luke trilled his fingers on the table, struggling to remain calm. He needed more to do in the country than search for a wife. Settling the old land dispute was it. He hadn't thought the idea would receive such a hostile response. 'We need the water to irrigate the west field. Without it, we can't expect to have a profitable enough harvest next year to cover our losses from this one.'

'I'm well aware of what we need, more so than you.' Edward pointed his knife at him. The conflict between them had returned with Luke from Spain with a vengeance. Except this time it was different. He and his brother were more equal now than in the past and Edward didn't like it any more than Luke did. 'This isn't school. You needn't try and outdo everyone.'

'You were the only one I ever outdid and only because it was so easy.' Luke speared a piece of ham and stuck it in his mouth with a smugness he didn't feel. In the heat of more than one battle, when he thought he wouldn't come home again, he'd longed to end the old rivalry between him and Edward. Now he was here and all he could do was argue with him. It wasn't right, but he seemed powerless to put an end to it.

Alma exchanged a troubled glance with their mother, who flapped a silencing hand at her sons. 'Boys, it's too early for this. If Luke wishes to try to settle the dispute, then he may. After all, it's cheaper to pay a surveyor than a solicitor and if it benefits us, then good. In the meantime, we must make a decision about the Huntford house party. Edward, will you and Alma attend?'

'We will if you want us to.' Alma set her fork aside, her food hardly touched. The circles under her eyes were far darker than they should have been, even after a late night. She rose and made for the door. 'If you'll excuse me.'

'I'd better see to her.' Edward stood, his square chin stiff in the air as he marched to the door. He matched Luke in height, but had their mother's hazel eyes and their father's black hair. 'I wouldn't want anyone accusing me of failing as both a husband and an heir.'

Once he was gone, Luke's mother shook her head. 'Alma tries so hard to be brave and I tell her not to worry. Since we have you, there's no reason to despair.'

Luke resisted groaning at having his value to the line stated so plainly. He rose, the tiff with Edward, as well as the memory of Miss Radcliff and the sleep it had stolen from him, crawling under his skin as much as his change of situation. Luke wasn't likely to ever be the earl, and he didn't want to inherit if it meant his father and Edward's deaths, but he wasn't sure he wished to foist the responsibility for Pensum Manor's future on some unsuspecting son either. He'd seen the demands it had made on his family and the way it had treated him. It wasn't something to envy. 'I'm riding over to visit Lord Helmsworth.'

'Luke, say you'll come to the house party.' His mother reached up and laid a hand on his arm. 'You don't know how much I want to be a grand-mother, to have Pensum Manor filled with the giggles of small children as when you and your brother were small.'

He was amazed she could remember the laughter and forget the awful rows he and his brother used to have. Time hadn't made them less intense, only more chilling.

'All right, I'll go.' He'd rather spend time in a French prison than with the Huntford girls, but visiting them would allow him to make sure Miss Radcliff was well and Miss Huntford was uphold-ing her end of the agreement.

He left the dining room and made for the sta-bles. He shouldn't concern himself with the wel-fare of a governess, but he hadn't allowed any of the weaker men in his regiment to be bullied by fellow soldiers or even officers. He wouldn't leave a poor governess to suffer under an indifferent, if not hostile employer. Nor would he allow anyone's prejudices to stop him from coming to know her better. He couldn't pursue her, but there was no reason why they couldn't be friends.

'Major Preston is coming here?' Frances wailed from across the breakfast table after her mother made the announcement.

He'll be here. Joanna stared down at the scuff mark on the toe of her half-boot to hide the flush creeping over her cheeks. She unclasped her hands from in front of her and allowed them to dangle by her sides. It shouldn't matter to her if Major Preston was coming or not. His doings were not her concern, but the news made standing still difficult.

She waited behind her three other charges for them to finish their food so their lessons could begin. Since the family ignored her at breakfast, and most of the day, her worry quickly passed. She could drop dead of the pox behind them and they weren't likely to notice.

'All of the Inghams are coming.' Lady Huntford didn't look up from her morning correspondence, taking little note of Frances's distress. Her blonde curls, like her daughter's, were tight beside her full cheeks and small eyes. Bearing six children had made her stout, but not fat, and her lack of interest in anything besides gossip and dresses gave her wide face a perpetually bored appearance. 'I thought you'd be pleased—after all, you were with him for some time last night.'

'I wasn't with him.' Frances all but pounded her thighs in frustration.

This was enough to make Lady Huntford finally put down her letter and look at her daughter. 'Then what were you two doing in the hallway?'

Frances looked to Joanna, who dropped her gaze to the back of the chair in front of her, noticing a chip in the finish. The chit didn't deserve her help. Her silence meant Frances was forced to invent her own excuses for her mother.

'We were talking. Miss Radcliff and I had stepped out for some air and he happened upon us. We discussed, uh, well, it was—what were we discussing, Miss Radcliff?' Frances appealed to the woman she'd declared her enemy for her salvation.

You acting like a harlot with Lieutenant Foreman.

'His return from Spain.' It galled Joanna to use her private conversation with him to defend

Frances instead of telling Lady Huntford the truth. She doubted how much good speaking up would do anyway. Lady Huntford would probably blame her favourite daughter's misguided attempt at romance on Joanna.

'Of course, I forgot he was telling us about Spain,' Frances rushed. 'An awful topic.'

'I don't imagine you'll be forced to discuss it much with him since he's resigned his commission.' Lady Huntford sniffed before turning in her seat to face Joanna. 'I noticed you were speaking a great deal with him. What were you thinking dominating so much of his time?'

'He approached me, Lady Huntford, and asked about Frances.' Joanna hoped she wasn't struck down for lying. 'I answered his many questions about her.'

Lady Huntford's eyes widened. 'What an unexpected surprise. You should have told me about it at once and not kept it a secret. You'll do no such thing in the future, do you understand?'

'Yes, Lady Huntford.' It seemed Frances wasn't the only one to be nearly caught out this morning. Joanna glanced at the young lady who frowned into her plate. The two of them hadn't been alone together since they'd left the ball last night. In fact, Frances had all but avoided Joanna, upholding her end of the bargain with Major Preston. His threat would be more potent while he was here, sleeping in a room below Joanna's, eating at this very table, walking the halls where she might glimpse his confident stance and dominating eyes.

Stop thinking about him!

Lady Huntford fixed on her eldest daughter, her voice snapping Joanna out of her daydream. 'It appears we have even more reason for you to try and impress him.'

'I don't see why. He's only the second son and it could be years before he inherits, if he does at all. A woman might waste her life waiting for nothing.' Frances crossed her arms over her chest in a huff.

Joanna balled her hands into fists at her sides, her nails biting into her palms. After last night, and the quick way Major Preston had defended her, Frances should be grateful. Joanna would give her eye teeth to be able to speak freely with him. All Frances could do was cast him aside and pout over her rake of a lieutenant. Her behaviour disgusted Joanna, but she buried it deep down, afraid it would show in what she did or said. Her one consolation was Major Preston having seen Frances's true personality. She doubted a man as honourable as he would take a genuine interest in a woman like Frances. Though if he didn't, why had he accepted the invitation? Lady Huntford had lamented the lack of a response from the Inghams for days. Joanna wondered what had changed his mind and if it had something to do with her.

Of course not. She was nothing to no one. Not even her mother or father, who'd cast her on the charity of Madame Dubois instead of raising her themselves, had wanted her. It was foolish to think the second son of an earl would defy his parents' and society's expectations to woo her. His concern for her well-being last night had been a fluke, like Catherine completing her French lessons without an argument yesterday. While Major Preston was staying at Huntford Place, he wasn't likely to be kind or attentive to Joanna, but to ignore her like everyone else did. There was no reason for him to behave differently when there'd be so many other eligible ladies here to hold his attention.

Lady Huntford gathered up her correspondence and beckoned her eldest daughter to follow her.

'Come along, we must choose the gowns you'll wear. We can't waste this opportunity.'

'What about me? Can I attend the house party?' Catherine sat up straighter in her chair in eager anticipation.

'Of course not. You're not out yet.'

'Even if you were, he isn't likely to favour you,' Frances sneered at her sister as she trudged after their mother.

Catherine slumped over her breakfast, struggling to hold back tears. Unlike her sister, Catherine had her father's dark hair and long face with thin lips which seemed perpetually fixed in a downtrodden frown. Her one blessing was lacking the petty streak which permanently marred her older sister's personality and beauty. At eighteen, Frances was only two years older than Catherine. Given their closeness in age they should have been friends, but Frances's churlish nature, and Catherine's more retiring one, discouraged it.

The grand clock in the entrance hall began to chime nine times.

'Come, girls, it's time for your French lesson,' Joanna urged, feeling sorry for Catherine and wanting to distract her from her sister's insults with activity.

'I'm too old to be hustled into the schoolroom by a governess.' Catherine's defiance weakened Joanna's pity.

Anne, the blonde seven-year-old, turned around and stuck her tongue out at Joanna. 'We'll tell you when it's time for our lessons.'

Ava, her twin sister, ignored Joanna and continued to eat her half-burned toast.

Joanna stared at the back of their three heads and the bows wound through their curls. The twins were no better behaved or obedient than their eldest sister. She wondered how she would get them to the schoolroom when, to her surprise, it was their father who interceded.

'Girls, get up at once and stop being contrary,' he commanded as he strolled into the room, his large, black hunting dog muddying the carpet as it trotted beside him.

With deep pouts the girls shoved away from the table and stood up to form something of a straight line in front of Joanna.

'That's how you command charges, Miss Radcliff,' Sir Rodger tossed at Joanna as he took his place at the head of the now-empty table. 'One would think you'd have learned such things at that school of yours.'

Joanna's cheeks burned at the insulting rebuke and the sniggering it elicited from the girls. After their father's public reprimand, they'd be even more difficult to deal with once they got back to the schoolroom.

Gruger, the withered old butler, shuffled in and tossed the London newspaper down beside his employer's plate with no attempt at ceremony. Sir Rodger didn't correct the surly man with the pocked and wrinkled face, but picked up the paper and snapped it open in front of his face. Gruger shuffled out, mumbling insults about the cook under his breath.

'Come along.' Joanna led the girls upstairs to another day of fighting to get them to obey her and to do their work. With each step up the curving staircase in need of a polish, past the maids gossiping while the ashes remained in the fireplaces, she wished she could slip off to her room and pour out her heart to Rachel, or Grace or Isabel like she used to do at the school. It wasn't likely anyone would notice her not working since half the staff hid in corners and shirked their duties, but what they did or didn't do wasn't her concern. Her pride in her work and her responsibility for the girls was what mattered and she would see to them, even if it proved as difficult as shooing Farmer Wilson's cow out of Madame Dubois's garden.

The single comfort she found in the long trudge down the halls kept dark to save on candles was the knowledge Major Preston would soon be here. While they crossed the second floor and made for the steep and unadorned third-floor stairs, her excitement faded. He wasn't coming to visit her, and even if he was she had no interest in a dalliance which might result in a child as Grace's had done. After the way he'd assisted her last night, she doubted he'd be anything but well behaved around her. Still, the strange feeling in her chest at the memory of him beside her at the ball made her wary. It wasn't so much his weakness she worried about, but her own. She'd already made one mistake in talking to him at Pensum Manor and allowing his kindness and humour to make her forget herself in a room full of people. She feared what might happen between the two of them during some chance meeting in a darkened hallway.

Nothing will happen. She was too sensible of her place and all Miss Fanworth's old warnings about gentlemen to be corrupted by a man's fine words. She would do her duty and if she found herself alone with him, she'd smile, nod and continue on her way, no matter how much she wanted him to flatter and protect her as he had at the ball.

Chapter Four

'Miss Radcliff.' Sir Rodger waved her over to him with a book as she came downstairs from the schoolroom. Frances and Catherine were upstairs with their mother discussing the house party while Ava and Anne were with their nurse, giving Joanna a brief rest from her duties.

'Yes, Sir Rodger?' She'd hope to take a walk in the garden. It appeared her plans were about to be waylaid by her employer. She wondered what he wanted of her. He'd barely said two words to her during her time here except to scold her in front of others or question the quality of her education.

'Since it appears you have nothing to occupy you at present, I'd like you to return this book to Vicar Carlson.' He handed her the tome, the blue cuff of his favourite coat sprinkled with food stains. With his wild grey hair frizzed out on either side of his head, he appeared more like some forgotten grandfather than a wealthy baronet. His dog sat beside him, its drool dripping on the stone floor. 'While you walk, think about how you can better manage the girls. I won't pay for a governess who has no control over my daughters. Do I make myself clear?'

Joanna's fingers dug into the leather binding. She wanted to tell him the girls' obstinacy wasn't her fault but his since he rarely reprimanded them. Instead, she summoned up her best prim-and-proper governess stance to answer with all the deference required of her position. 'Yes, Sir Rodger. I'll deliver the book at once and consider what you've said.'

She dipped a curtsy and walked away, indignity making her insides burn as she left the house and headed down the drive. Sir Rodger employed slothful maids, a crotchety butler and a cook who couldn't warm bread, yet he threatened to fire her? She snapped a thin branch off a poorly pruned topiary and swiped it at the air in front of her. It would take nothing short of an exorcism to drive out the wilful streak in the Huntford girls. She'd already employed every trick Madame Dubois and the other teachers had taught her, but nothing had worked. Without the support of their parents, there was little Joanna could do to make them mind. Her failure was almost assured.

She made the sharp turn on to the small path which led into the woods and to the narrow road traversing it. The woods covered the corner of land marking the boundaries between Huntford Place, Pensum Manor and Helmsworth Manor. She and the girls often walked here during their daily outings to study botany and geology. They were no more obedient outside than inside and it was always a chore to bring them home in time for supper, or with the twins not covered in mud.

Why didn't Madame Dubois better vet the Huntfords before she sent me here? Or perhaps she'd been so eager to relinquish responsibility for Joanna after nineteen years, she hadn't cared. Her parents hadn't cared when they'd left her on the school's doorstep as an infant without a clue as to who they were, so why should anyone else?

Joanna stumbled over a rock, the old rejection burning in her chest. It was an uncharitable thing to think of Madame Dubois who'd taken her in and been so kind to her, but she couldn't help it.

The loneliness which used to fill her every Christmas when the other girls would go home for the holidays while she remained at the school came over her again. The teachers had done their best to raise and guide her, but with so many students, Joanna had received no special attention, nor had she sought it. The teachers had always praised her for her independence, not realising it wasn't independence at all, but resignation. There hadn't been any point asking for something she wouldn't receive.

The teachers might not have cooed over her, but they'd imparted their knowledge to her, preparing her for her present position. Sadly, it was nothing like what she'd been led to believe it would be, or what she'd hoped. When she'd viewed the house from the mail coach on her first day here, she'd been so excited, expecting to at last experience what it was like to be a member of a true family. It had all been a silly dream, like the one she used to have about her mother returning to claim her.

Joanna flung the branch away. It would be a blow to her and the school if she was dismissed and forced to return to Salisbury without a reference. All the many years of effort, time and work Madame Dubois, Miss Fanworth and the other teachers had put into her would be ruined because of her inability to maintain her first position. In the end she might not have a choice but to leave. Sir Rodger had made his unrealistic expectation of her clear and she didn't see how she might meet it.

She reached the small brook cutting across a dip in the road and paused on the sloping and muddy bank. Further away, outside the woods, she could hear the river it came from rushing along its banks. A line of flat stones split the small current which ran clear, showing the smooth pebbles and mud at the bottom of the bed. She wanted to sit down on the bank, drop her head in her hands and watch the water flowing past until nothing else mattered.

No, I can't give up. There had to be a way to succeed, she only needed to find it and soon. She stepped on to the first rock and then the next one. She almost slipped off the third when it tilted beneath her weight. She threw out her arms to regain her balance, then hurried to the far bank. She didn't need wet boots on top of her present troubles.

Reaching the other side, her resolve began to fade. She didn't want to continue with this errand, or her time at Huntford Place. Finding a way to make the girls behave seemed as impossible as finding her mother, but she couldn't give up. She'd write to Miss Fanworth about what to do and ask her not to tell Madame. Perhaps she'd have some suggestions for Joanna.

In a clearing up ahead, the grey-stone vicarage with a tilted chimney releasing a tendril of pine-scented smoke came into view. Over the low roof rose the square spire of the church behind it, squat against the scattered clouds filling the September sky. This wasn't the church she and the family attended on Sunday in town, but a living on Helmsworth Manor which served the Marquis of Helmsworth, his staff and the tenants in the small village a mile off.

She heaved a large sigh as she entered the front garden, too upset to summon her usual steadfast cheerfulness. Let Vicar Carlson see her surly and ill-tempered, she didn't care. A tangle of chrysanthemums, mallow and weeds choked both sides of the slate walk leading to the sturdy door. She knocked lightly on the wood and listened for the answering footsteps of the vicar or a housekeeper from inside. The rustle of the wind through the surrounding trees were the only noises which greeted her.

She leaned off the steps to peer in the front window. Inside was as untidy as the garden with stacks of books piled on every surface. It appeared more like the messy studio of their old art master, Signor Bertolli, than the neat and orderly abode of a vicar. Leaning away from the window, she caught her pinched expression reflected in the glass.

Taking another deep breath, she forced the crease between her eyes to soften and the impassive look she'd perfected during the last four weeks at Huntford Place to return. No one needed to know anything was wrong with her, especially not a stranger. Even if they did, they wouldn't care. Few people gave a second thought to a lowly governess.

A few more minutes passed while she waited for someone to return. She tapped the book against her hand. It was clear there was no one here. She could leave the book on the step and be on her way, but she couldn't risk it being damaged. Sir

Rodger had given her an errand and she must do it well. She didn't want to fail at every task she'd been set to here in Hertfordshire.

She tucked her skirt under her legs, about to sit down and wait, when the whinny of a horse from behind the house caught her notice. She followed the vicarage around to the back. A horse was tied to a tree in the small graveyard between the house and the church. An older man stood before one of the headstones, staring down at the brown grass surrounding it. He was heavyset but tall, with grey hair slicked back above a proud forehead. Sadness left deep creases in the smooth skin and drew down the lines around his mouth, adding years to his face. He held his hat in one hand as he reached out to trace the etched and weathered headstone in front of him. It was pitched to one side from age, but the small bunch of violets laid on its curving top set it apart from the others.

He hadn't seen her and she didn't want to interrupt his contemplation. She was about to go, but he clenched his fist in his mouth in a stifled sob. She was afraid to approach him, to interrupt his grief, but she couldn't leave him alone any more than she could have the new girls who used to cry during their first night at the school.

She approached him, the dry grass crunching beneath her boots and announcing her presence. 'Are you all right, sir?'

'Yes, just an old man weeping over the past.' He rubbed the moisture from his eyes with his fingers then dropped his arm and at last looked at her.

Joanna gasped. His eyes were the same colour as hers and just as vivid.

'Jane?' he whispered, dropping his hat. His face went white beneath his grey hair with the same shock Isabel had worn the time she'd come down from the attic claiming to have spied a ghost. In the end it had been nothing more than an old dress dummy covered in dust.

'No, I'm Miss Radcliff, the new governess at Huntford Place.' Joanna was eager to ease his alarm the way she'd eased Isabel's.

He continued to stare at her and she studied his round face and the slender nose set over full lips. Something about him seemed familiar but she'd never seen the gentleman before.

'Of course you are, how silly of me.' The slight ruddiness along his cheeks returned as he plucked his hat off the ground and settled it over his hair. 'You must forgive an old man his foolishness. You reminded me of someone I loved very much.'

Joanna took a cautious step back.

'My daughter,' he clarified. 'You look very much like she did at your age, with the same hair and eyes. The resemblance is remarkable.'

He rubbed his round chin, his previous melancholy threatening to overcome him again.

'I'm so sorry to disturb you, but Sir Rodger asked me to return this book to Vicar Carlson. Do you know when he'll return?' Despite the stranger's kindly manner, she wanted to be done with this errand, to enjoy the solitude of the long walk back to Huntford Place. She needed the quiet to gather herself before she was thrust back into the pit of she-vipers and their indifferent parents.

'Vicar Carlson? Why, that's me.' He didn't seem too sure but it wasn't her place to question a clergyman.

She handed him the book. 'I won't disturb you any longer. I'll be on my way.'

'No, please stay. You seem troubled.'

She ran her foot over the patch of tall grass in front of her, trying to bite back the worries which had followed her through the forest. At school there'd always been Grace, Rachel or Isabel to commiserate with. She'd written to them, but with each of the girls facing their own trials in their new positions, she'd understated hers. She didn't want to burden them with her problems. She needed to speak to someone, anyone or she'd run mad.

'I'm having difficulty in my new position.' It was all she was willing to hazard with this stranger. 'The girls won't listen and Sir Rodger is threatening to dismiss me if I don't control them, but I can't.'

He winked at her. 'Dealing with the Huntford girls, I'm not surprised. They could use a firm hand and much better parenting. I had the entire brood at a Christmas party once, a long time ago when they were very young. They nearly tore up the music room with their wild behaviour.'

'The twins almost set the curtain in the sitting room on fire yesterday. They're unwieldy heathens.'

Vicar Carlson tossed back his head and let out a laugh as rich as a church bell.

She clapped her hand over her mouth, horrified

by what she'd just said. He might tell Sir Rodger and she'd find herself on the next mail coach to Salisbury. 'I'm sorry. I shouldn't talk about them so, but be grateful to have a position.'

She didn't feel grateful, but exhausted.

'Don't be sorry for speaking the truth. I promise I won't say a thing to Sir Rodger about his precious offspring,' he reassured her with all the authority of a man used to speaking from the pulpit. 'It's the duty of a vicar to help those who are burdened.'

'Burdened doesn't begin to describe it.' She paced back and forth, hands flapping at her sides with her agitation as she explained to him everything about her conversation with Sir Rodger. His willingness to listen unleashed the torrent of words she'd kept inside her for the past month. She even told him of Frances's two instances with Lieutenant Foreman and the impossible position she now found herself in. 'If I'm sent home, the people who cared about me the most will be disappointed.'

'You mean your family?' he prodded.

'I don't have a family, not a real one. My parents, whoever they were, left me for the school to raise when I was a baby,' she nearly whispered the words as she stopped to face him. It was the first time she'd admitted her illegitimacy to a stranger. It wasn't something Madame Dubois or any of the teachers had ever mentioned. A few days before leaving the school, Madame Dubois had cautioned her about revealing it in her new position, though the warning hadn't been necessary. Joanna knew how the world viewed illegitimate children. 'The teachers at the school raised me.'

'And you must be about nineteen?' He scrutinised her with the same curiosity as when they'd first met.

Joanna nodded, wondering what her age had to do with anything, but she didn't care. For the first time since her arrival in Hertfordshire, here was someone besides Major Preston who sympathised with her plight. Unlike the major, who was all but forbidden to speak to her, Vicar Carlson could listen and perhaps help. 'What am I going to do?'

'As someone who's supposed to guide his flock...' he flapped his hand at the church as though he wasn't certain this was his duty '...I'll tell you what you can do. Headstrong girls like to be in charge. Of course they can't be with the governess, but they'll try. The trick is to give them choices, but make sure they're deciding between two things you want.'

'Like studying French or Geography?'

'Exactly. Make them think they're in charge, even when they aren't.'

'I've never heard anything like this.' And if it helped, it might be her last hope of staying on and making Madame Dubois proud.

'I used to do it with my daughter, though it didn't always work.' He looked to the headstone with the violets. Sadness crossed over his expression like a cloud in front of the moon. 'After my wife died, I spoiled Jane. It made her headstrong. The older she grew, the more obstinate she became, like me.'

'I'm very sorry.'

He smiled at her, tender like the fathers used to be with their daughters before they left them at the school. 'Don't be. Her troubles are passed now, but yours aren't and we must focus on those.'

He offered her a few more suggestions on how to deal with the girls.

Then, in the distance, the bells from the village church began to ring. She didn't want to leave the vicar or the tranquillity of this corner of the world, but she must. 'I'm sorry, I have to go. Thank you so much for your help.'

'It was my pleasure. Please, feel free to return whenever you want. I'm often here reading during the day. I like the quiet. And good luck with your students.'

'Thank you and goodbye.'

Joanna hurried down the path towards Huntford Place. The shadows of the trees didn't consume her as they had on the walk here. It was the light coming through the branches she noticed instead. She didn't dread facing the girls, but looked forward to it with a new resolve, eager to try Vicar Carlson's suggestions, confident for the first time in days she might at last settle into her position.

She was well along the path when male voices from somewhere up around the bend caught her notice.

'Why are you trying to stop me from visiting him?'

'Because you don't understand the situation.'

Joanna crept cautiously forward and peeked around a thick oak tree in the bend of the road. Up ahead, two men had dismounted and now stood arguing while their horses grazed nearby. Joanna's fingers tightened on the smooth bark. It was Major Preston and his brother, Lord Pensum.

'If you expect me to linger in your shadow, doing nothing except waiting for providence to make me an earl, you're mistaken,' Major Preston countered.

'Now you know what it's like to be me.' His brother grabbed the reins of his horse from where they dangled below the animal's nose. Lord Pensum stepped into the stirrup and threw one leg over the top of his horse. 'You think I have all the advantage, but I don't. Then again you've never been able to look beyond yourself and all your need for aggrandisement to realise it.'

I shouldn't eavesdrop. Trying not to be seen, Joanna crept through the thick underbrush filling the U-shaped bend, determined to slip past the feuding brothers. She winced with each snapping twig and rustle of leaves, trying not to draw attention to herself, but it was almost impossible. She was just on the other side of the large oak tree, about to step onto the path, when someone grabbed her by the waist and pulled her back. Lord Pensum galloped by on his grey horse, narrowly missing her as she hit the solid chest of the man behind her.

'Are you all right?' Major Preston's chin brushed her temples as he spoke, his voice as tight as her insides.

His firm arm against Joanna's stomach made her heart beat faster than the near collision with the horse. She leaned deeper into him and his fingers twitched against her hip. She reached behind her, ready to grasp his thighs and steady herself like she would against a wall after a shock. Before her fingertips could touch the buckskin of his breeches, she clutched the side of her dress, her breath catching as he shifted against her. She peered up into his dark eyes made more severe by the alternating shadows and sunlight piercing the branches overhead. If she tilted her head, closed her eyes, she might experience his firm lips against hers.

'Miss Radcliff?' Major Preston nudged, easing his hold on her.

'Yes, I'm fine.' She stumbled out of his grasp, mortified at almost losing her head over him. 'Much better, in fact, for not being ground into the forest floor.'

'I'm glad I could keep you from becoming one with the fallen leaves.' He smiled as he bent over to pluck his hat off a bush. His breeches pulled tight over his buttocks when he dipped down then rose, towering over her like the oak above them. 'May I escort you back to Huntford Place?'

Joanna jerked her attention from his thighs to his face. To walk with him would mean the opportunity to listen to his commanding voice and enjoy more of the conversation they'd indulged in last night. It also risked them being seen together. It might be innocent, but people wouldn't regard it as such and her position with the Huntfords was already at risk.

'I can't.' She slipped through the last few brambles to return to the path. 'I must be getting back.'

'I promise to only go as far as the edge of the woods, and then I'll leave you to continue on. I wouldn't want to place your reputation or employment in jeopardy.'

She hesitated. Being alone with him was dangerous, but she wanted companionship and something pleasant before she returned to the annoyance of her work. 'Yes, company would be lovely, especially if any more galloping horses should happen by.'

'Then allow me to fetch mine so we'll be equally matched should we encounter any.' He laughed as he pushed through the brush. The stiff branches raked his long legs before he slipped behind the tree. He soon rounded the turn, leading a large white horse with a patch of brown above his nose.

'A magnificent animal,' she remarked. 'Not at all the mill-horse you painted him to be at the ball.'

'Careful what you say around Duke, I don't want it going to his head. He's already difficult enough to control.' He patted the animal's side and it gave an indignant snort.

'I don't believe a word he says about you.' She reached up to stroke Duke's long nose, making the skin beneath his hair twitch.

'Now you've done it, he won't listen to me for the rest of the day.' He clicked the horse into a walk and the three of them set off towards Huntford Place.

They walked side by side in silence, the twittering birds and the rustle of leaves settling in between them. It wasn't an awkward or uncomfortable quiet, but familiar, as though this wasn't the first time they'd enjoyed the forest alone together. With each of his sure steps, Joanna was keenly aware of the shift of his muscles, the crinkle of his leather gloves as he tightened or loosened his grip on the reins. It wasn't the easy movements of a man at peace, but the constant fidgeting of one with something on his mind. Whatever troubled him, it was none of her business. However, she hadn't been this conscious of another person since the nights at school when she could tell which one of her friends was upset by their constant turning beneath the coverlet, or a sob stifled by a pillow. She couldn't pretend to ignore his difficulties any more than she could have her friends'.

'I didn't mean to intrude on you and your brother,' she offered. 'Is everything well?'

'It is.' Major Preston banged his hat against his thigh to free it of dust and leaves. 'Except we differ on how to resolve a long-standing conflict with Lord Helmsworth.'

'Is it massive enough to divide brothers?'

'It is when it threatens the income of Pensum Manor.' He turned his hat over in his hands, pausing before he settled it down on his hair. 'Miss Radcliff, what I'm about to tell you isn't commonly known and would, like the revealing of Miss Huntford's secret, do a great deal of damage to my family.'

'I won't tell anyone.' She wouldn't do anything to harm him. He'd been too kind to her, and the thrill of being taken into his confidence was as powerful at the grip of his hand on the reins.

He explained to her the dispute about the land as his feet covered the imprints of his brother's horse's hooves in the packed dirt. 'My family isn't as wealthy as we've allowed society to believe. My brother is worried that if we reveal our desperate need for access to the river on the disputed land, Lord Helmsworth might use the information to place pressure on our creditors to strangle us.'

'Is he really so mean?' She'd heard a little about him from Sir Rodger and Lady Huntford. He seemed more eccentric than spiteful, preferring to keep to himself at his estate and never venturing to London.

'Not the gentleman I remember from his Christmas parties when I was a boy. He changed after his daughter's death. It made him irascible and less willing to listen to reason, like Edward.' He plucked a thorn from his breeches and flicked it away. 'My brother thinks I can come home, sit around and watch the seasons change, but I can't. He's been handed everything by right of birth, he doesn't understand what it is to earn achievement or what it gives to a man, and what it's like to leave it all behind.'

'Maybe he does realise it and that's why he fights with you.' They came to a narrow pass in the path between two large yew trees. He stopped to let her go ahead before joining her with Duke. 'Perhaps he wonders if he's worthy of having so much responsibility placed on him because he's the heir and not because he's earned it. Failing to have a child might reinforce his lack of value beyond his place of honour in your family?'

He didn't answer straight away, but it was clear from the slight twist of his lips that he was mulling over what she'd said. It would be nice to think she might make a difference to someone while she was here. The Huntford girls certainly weren't benefiting from her presence.

'I suppose it's possible. I've never considered it from his perspective.' Duke's harness jingled as he tossed up his head before settling back into his steady gait. Luke switched the reins to his other hand and patted the horse's neck.

'Perhaps if you put your grievances against him aside, he might, too. After all, it takes two people to maintain a quarrel.'

He met her eyes, the brown in them appearing lighter with his earnestness. 'What you suggest isn't easy to do, not after so many years.'

'It might be easier if you appreciate how fortunate you are to have him. Not all of us have family to argue with. Sometimes, when Frances and Catherine are sniping at each other, I want to grab them by their scruffs and shake them until they realise how lucky they are to have one another.' She raised her fists before her as if she held the girls. Then she opened her fingers and dropped her arms to her sides. 'All I've ever had were the teachers and my friends.'

'What happened to your parents?'

'They died when I was very young.' She didn't dare tell him she knew nothing about them. She never had. They'd left her on the school's front steps with only the ripped piece of paper with her name on it and a blanket. She'd learned long ago not to ask Madame Dubois about them since there were no details Madame Dubois could give her and nothing she could do to change the truth. 'They entrusted me to the teachers to raise.'

'Then the school has succeeded.' He fixed her with an appreciative smile which made her prouder than when she'd won first prize for French. 'You're a very wise young lady, Miss Radcliff. Miss Huntford doesn't realise how lucky she is to have you.'

'I don't think she viewed my interrupting her liaison, or any of my efforts to influence her, as lucky.'

'It's certainly something to write to your headmistress about.' He laughed, the deep sound silencing the birds.

'Heavens, no.' She didn't want Madame to believe anything was wrong here, or to think Joanna wasn't living up to her expectations. It was better to pretend everything was well and not to complain. There was little anyone could do about it even if she did.

They reached the brook and Major Preston led his horse across, skipping every other stone while Duke splashed through the water beside him. Once on the far side, Major Preston turned the horse in a wide circle to watch her cross. 'Do you need my help?'

'No, I can manage.' Joanna took up the hem of her dress and stepped onto the first stone. She fixed on him as she moved to the next one. The force of his presence drew her across the water more than the need to return to her duties. She envied whatever lady caught his interest at the house party for she'd be very lucky to have him for a husband. Marriage and a family were so far outside Joanna's reach, she didn't dare imagine obtaining it, especially not with a man like Major Preston.

Her foot landed on the loose stone in the middle, pitching her forward. In a flash, Major Preston rushed to her, catching her about the waist before she could hit the jagged rocks sticking up out of the stream bed. Her back arched over his forearm as they stayed linked together above the splashing water. She grasped his arms, bracing herself against the anticipation building deep inside her from the pressure of his fingers against her back. Staring up into his concerned face, the blue sky bright above him, for the first time she understood why Grace had given in to her urges, despite the risks. A moment with a man like Major Preston could make a woman forget the danger of his touch and his flattery.

She didn't move, nor did he try to right her. As they held on to one another, the flowing water indifferent to them, she wondered if what she'd thought impossible a few steps ago might be within her grasp. Even if it was, surrendering to him would mean defying everyone and every responsibility waiting for them outside these woods, and there was no guarantee the passion would last. Duty to his family commanded him, as did her duty to Madame Dubois. They might withstand it for a short while, but eventually it would wear away at them like the water did the mud under the loose stone.

'It seems I'm meant to protect you from a number of dangers today.' His frown eased into a smile. 'Are you all right?'

'Yes.' The forest spun as he righted her. *No.* She wasn't the same Joanna who'd started across the stream.

He held her hand as he led her over the remaining stones to the bank. Leather and cotton gloves separated their skin, but it couldn't smother the heat of his firm grip which drove away the cold which had surrounded her since her first day in Hertfordshire.

On the other side he let go and she straightened her pelisse from where his grasp had twisted it and silently shook herself out of her foolishness. There was no connection between them, there never had been and there never could be.

The bells of the church rang out over the countryside again, marking the quarter-hour, and panic replaced the fading passion, making her stomach flutter.

'I must get back at once.' With half a forest between her and Huntford Place, she wasn't sure how she'd reach the house in time to collect Catherine from the drawing master or the twins from their nurse.

'It'll be quicker if we ride.' He stepped into the saddle and tossed his thick leg over the curving leather. With his back erect and his feet set firmly in the stirrups, he was the very image of the gallant knights she'd read about in so many stories. Then he held out his hand to her, entreating her to join him.

She hesitated, as shocked by his offer as the muscular curve of his arm beneath his fawn-coloured coat. The young maids in her old books might have won the hearts of princes, but this wasn't a fairy tale. Nothing in her life was. She should run for the house, but her feet wouldn't move. Instead, she slipped her hand in his and raised her foot to cover his in the stirrup. With a powerful tug, he pulled her up so fast she let out a surprised yelp before he settled her across the saddle in front of him.

Their closeness made her dizzier than being up so high. She held on to the edge of the leather saddle as he slipped his arms on either side of her, took up the reins and kicked the horse into a canter. The wind whipped her cheeks, dampening the heat spilling through her from the steady rocking of their bodies together in motion with the stallion beneath them. Each landing of the horse's hooves against the ground made Major Preston's chest press deeper into her shoulders. She'd never experienced something as thrilling as riding this fast, or having Major Preston behind her. His breath caressed her cheek as he stared straight on. His thighs were solid beneath her, every shift of his muscles as he commanded the animal radiating up through her skirt. His arms kept her anchored in front of him, stiff and tight with his control of the reins. The horse turned and she lost her grip on the smooth leather. Without thinking, she clutched his leg to steady herself and felt the low rumble of a groan through his chest. She was too afraid to fall, to snap herself out of this dream to let go, or do anything but sink into him and the steady, rocking gait carrying them through the woods.

The trees were a whirl of green, gold and brown on either side of them as the horse hurried on. Then at last they began to thin and the faint outline of Huntford Place appeared through the naked branches up ahead. The red brick was dulled by years of dirt and weather and covered by ivy turning brown with the coming winter. Joanna sat up straighter in the saddle as Major Preston tugged the horse into a walk, ending the heady exhilaration of their ride.

'I'll leave you here.' He pulled the horse to a halt and leaned into her one last time before dismounting. He reached up and she slid into his outstretched hands, exhaling as he gripped her hard about the waist. As her feet touched the ground, the horse shifted, knocking her into his chest. She clutched his waist to steady herself and his fingers stiffened on her. The pungent scent of leather and cedar clung to him, heightened by the subtle press of his hips against hers. Her insides ached with their closeness and she wished she could climb back up in the saddle with him and be like Grace and ignore all the consequences, but she couldn't. Despite Grace having been so happy during those brief months with her young man, in the end her passion had caused her more heartache than joy. The same thing would happen to Joanna if she forgot herself with Major Preston. Things were difficult enough without her making them worse.

Joanna stepped out of his grasp, recovering her sense of decorum. 'Thank you, Major Preston, for everything, but I must go.'

'Don't allow Miss Huntford or any of them to push you around, or make you feel low,' he encouraged. 'You're better and smarter than any of them.'

She shrugged. 'And yet they pay my wages.'

'Which, if I know Sir Rodger, are poor.'

She couldn't stop the laugh which sprang out of her. 'Beyond meagre.'

'Then you have little to lose by telling Sir Rodger the truth about what his progeny are up to?'

She sobered at his suggestion. 'You're wrong. I have a great deal to lose by telling him things he doesn't wish to hear.'

'There were many senior officers who didn't want to hear what I had to say and I still told them. It benefited me, and them, more than it hurt me. It could do the same for you.'

'Says a gentleman with family and some station. We aren't all so fortunate.'

Instead of chastising her for rebuking him, he smiled as though he'd won a victory. 'I was worried they'd crush someone as insightful and genuine as you, but I see you have great strength. You'll do well, Miss Radcliff, I have no doubt of it.'

She didn't share his confidence and, with a half-smile of regret, she hurried off to the house. The closer she drew to it, the more the delight of being with Major Preston faded. Despite his faith in her, and Vicar Carlson's suggestions, she wasn't sure all would be well. Major Preston was correct, she should speak up about the girls' behaviour, but she couldn't. Isabel used to speak up and all it ever did was get her in trouble. It wasn't like Joanna to do the same and she wouldn't. Silence had served her well in the past and it would do so again. It would allow her to keep her position and make Madame Dubois proud.

Luke didn't call Miss Radcliff back. In the Army, he'd been governed by the hours of camp life and regulations. He might be done with them now, but Miss Radcliff wasn't free of those commanding her. Luke stepped back into Duke's saddle, but didn't ride for home until Miss Radcliff was out of the woods, across the lawn and inside Huntford Place. Even then he lingered, watching the dark and obscured windows, hoping to catch another glimpse of her. All borrowed traces of the debutante from last night had been scrubbed from her as she'd stood in a sturdy grey pelisse and half-boots, but it hadn't dimmed her natural beauty. It wasn't the wisdom she'd offered him which kept him riveted to the old house, but the impression of her body against his. It left him so agitated it made Duke dance and snort beneath him.

When he'd grabbed her by the waist in the woods, he'd thought of nothing but saving her from being struck by Edward's horse. When she'd pressed back into him, her buttocks shifting against his thighs as she'd peered up at him, her rose-coloured lips parted in surprise and wanting, he'd almost forgotten himself. Once he'd let go of her, he'd dismissed his reaction as the natural response of a man to a beautiful woman after so much time without one. Then she'd tripped on the rock.

He opened and closed his fingers over the reins, the weight of the leather insignificant compared to the memory of Miss Radcliff in his arms. Her near pitch into the water had frightened him the way one of his men rushing headlong into a barrage used to do. He'd wanted to protect her from the sharp rocks as much as he wanted to shield her from the petty meanness of the Huntfords, but he couldn't, nor was it his place to do so.

He jerked Duke round and kicked him into a gallop. The tightness of his thighs against the horse's flanks, his body hunched low over the animal's neck, helped stave off the tension coiling inside him. The weight of Miss Radcliff, the arch of her back over his arm had been as natural as his coat across his shoulders. Her stunning blue eyes had held his, sparkling like the water flowing behind her. It had taken every ounce of strength he'd possessed to set her upright and lead her to the bank instead of claiming her lips, but he'd had no choice. He wasn't Lieutenant Foreman, ready to ruin a young lady of lesser rank to satisfy his desires, nor would he allow emotion to guide him. Even in the heat of battle he'd made every decision based on facts, the lay of the land, the strength of his troops and the French's, not fear or panic. He'd do the same here.

Up ahead, the road forked. Luke pulled Duke to a stop, making the horse rear up at the sudden command before dropping down on to all fours. The path going left led to Lord Helmsworth's. The one pointing right went back to Pensum Manner. His brother's accusations, the desire to show Edward he was wrong and for Luke to achieve something of merit while he was here almost made him turn left. Edward was the one person who could undermine Luke's sense of reason and make him react with his gut instead of his logic. Today it was Luke's command over his emotions as much as Miss Radcliff's advice about family which made Luke tug Duke to the right and head for home. It would sting like hell to endure Edward's glee at Luke not meeting with Lord Helmsworth, but he'd let him rejoice and not say a word. Miss Radcliff was right, it was time to focus on what was important and end the old rivalry. Luke might not have returned home on his terms, but he'd returned. It was more than the many men lying in graves in Spain could say. Besides, there was always tomorrow to approach Lord Helmsworth and perhaps see Miss Radcliff again.

Lord Johan Helmsworth strode through the massive front doors of Helmsworth Manor. The meeting with the young lady in the graveyard had nagged at him during the entire ride home. Her image continued to haunt him beneath the frieze of Apollo in the entrance hall, past the paintings of the former Marquises filling the long main hall. Half of them watched him with the vivid blue eyes so prevalent in the family, Miss Radcliff's eyes.

He clasped his hands behind his back and knocked the single ring he wore on each hand together in time to his steps. In Miss Radcliff's trusting, oval face, he'd caught a glimpse of his past. Memories of carrying Jane high on his shoulders while he'd showed her the horses in the stable rushed back to him as strong as the smell of cut hay in the fields carrying in through the open windows. When he'd sat with Miss Radcliff, giving her advice, it had reminded him of the time he'd sat with his daughter explaining to her how the little spaniel she'd loved was gone, not destined to live as long as her. In the end, she hadn't lived as long as she should have either.

He paused in the hallway and rested one hand on a side table to brace himself. The pain was as fresh today as nineteen years ago when she'd passed. It didn't send him into dark moods like it used to, but it still hadn't eased after all this time.

The shifting of papers in the study up ahead forced him to take hold of himself. Straightening, he took a deep breath and strode inside.

'Lord Helmsworth, you've returned. We need to discuss the issue of the property dispute with the Inghams,' Mr Browning, the bespectacled solicitor, greeted, setting aside a leather satchel filled with the business he intended to discuss with Johan during their regular meeting. 'I received a letter from Major Preston. He'd like to speak with you in regards to the issue of the river land.'

'The young whelp returns home and thinks he can fix twenty years of troubles,' Johan grumbled, in no mood to entertain the Inghams' whining on today of all days.

'This issue has gone on for entirely too long.'

'And it will continue. I won't have one of those Inghams in here thinking he can steal my land from me, no matter how many medals he wears.' He thumped the top of a burled escritoire as he passed it. 'I lost enough to an Army man nineteen years ago. I won't lose more.'

Johan stopped in the centre of the room and stared up at the portrait of his daughter and wife together in front of a view of the columned entrance to Helmsworth Manor. It had been painted the year before his wife had died, when Jane was eight. Beside it was a small portrait of Jane at seventeen, the year she'd come out. She was resplendent in her pink gown, the sash of which curled around her shoulders as if caught in a breeze. She smiled with all the expectation of a young lady poised to find her place in society. It was a far cry from the one who'd stood in here railing at him a mere six months later. They'd argued fiercely after Johan had withheld his permission for Jane to marry. Being under twenty-one, she'd needed it. Unlike her, Johan had seen through Captain Handler's designs on her and her fortune and had cut her off, hoping it would end things. It had only made her more obstinate in her desire for the wretched man and her stubbornness had increased his. All Johan's attempts to make her listen and obey had, in the end, driven her to run away with the Captain. He hadn't wanted to deny her love, but to keep her safe from the heartbreak and ruin she'd ultimately suffered. He'd failed.

The old guilt washed over him, joined by another. He shouldn't have impersonated a man of the cloth, or lied to Miss Radcliff simply to speak with her, but it had been necessary. If he'd revealed his true identity, Miss Radcliff would've dipped curtsies as though he were a king, mumbled her apologies and kept quiet. The young lady had spoken with him like Jane used to do before she'd turned against him in favour of the wicked spendthrift Captain Handler.

'Let's get to our business.' The leather armchair by the fire crinkled beneath Johan's weight as he sank into it. He motioned for Mr Browning to take the less worn one across from him.

The solicitor obliged, setting his satchel on the floor beside him and removing a few papers. 'Lord Faston has vacated the London town house. I'll advertise for a new tenant, unless you intend to go to London soon. I understand Parliament is poised to convene a special session to deal with the Luddite uprisings in the north.'

'I haven't taken my seat in the House of Lords for nearly twenty years. I have no intention of doing so now. Go ahead and let it,' Johan answered with a flick of his hand, unwilling to reside in the London house even for the King. The stately home in Grosvenor Square had been his wife's before she'd married him and he'd retained it partly for the rent, but mostly because he couldn't bear to let it go. He'd intended it as a wedding present for Jane. How he wished his wife had been alive to guide their daughter through the pitfalls of men and balls. Johan hadn't had the talent for it.

'You seem troubled, my lord. Is there anything I may do?' The fortyish Mr Browning had assumed his father's clients when the elder man, who'd been with Johan for years, had at last grown too old to oversee the affairs. The son was sharp and as good a sounding board as his father had been.

'I had a strange encounter today.' Johan pressed his fingertips together in front of his face. 'I met a young woman while I was at the vicarage. The instant I saw her, I thought she was Jane. You would've, too, if you'd seen her. She had Jane's eyes, the Helmsworth eyes.'

The papers went limp in Mr Browning's hands. 'A girl with the Helmsworth eyes?'

'Yes. The resemblance was remarkable.' And unsettling. He'd gone to the graveyard as he always did on Jane's birthday. He hadn't expected to be startled by what he'd first thought was a ghost, nor had he been afraid. For a moment he'd rejoiced, thinking the longed-for reconciliation would finally come to pass. Then the sweet young girl had proven she was as real as him.

'What was her first name?' Mr Browning asked, sliding forward on to the edge of his seat.

'I don't know, she only told me she is Miss Radcliff.'

'How old was she?'

'Nineteen.'

The room grew quiet, filling with the crackle of the fire in the grate. Mr Browning, for the first time in a long time, did not continue with his business or offer Johan advice. Johan regarded the man who sat staring at the flames. He was deep in contemplation, fingers against his chin, and it wasn't over leases or rent.

'What is it, Mr Browning?' Johan prodded.

The solicitor dropped his hand and faced his employer, more serious than Johan had ever seen him before. 'There's something I must tell you, Lord Helmsworth. Afterwards, you may view me, your daughter and everything in a different light.'

The younger man had been friends with Jane in her youth, one of the few gentlemen Johan had trusted around his headstrong daughter once she'd entered society. Mr Browning had been too in love with the woman who'd become his wife for Johan to worry about his falling for Jane. He wondered if he'd been mistaken about the young man. 'Then don't tell me. I'm burdened with enough troubles already.'

'I must, because I can't help but feel it somehow involves what you've told me about the young lady you encountered.'

Johan picked at the nail-head trim on the arm of his chair. 'How so?'

Mr Browning cleared his throat once, then again

before at last finding his voice. 'Lord Helmsworth, the day before Jane died, she summoned me on the pretext of preparing her will. During our interview, she told me the truth about her illness. She didn't die of an infectious fever, but childbed fever. A few days before she'd returned to you, she'd given birth to a little girl. It was why she wouldn't allow Dr Scopes to examine her when she fell ill. She was afraid he would notice. She hadn't realised the severity of her illness.'

Johan's fingers dug into the cracked leather as the room around him shook with the man's revelation. Jane had had a child and she hadn't told him. He sank back against the chair, the distance between him and his precious daughter seeming to reopen. 'Why didn't she tell me?'

Mr Browning tapped his knee, pausing before he continued. 'I urged her to, but she refused, afraid you'd reject her again. She thought she would recover and then once you two were properly reconciled, she could reveal the truth to you. Despite your objections to Captain Handler, and your falling out, she never stopped loving you. She even named her baby girl Joanna, after you.'

Johan dropped his head in his hands and closed

his eyes, struggling to hold back his anguish. Even in the end when her life had been in peril, she'd still held back from him, afraid he would push her away again. Losing Jane had ripped his heart from him. Having her come home to die a few days later had left the rift between them unsettled for good, until now. He looked up at the younger man. 'What happened to the baby?'

'I don't know. Captain Handler was killed in battle in Europe before he and Jane could marry, leaving her with child and penniless in Austria. She found her way back to England, landing in Portsmouth. She had the child somewhere near Salisbury and entrusted it to an officer's wife who'd helped her in her travails before Jane continued on to here. She'd hoped after reconciling with you to return for the baby, but she never had the chance. It was her dying wish I find the child and see to its future. I did my best, but the officer's wife, Mrs White, had left with her husband to rejoin his regiment in Austria. Her husband died in battle. I don't know what happened to Mrs White, or the child. I'd intended to find the girl and bring her to your attention, but when I was unable to discover anything and you being in such deep mourning, I didn't wish to make matters worse.'

Johan understood and couldn't blame the solicitor for acting the way he had. It had been a year after Jane's death before he'd been able to leave Helmsworth Manor, his grief consuming him until his sister, and many others, feared he might harm himself. To discover there'd been a granddaughter, one he couldn't find, might have pushed him over the edge he'd feared crossing for so long.

He was no longer the same broken and sad father, but an old man in his dotage who could right some of the old wrongs.

'I want you to investigate Miss Radcliff's background and see if there's any connection between her and this Mrs White. If I have a granddaughter, whether she's legitimate or not, I want to know about it.' He'd failed Jane during the last year of her life, driving her away with his anger. He would do right by her child.

Chapter Five

Joanna watched from the third floor schoolroom window as Lady Huntford's house party guests began to arrive. Behind her, the girls sat around the table reading aloud from a French grammar book. A line of carriages stood in the drive, the horses kicking up pebbles and dust. One by one, each vehicle pulled up to the door and discharged its passengers, who greeted Lady Huntford and Frances with smiles, hugs and loud chatter.

Huntford Place was not very large and neither was the house party. Judging by the women in attendance, Lady Huntford had chosen the plainest ladies of Frances's age to give Frances the advantage. A smile crept over Joanna's lips. If Lady Huntford knew how little regard Major Preston held for her daughter, she wouldn't have gone to so much expense or bother, but Joanna wasn't about to tell her. The woman was cutting enough in her censure without Joanna voluntarily risking more.

She rubbed the back of her stiff neck, trying to drive away her exhaustion. All night she'd lain awake in her attic room, staring at the slanted and water-stained ceiling and thinking of Major Preston and his impending arrival. The memory of his firm chest against her back had bothered her more than the lumps in the mattress. She dropped her arm and tried to recollect their conversation and not the more physical aspects of their meeting the other day. He'd considered her opinions as though they'd mattered, despite the difference in their stations, making her feel valued for the first time in a long time. Her desire to experience it again, and the frustration of knowing she couldn't, had kept her awake until the darkness outside her window had begun to lighten.

She'd risen before the sun and set out into the Huntford Place garden for a walk, determined to settle her tumbling thoughts. Any hope of dealing with the girls or continuing to implement Vicar Carlson's ideas had depended on her regaining control over herself, and she had, until the Inghams' carriage rolled into view.

They were the last to arrive and, as their black carriage came to a stop at the front door, the top of it almost brown with road dust, the crowd waiting to greet them swelled. All the eligible young ladies and their mothers clustered around the front entrance while their fathers and brothers remained cloistered in Sir Rodger's study, probably drinking port and listening to him complain about the expense of the weekend party.

Joanna touched the cold glass separating her from the outside and held her breath as the door to the carriage opened. Lady Ingham stepped out first and Joanna near groaned in disappointment. Lady Ingham was followed by Lord Ingham, then Lord and Lady Pensum, and they all made for their hostess. Major Preston was the last to appear.

He didn't look at the swooning crowd of young ladies on the front steps. With one hand, he shaded his eyes against the late morning sun cresting the roof and gazed up the long front of the Stuart-era house.

He's searching for me.

The voices of the girls reciting their French at

the table behind Joanna faded. She stared down at him, not sure if he could see her. She wanted to push open the window and call out to him, or at the very least wave, but she remained still, her fingers stiff on the sill. He was here and she was trapped away like a fairy princess in a tower. Except she wasn't a damsel a man of his rank might fight for, but a servant.

Lady Huntford stepped forward, eager to pull Major Preston into the circle of her influence. She flicked a quick glance up, trying to see what he did. Joanna jumped back from the window before her employer could notice her. It was a warning to Joanna to mind herself while he was here. Major Preston was not for her.

'What's wrong with you?' Catherine asked from the schoolroom table. The commencement of the house party had increased the girl's petulance and made Joanna's job even more difficult today. 'You act as if you've seen a ghost.'

'Perhaps, I did. Mrs Winston tells me there are all sorts of spirits in this house, especially close to your room.' Joanna tapped Catherine playfully on her long nose.

Catherine's eyes widened in horror before she

brushed Joanna's hand away. 'That's just the nurse's excuses for not coming up here to make sure the maids have cleaned.'

'I hope you're right. Now finish, it's almost time for our botany lesson in the garden.'

She strode around the table to check the twins' French grammar, doing her best to put Major Preston out of her head. Unless Lady Huntford asked Joanna to be Frances's chaperon during some event, there would be very little interaction between Joanna and any of the guests. As she leaned over to correct Ava's verb conjugation, bringing an irritated wrinkle to the girl's forehead, Joanna prayed she'd be called on to chaperon.

Luke climbed the stairs, following the footmen carrying the portmanteaus for him and the other three bachelors who'd been invited to the weekend party. They were the brothers of the young ladies being trotted out for Luke's inspection. These men were welcome to them. Unless one of the ladies demonstrated more character than they had in the front drive, Luke wasn't likely to find a wife here. The weekend had barely begun and already it felt like a waste, except for the chance to encounter Miss Radcliff.

Despite reaching each corner of Huntford Place and expecting to find her on the other side, he'd convinced himself her presence in the house made no difference to him. He was wrong. She was the entire reason he was here and it was a mistake. His family needed him to marry a woman with money, not be distracted by the governess.

He paused on the stairs to take in the house. The wooden banister beneath his hand was rough from too much use and too few polishes while the sun coming in through the leaded diamond windows along the staircase highlighted the faded carpet beneath his boots. With parts of Pensum Manor in need of refurbishing, Luke couldn't complain too much about the lack of upkeep in Huntford Place. What he could complain about was the lazy footmen commanded by the indifferent butler. The lanky men in their tired livery dumped his and the other gentlemen's things in each room as Gruger with his bent shoulders, pointed nose and sprouting head of grey hair, unceremoniously threw open the four bedroom doors at the end of the hall near the stairs leading to the upper floors.

'I've seen better accommodations in an Army camp,' Luke grumbled aloud at the doorway to his room, his hands on his hips in disapproval of his portmanteau lying on its side in front of the narrow bed.

'Wait until dinner.' A light female voice carried over him. 'I'm sure your camp cooks provided better food, too.'

He turned to find Miss Radcliff standing on the landing behind him in a most proper governess attitude. She held her hands tight in front of her, back straight, shoulders set, ready to rebuke anyone who dared to step out of line. The seriousness of her stance was betrayed by the impish smile softening her face which echoed with the sprightliness he'd enjoyed in the woods. It undermined her stern control as much as the twins behind her tugging at one another in an argument while their elder sister made moon eyes at Mr Chilton.

She turned and let out an exasperated sigh. 'Girls, mind your manners.'

The twins took one last swipe at each other before settling into their line. Even the older girl wandered back to her place, tearing her besotted gaze off Mr Chilton as he closed the door, his grumbling about his room as audible as Luke's.

'Out to the garden, girls,' Miss Radcliff instructed, leading her charges to the stairs like a mother hen does her brood, except the girls were far more wayward than compliant chicks.

'I'm not a girl,' the oldest one complained.

'Stop pulling my bow,' one of the twins whined before hitting her sister hard on the arm.

'Good luck,' Luke called after her, stepping up to the banister and leaning over it.

She peered at him over one shoulder, her eyes highlighted by her dark lashes and white skin. She mouthed 'Thank you' with her pretty lips before she ran out the door after her wild pupils.

Luke thumped the creaking railing, pondering a walk in the garden instead of setting his things to right in his room. He hadn't brought a valet. After seeing to himself in the Army, he didn't see the need to bother or to incur the expense. With the younger Huntford girls present and the excuse of exploring the grounds, Luke might enjoy a few moments of conversation with Miss Radcliff.

Luke turned to fetch his redingote, then stopped. Mr Selton leaned against the door frame to his room with a smirk of congratulations as if he'd surprised Luke in the pantry with a comely maid. Luke's experience with the tall young man with a face as pocked as a church carving was limited, but it was clear he'd noticed the exchange with Miss Radcliff and taken it for more than a friendly greeting. Luke silently dared him to say something about either him or Miss Radcliff. Mr Selton didn't meet the challenge, but pushed away from the wood, strolled into his room and closed the door.

Luke strode into his room and to the one long window on the far side with a view of the barren front drive. His frustration with coming here was beginning to rival that of his coming home. The one woman whose time he wanted the most was the one woman he must avoid. If a brief exchange could capture the attention of Mr Selton, Luke being seen with her in the garden might create a scandal. In the future, he'd have to better mind himself in her presence.

'Why must Frances have all the fun while I'm stuck here?' Catherine flung a stone in the algae-filled goldfish pond in the centre of the garden.

The twins were busy pulling up long weeds and whacking each other with them. Joanna didn't stop them, hoping they'd wear themselves out and be a little more compliant when they returned to the schoolroom.

'When you come out next year, you'll be able to enjoy things like house parties.' Joanna glanced again at the French doors leading into the back sitting room, hoping to see Major Preston emerge from the house, but there was no one there. With the twins screaming like banshees, no adult was likely to venture into the garden. She should be glad. No matter how jovial he was, or how handsome he appeared in his dark blue coat, it wasn't her position to speak with him.

'Father isn't likely to spend the money on a Season for me. He's never done anything for me, only for Frances,' Catherine despaired, her head lowered in defeat. 'You don't know what it's like to be ignored. No one will ever love me.'

I know exactly what it's like. But this wasn't about her and her troubles, but those of her charge.

'Keep your chin up,' Joanna encouraged, using her fingers to lift the girl's crestfallen head. She pitied the young woman. Unlike her sister, Catherine's petulance was not from being spoiled, but from a lack of attention. 'Remember, a kind word and a pleasant personality will attract a gentleman as much as beauty.'

'How can you be sure?'

The image of Major Preston at the ball came to her. He'd had so many ladies to choose from for conversation, yet he'd singled her out. It wasn't because of money, or looks, but for a much deeper and more meaningful reason she'd caught in the holding of his breath as he'd cradled her over the stream. 'I've seen it happen more than once. Besides, when Frances finally finds a husband, your mother will have no one to dote on except you.'

'Mother doesn't dote, at least not on me.'

'But she'll help you find a husband. It's a mother's duty to do so.' Joanna smiled, encouraging Catherine to do the same. Deep inside, Joanna wanted to mope as much as the girl. As dismissive as Lady Huntford was to Catherine, she would guide her through a Season, arrange her marriage and show at least the minimal amount of concern. There was no one to do the same for Joanna. Her parents had abandoned her and Madame Dubois had sent her out in the world to make her way the best as she could. Her headmistress might offer advice and suggestions, but it wasn't her place to help Joanna find a worthy gentleman. Hidden away in schoolrooms, Joanna wasn't likely to do it on her own. Over time, her pupils would change, as well as the attic rooms she occupied and she would grow old and withered along with the one dream she'd carried with her since childhood, to have a family of her own. It made her want to complain as much as Catherine, but she couldn't. The young lady needed her comfort and encouragement as much as the new pupils at the school used to. It was her duty to help her and she would.

Luke and the other gentlemen entered the sitting room with the faint scent of tobacco and port still clinging to their coats. The evening meal had been more painful and tedious than a long march. He'd sat between the vapid Miss Carlton and the almost-hostile Miss Huntford, trying to choke down the overcooked venison until Lady Huntford and the other ladies had taken their leave. The male camaraderie after dinner had been a fortifying respite from the sea of hungry sharks which was the ladies, and now it was over.

Every female eye fell on the arriving gentlemen and there was a notable dip in the conversation before the men fanned into the room to revive it. Luke wanted to retreat to his bedroom, but he pressed forward. He was a guest and he must be polite to his host and hostess. It was yet another of the new constraints wrapping around him and trying to choke the life from him.

He approached a group of gentlemen discussing hunting, resigned to another tiresome hour or two before he could retire. Then, a sight as cherished as a breath of fresh air after hours in the hold of a transport ship greeted him. Miss Radcliff stood at the back of the room, almost hidden by the shadows cast from the large plant stand supporting a drooping fern. She remained outside the circle of guests, ignored and quiet, but watching with intelligent eyes which took in everything, including him. The faint flicker of the candles on a nearby table caressed her face, giving her skin a creamy glow. Even in the dim light, she was as beautiful as she'd been beneath the trees. He opened and closed his hand, the weight of her body in his arms as fresh now as when he'd left her. He shifted forward, ready to make for her, then stopped. Showing her favour would draw the ire of the other guests, especially his hostess. He would have to be more subtle in his engagement.

He began to weave his way to her. It took more effort to slide past the mamas in their *bergère* chairs without being waylaid than it did to get his regiment through a steep mountain pass. He was just beyond them when the ladies began their assault.

'Major Preston, would you like to turn my music?' Miss Bell asked from where she sat at the pianoforte as he squeezed between it and a side table.

'My inability to read music would ruin your beautiful playing,' he answered with a bow before continuing on. He was barely two feet away before the voluptuous Miss Selton stepped in front of him.

'Might I draw you? I've saved my sharpest pencil for you.' She leaned close to him and her generous breasts nearly spilled out of the top of her bodice brushing his arm.

'I'm not much of a subject for portraiture,' he answered. 'Mr Chilton has a much more classical profile.'

He motioned to the sturdy gentleman sitting in the chair beside them.

Mr Chilton rose, more interested in Miss Selton's talent than Luke. 'I'd be happy to sit for you.'

Miss Selton wasn't as enthusiastic. She threw Luke a disapproving frown before leading Mr Chilton to the table near the fireplace with better light and her drawing things spread out across the top of it.

Luke left them to dodge Lord Selton and Sir Rodger, stepping over Sir Rodger's large, black hunting dog which snored on the hearthrug in front of the fire.

'Major Preston, what do you think of the Luddite uprisings?' Lord Selton asked.

'We must see these men have other work if they're losing their positions to machines,' he answered before continuing on.

He hadn't done this much manoeuvring since the last time he'd drilled his troops. It seemed like a full half-hour passed before he casually came up beside the fern stand, the plant between him and Miss Radcliff. By then, the husband-hunting ladies had taken to colluding together by the fireplace to devise some amusement for the weekend while their mamas resumed their gossip or sat at the whist table to partake in the play.

Luke perched his elbow on the high wood and surveyed the room as if Miss Radcliff held no interest for him. In fact, he was aware of every shift of her dress, the faint inhale and exhale of her breath, and the clean scent of soap and lavender surrounding her.

'I see they let you out of the garret,' he joked in a low voice.

She shifted on her feet and glanced from Lady Huntford to Frances whose attention was fixed on the red-haired Mr Winborn sitting beside her. 'Lady Huntford would rather speak with her friends than chaperon her daughter. It's why I'm here.'

'A monumental task if I remember.' He didn't face her as he spoke, careful not to draw attention to their conversation.

'Such as you escaping those mamas. They almost had you captured.'

'Like a French patrol once did, but I outflanked them, too.'

Miss Radcliff smothered a smile. This small show of delight intrigued him more than anything else in the room. 'Your battle plans are very impressive.'

'Not so much as the sight of you.' Or his ability to stop offering her the most inappropriate compliments. 'I'm sorry, I spoke out of turn.'

'It must not happen again.' She clasped her hands in front of her as she had on the stairs, the joking young lady replaced by the stern governess.

'It won't,' he promised, though he couldn't bring himself to abandon her enticing humour for any of the droll conversation taking place around them. 'Is Miss Huntford keeping her end of the bargain?'

'Yes.'

'Good, because I've been worried about you.'

She trilled her fingers over her other hand, but didn't soften her stance. 'There's no need to be. I'm perfectly fine.'

He didn't believe her. He'd led enough men from a number of different backgrounds to recognise when they were settling in with the regiment and when they weren't. 'I want you to know that, should you need any additional assistance, you can call on me, as a friend.'

She unclasped her hands and fingered a feathery

leaf of the fern, trying to appear as if it, and not him, held her attention. 'A very kind offer, Major Preston, but you know it's impossible.'

'You think the son of an earl can't have friends outside his station? I consorted with all manner of men in the Army.'

She glanced up at him through her lashes, making his heart stop. 'This isn't the Army and I'm not a man.'

Despite the plain brown dress covering her figure and the equally drab ribbon holding back the richness of her light brown hair, there was no mistaking her for a grimy soldier. He longed to see her in a dress like the one she'd worn at the ball, her eyes sparkling with mirth instead of constantly flicking past him to worry about her employer. Yet, for all his desires, she was correct. If he were still a major, he might come to know her better without raising much scandal, but he wasn't. The divide between them was as deep as one of the gorges in the Pyrenees. When the house party ended, there'd be no chance to approach her or any reason for them to speak. She would go on to lead her life and unless he married Frances Huntford, which was unlikely, their paths wouldn't cross again. 'You're right, it's not fair for me to ask you for something you can't give.'

'Don't think I'm ungrateful for your offer. If I was of your class, I'd most certainly be your friend.' She smiled and his chest stilled at the beauty it brought to her face, then she looked past him. She laced her hands in front of her again and her expression changed from interested delight to the bland deference expected of a woman in her position. 'I believe the other young ladies are about to launch an attack.'

Miss Chilton, Miss Bell and Miss Selton swarmed up to Luke along with Miss Winborn. Only Miss Huntford was absent, remaining by her mother despite Lady Huntford shooing her to join the ladies.

'Major Preston, we've decided to put on a theatrical while we're here, *Hero and Alexandra*. You're perfect for the lead,' Miss Selton gushed to the agreeing tittering of her companions.

Luke tried not to wince. Out of the corner of his eye, he noticed Miss Radcliff sliding away, determined not to be seen by the ladies trying to corner him. He wished he could join her. It wasn't their attention he wanted, but hers.

'I'm a very poor actor, but I understand Mr Winborn is quite talented.' He motioned to the red-haired gentleman as he passed.

Caught off guard, Mr Winborn jerked to a stop, making his port slosh up one side of his glass. 'I wouldn't say talented, but I've shown some flair in my fair share of lead roles.'

He puffed out his slender chest, ignoring the disappointed frowns of the ladies.

'Great, then it's decided.' Luke waited for the group to flutter off, but they proved as stubborn as a bloodstain.

'Major Preston, you must have a part in the play,' Miss Winborn insisted with a most unattractive pout.

'I'll watch and applaud.' He hadn't left the Army to become a house-party peacock.

'He'll be glad to accept a minor role.' Edward dropped a heavy hand on Luke's shoulder and gave it a warning squeeze.

'And so will you.' Luke rolled his shoulder to dislodge Edward. He might be forced to partake in these idiotic distractions, but he wouldn't do it alone.

'Of course,' Edward agreed through clenched teeth. Beside him, Alma did her best not to laugh.

'We'll start rehearsals tomorrow morning.' Miss Selton clapped her hands together in front of her, more he thought to show off her breasts than to celebrate. Then she linked her arm in Mr Winborn's and drew him away, followed by the other ladies.

Luke looked for Miss Radcliff. She stood across the room behind his hostess, as distant as when he'd first entered the room. He shifted on his feet, anger and annoyance mingling like smoke and flame in the fire. She shouldn't be forced to linger in corners while insipid women like Miss Selton commanded the room. Miss Radcliff should be brought into the candlelight to laugh and smile like the others, but it wasn't her lot. Her parents had abandoned her to be all but reviled by young ladies who thought of nothing except laces and landing a husband. It was as unfair as the officers who used to be passed over for commissions because they didn't have the right family or connections. Luke had argued vociferously for those men, sometimes winning, but most times not. The culture of the Army was too entrenched against men of modest backgrounds. So was society. Nothing he could say in Miss Radcliff's favour would change anyone's mind, or help them see her as more than a humble servant. All it would do is cast aspersion on her and create more gossip for the mamas to chew on.

Luke caught his mother's eye and she motioned for him to join her at the whist table. He fingered the bugle badge pinned to the lapel of his coat. Guilt stung him. Soon, his regiment would be enduring the encroaching cold as they settled into their winter quarters while he played cards and performed in theatricals. Already, his time with them and the danger they'd shared was beginning to fade, replaced with frivolities as useless as his place in the family and thoughts of Miss Radcliff. In the last few days, he'd mulled over her precarious situation more than his soldiers'.

Sick to his stomach, Luke marched across the room to join in the game. He'd play along for now, but Edward was correct. At some point, after Luke did his duty, he'd be free to return to his regiment and he would. It was the one thing, beside Miss Radcliff's presence, which kept him from leaving the house party.

* * *

Joanna watched Major Preston play cards with the other ladies and envied them. The part of her eager to be special wanted to garner more of his attention. The practical girl who'd learned not to base her life on dreams made sure she kept her head. Tonight wasn't the time to set the room alight with speculation and see herself dismissed.

'You must go play cards with him,' Lady Huntford commanded her daughter from where they sat on the sofa in front of Joanna.

'I don't want to.' Frances pouted. She was the only eligible lady who hadn't thrown herself in Major Preston's path tonight.

'We aren't spending all this money for you to speak with Mr Winborn whom you may see whenever you wish. Now come with me.' Lady Huntford took Frances by the arm and all but pulled her off the sofa. 'Miss Radcliff, you're no longer needed. You may go, but don't tromp through the room like a bull and be discreet about it. I don't want everyone to think I employ an uncouth governess.'

'Yes, Lady Huntford.' Joanna responded, trying not to grit her teeth. No one at Madame Dubois's had ever been this rude to her. She wasn't sure why Lady Huntford felt the need to be or to worry about what others thought of Joanna. The entire time she'd been here, no one had noticed her except Major Preston. She doubted anyone would be conscious of her leaving, except him.

As Lady Huntford dragged a reluctant Frances to the card table, Joanna circled the edge of the room, stepping around Sir Rodger's dog as it chased rabbits in its sleep. She should be glad to be dismissed, to be able to sleep before tomorrow's duties descended on her, but she was reluctant to leave. She passed by the whist table, subtly studying Major Preston. She admired the fine set of his nose, the sharp arch of his eyebrows and the soft wave of his hair brushed back from his strong forehead. She stopped when his eyes rose to meet hers and the two of them remained linked in their silence.

He wants to be my friend. It was a foolish request, but she appreciated the gesture. *I should have accepted it.*

She needed all the allies she could muster here in Hertfordshire, even if she wasn't sure what one like Major Preston could offer her. Despite her refusal, he'd come to her aid if she asked him, she was certain of it. What else might he grant her if she asked it of him?

Then Lady Huntford made a fuss, insisting Lord Selton rise so Frances could sit beside Major Preston. The shuffling of seats at the table pulled Major Preston back into his world and isolated her once more in hers.

Joanna left the light of the sitting room and headed down the dim hallway to the front stairs. She trudged up the first flight, having to feel her way along the wall to the back stairs at the end. Even with a house full of guests unfamiliar with the rambling layout, Sir Rodger was too miserly to light more candles. Perhaps he, more than Lady Huntford, could see the waste of this weekend and how he wasn't likely to gain more from it than a pile of bills.

It wasn't the dark which concerned her as she climbed the cold and winding flight of stairs to her room, but the subtle change in her situation. Before yesterday, she'd had no friends in Hertfordshire. Now, she had two. Vicar Carlson she trusted. She wasn't sure how to consider Major Preston. The son of an earl shouldn't be concerned about the well-being of a lowly governess, and she shouldn't be flattered by his attention. She'd been warned about overly interested gentleman by Miss Fanworth. It was to her peril if she chose to ignore it. The kindly teacher wasn't here to help her the way she'd helped Grace, if, in a moment of weakness, Joanna forgot herself. Madame Dubois might have taken her in as a foundling, but she wasn't sure she'd welcome Joanna back if she ruined herself. Madame Dubois was understanding about many things, but Joanna doubted the strength of young passion was one of them.

At the top of the stairs, she shivered as she crossed the long, bare hall to her room. This narrow and desolate space was so different from Madame's school, where woven rugs covered the upstairs floor, bright light filled it in the day and the laughter and chatter of girls echoed through it in the evenings. The only sound she heard here was the faint snoring of a maid from behind one of the many doors. When Joanna reached her room Rachael, Grace and Isabel wouldn't be there to greet her with smiles, sympathy and humour. The only thing waiting for her was the peeling plaster walls and loneliness. She would go to sleep in the dark without friends or anyone here who truly cared about her.

Major Preston cares. She breathed into her hands, trying to warm them. Despite the risks in cavorting with Major Preston, his presence offered her something she hadn't experienced in a long time—hope. If a man like him could value her company, perhaps some day another would, too, one of more modest means who'd be free to love her without hesitation and whom she could love openly in return.

She slipped into her room which was no warmer than the hallway. The moonlight falling in through the single window washed out what little colour remained in the thin coverlet draped over the rickety bed. She wandered past it and to the window. The drive outside was just as bare as her room before the darkness of the woods enveloped it on either side.

Raising her fingers to the window, she pictured Major Preston emerging from his coach and searching for her. If only the man who might some day come to love her could be him. With a sigh which fogged the window, she pushed away from the glass and began to prepare for bed. It was reality she needed to face, not dreams. Thanks to him, tonight, the reality she might one day have a family of her own didn't seem so unobtainable.

Chapter Six

'No, no, no, you're not saying it right. Try again.' Miss Selton raised her hands in exasperation at her brother's poor interpretation of a Greek god.

Luke leaned against the large stone fireplace where a weak flame was limply trying to heat the large room and exchanged an amused look with Miss Radcliff. She sat across the ballroom-turned-theatre near where the mishmash collection of props had been dumped by grumbling servants under Miss Selton's direction. The young lady had even managed to have the lazy staff remove the sheets from the furniture and make a half-hearted attempt to sweep away the dust covering the stage where the musicians, if there had even been a ball at Huntford Place, might play. He was amazed at her accomplishment since Luke could barely get fresh water in his washstand jug. It was the one mark in favour of Miss Selton, along with her having insisted Miss Radcliff stay for the rehearsal. Miss Selton, who'd taken it upon herself to both direct and play the lead, had assigned the younger Huntford girls small parts, necessitating Miss Radcliff's presence.

Miss Radcliff returned to reading the letter which had commanded her attention since she'd sat down to watch the rehearsal. A simple peach-coloured dress flowed over the curve of her knees, stopping just above her feet. The long sleeves covered her arching arms as she held up the missive which appeared to amuse her more than the rehearsal. Her eyes glittered with a mirth which increased each time she glanced up to take in the ridiculous actors. In the midst of the chaos around her, she was calm and serene, but the hint of an imp showed itself in more than one reserved smile.

The glow he'd admired from across the room was the only reason he'd remained here instead of leaving to ride Duke. He'd attempted to avoid the play by lingering in his room this morning, but hunger had got the better of him. Not wanting to starve and unlikely to receive a plate of food from the surly butler, he'd been forced to venture downstairs for breakfast.

I've become soft already. He used to go for days without food in Spain, now he was wrapped up in a play because his stomach had become accustomed to regular meals. He'd hoped a late night of gambling and conversation would have kept people in their rooms this morning. He'd been wrong. The majority of the guests had risen early and he'd been accosted by the ladies the moment he'd entered the dining room. He and the other gentleman had barely had time to finish their eggs before they were ushered off to begin rehearsals.

In the end, it hadn't been so awful. Having the freedom to watch Miss Radcliff read, to enjoy the sparkle of humour softening her face almost made capitulating to his hunger pangs worth it.

Then her smile faded, and a small line settled between her brows as she turned the letter over to read the other side. On stage, Mr Selton stumbled over his lines again, drawing chuckles from the other actors, but Miss Radcliff didn't notice. She was so absorbed in the seriousness of her missive, even the twins sifting through the fake swords and shields searching for treasure had failed to capture her notice. Not even his studying her, wondering what the matter was, was enough to draw her away.

He pushed off the stone mantel ready to go to her before he stopped himself. He'd suffered hunger and not raided storehouses, endured a tongue swollen with thirst but refused filthy water. He would resist the draw of her and the risk of making everyone tut in disapproval at his behaviour as they had Mr Selton's inability to pronounce 'pungent'.

'Major Preston, would you like to share my book and study your lines?' Miss Bell approached him with a little too much eagerness. A number of guests had sent their servants back to their estates to retrieve their copies of the play, but there still weren't enough to go around. The lack of copies provided numerous opportunities for couples to step to one side and talk, especially Miss Huntford and Mr Winborn, who gossiped together at the corner of the stage, the open book in front of them all but forgotten.

'No, I'm quite content to watch the others.'

'I'll study with you,' Mr Chilton offered, but it

didn't raise her crestfallen expression as she followed him to a set of chairs near the window.

'At least try and look as if you want to be here.' Edward banged his copy of the play against Luke's chest.

'Is this better?' Luke threw his brother an overly large smile while holding a curt response behind his teeth. It was a wonder he hadn't bitten off his tongue in an effort to not quarrel with Edward as Miss Radcliff had suggested. If his unwillingness to engage Edward had dampened the anger threatening to flare up between them, it was difficult to discern, but he was determined to try.

Edward frowned at Luke. 'You should've accepted Miss Selton's offer to play the lead. It's obvious she has a preference for you.'

'You mean my chances of inheriting a title. You should be glad I'm not encouraging her. She's so determined, she might try and secure my inheritance faster, then you'd have to watch what's in your tea.' He smacked the book against Edward's chest, but held on to it, taking it with him as he crossed the room.

Curse them all and what they thought. It wasn't

like him to wait idly by while what he wanted was mere feet away.

'Will you help me practise my lines?' He held out the book to Miss Radcliff.

At last the letter lost its hold over her. She looked up at him, the faint trouble wrinkling her smooth forehead easing as she cocked her head and smiled.

'All three of them?' she teased while she folded the letter and slipped it in her pocket.

'It's a very demanding part. I'm playing the commanding general. Quite against type.'

'It will definitely be a stretch for you.' She took the book from him and her fingers brushed his. They paused at the meeting of their flesh and, for the first time since he'd entered the ballroom, it seemed warm and comfortable. Her eyes, framed by her dark lashes, opened wide with surprise. He lost himself in their brilliant azure and almost forgot all his duty to his family. Thankfully, she kept her head.

'I'm sure your authentic performance will outshine even the lead.' She pulled away with the book and motioned to the stage where Miss Selton indulged in an overly dramatic reading of her lines, her high voice echoing off the rafters.

Luke shook off his momentary and troubling infatuation. In Spain, when he'd gone into brothels to collect his wayward men, even after weeks or months without the tender company of a woman, he hadn't been as carried away or tempted to forget himself in a *señorita*'s arms as he was in Miss Radcliff's presence.

'It'll be the talk of the countryside for months. I might even be called to London by the Prince for a command performance.' He sat down in the chair beside hers, kicking aside a bent tin crown to make room for his feet.

'They'll fill newspaper columns with details of your stunning performance.' She shifted a touch on her chair, her back straightening as she tried to place some distance between them, reminding him of their potential audience.

'Will you be able to tolerate me when I'm famous?' he asked as she opened the book to the play and began to flip through the pages. At the turn of each one, she licked her fingers, her tongue flicking out to sweep the delicate tips and send a hard chill racing up his spine.

'I'll remind you of where you got your start.' She ran her finger down the page to the place with his part and he envied the paper. Her fingers were long, ending in small, rounded nails he wished he could feel along the arch of his back.

'Good, I don't want to get a big head.' Part of him was already straining because of her nearness. He shouldn't be here beside her, especially with Alma and Edward watching from across the room. He glanced at the other guests, wondering if they were scrutinising his time with Miss Radcliff, but they were too involved in the rehearsal to notice their surroundings.

'Go ahead and say your first line,' Miss Radcliff urged with a seriousness he imagined she employed in the schoolroom.

'I'm afraid I haven't learned them yet.' Instead of taking the book, he leaned in close to peer at the page, distracted by the curve of her breasts beneath the muslin and the flat fall of her stomach to where it led to thighs perched tight together against the chair seat. The heat from her cheek radiated off his and the scent of soap teased him like a bell sounding through a fog. He jerked back upright, the nearness too dangerous. 'As you can see, I have more than three lines.'

'How very fortunate for you and your admirer.' Miss Radcliff nodded to Miss Selton who approached them with quick, commanding steps.

'Major Preston, your character is on now and we have no one to be the nymph. Miss Radcliff, would you mind playing the part?'

'She's too busy for this,' Miss Huntford scoffed and Luke imagined it was Miss Selton taking over the running of things more than her invitation to Miss Radcliff which tweaked their hostess's nose.

'Nonsense, since your sisters are here we might as well employ her.' Miss Selton brushed off Miss Huntford with a flick of her dark-haired head. 'Miss Radcliff, it's only a few lines, say you'll do it.'

Aware of everyone watching her, especially Miss Huntford, she clutched the open book to her chest and pressed back against her chair. 'I don't think I should.'

'You must, otherwise the play will be ruined.' Luke took Miss Radcliff by the elbow and ushered her up on to the stage before Miss Huntford could open her mouth to protest. Her arm was soft beneath his grip and he slid his thumb over the smooth material to trace the curve of it. Her perfect lips parted with her surprise and he let go of her, just as startled as her by the intimacy passing between them.

'You stand here.' Miss Selton hurried forward to guide Miss Radcliff to her place on the stage.

Luke followed, trying not to notice the sway of Miss Radcliff's hips beneath her dress. What the hell had come over him? If he didn't regain control, he'd embarrass himself, and quite possibly her, in front of everyone.

Miss Selton tilted the book away from Miss Radcliff's chest and pointed to her lines. 'When he approaches, you say this. I know you aren't used to attention, but I'm sure you'll manage.'

She patted Miss Radcliff condescendingly on the arm before retaking her place. Miss Radcliff trilled her fingers on the edge of the book and Luke could almost hear the witty response coming to her lovely lips, but she pressed them closed, refusing to give voice to it. He wished he could hear it. It would be one of the most enjoyable parts of this morning. Instead, he resigned himself to listening to her deliver her lines in a clear, melodious voice before he answered with his.

When they were finished, Miss Huntford and Mr Winborn launched into their very lengthy scene which left Luke and Miss Radcliff alone together upstage waiting for their next cue. Not even Mr Selton took any notice of them as he stood on stage, his lips moving as he silently reviewed his lines.

'You shouldn't have encouraged my participation,' Miss Radcliff whispered, nodding across the room to where the twins were whacking one other with wooden swords in a manner no one would call playful. 'I have other duties to attend to.'

'I'm sure your work is the epitome of excitement and fulfilment.'

'Yes, every day is one of pure rapture and joy,' she offered wryly.

'Who was your letter from?' It was none of his business, but he wanted to know what had upset her.

She flicked the top edge of the book and he thought she wouldn't answer, determined to remain distant from him. At last she did. 'My friend, Rachel.'

'Is all not well with her? You seemed troubled.'

* * *

He'd noticed. Everything inside Joanna told her to stop sharing confidences with him. When he'd taken her arm, there'd been no mistaking the slide of his thumb as an innocent slip. The shock it had sent through her was a warning to not allow his kindness to make her forget herself, but she ignored it. Luke's concern melted her reserve and speaking with him was like speaking to Rachel, Isabel or Grace. There was no one else here who wanted to listen and she was tired of being alone.

'All is well with Rachel. She's caring for the children of Sheikh Malik of Huria.' She took the letter from her pocket and opened it. 'Her position appears to be a good one.'

'Unlike yours,' he finished for her, giving voice to a sentiment she feared to utter out loud in this company.

She glanced down at the letter in her hand, her friend's words too brief.

Dearest Joanna,
I never appreciated the rain and abundance of green in England until I arrived in Huria. The endless sea of sand turns everything here different shades of orange. Then the desert ends

right where the verdant oasis begins. Sheikh Malik's palace sits in the middle of this paradise surrounded by plants so rich in fragrance they rival one of my recipes.

The people of Huria are accustomed to the harshness of the desert, but I haven't adjusted to it or quite settled in with the Sheikh. While everyone here has welcomed me without reservation, he is more of an enigma than how people can live in this hot and desolate land. His wife's death has left him shaken and his children grieve for their mother. I do my best to help him and to comfort his children. They are the sweetest ones you can imagine.

I hope you are finding the same contentment with the Huntfords.
Your devoted friend,
Rachel

'Her description of Huria makes Hertfordshire seem dreary by comparison.' And Joanna's employment even more contemptible than before.

'Huntford Place is dreary. The decrepit staff doesn't add to its charm.'

Gruger shuffled by, pretending not to hear Edward asking for some refreshments to be brought to the ballroom. Joanna bit her tongue to keep from laughing out loud. She eyed Frances, wishing she knew the play better and how much more time she had with Major Preston before the scene ended and she must leave him.

'I envy Rachel, especially the warm climate. I've never been further than the seaside in Sandhills in Hampshire.' She raised her head to face Major Preston, refusing to give in to the melancholy threatening to steal over her. 'The sea there was so beautiful, especially how the waves curled over one another. Grace, Isabel and I went there with Rachel's parents. They assured Madame Dubois they'd chaperon us. They had the best intentions, but they were too wrapped up in each other to see much of the world around them, even us. We woke up one morning to discover they'd decided to go on to Brighton since they thought Sandhills was too dull. They left us with a note explaining their departure and a few pounds. We were forced to find our own way home and we did. We purchased outdoor seats on the last carriage to Salisbury and hung on all day, shivering in the rain. It was the grandest adventure I've ever had.'

'So far.' He tilted his head towards her, the question of something between them, friendship or possibly more, heavy in his piercing eyes. This wasn't the licentious interest Mr Selton had thrown at her this morning in the hallway, but something more intense and exhilarating. It reached into the lonely place inside her and pushed it back like a lit candle does the dark. It was everything she'd ever wanted to see in a gentleman's eyes and she couldn't have it because of his rank and hers.

The thrill inside her settled as she shifted away from him, but she kept her head up, refusing to allow sorrow or regret to ruin their time together. 'You're right. I don't know where my duties might take me. It could be Huria, or Austria or even the London stage after this performance.'

'You must invite all your friends to see your first performance, including me. We are friends, aren't we?'

She gripped the book tight. She should stop this flirting and rebuff him, make it clear to him there could be nothing between them, but she couldn't. He'd protected her at the ball, perhaps he could find a way to secure her continued employment if Frances or one of the other girls decided to make trouble for her. It was a great deal to ask of him and she wouldn't, at least not until she needed to. 'Of course we are and you'll be the first to receive an invitation.'

Beyond the stage, the din of the twins' wooden swords hitting the tin shields began to echo through the room.

'Thank you, Miss Radcliff, we no longer need you.' Miss Selton waved her off the stage, wincing with each ringing blow of wood against tin. She wasn't the only one irritated by the girls. Near the windows, Miss Bell pressed her fingertips to her temples at the noise. 'Be sure to memorise your lines.'

Joanna reluctantly handed Major Preston the book, avoiding his touch. Too many people were watching in their eagerness to see her silence the children. She hopped off the stage and crossed the long room, the gulf between her and the rest of the young ladies widening with each step. At Madame Dubois's, she and the other pupils, despite their varied backgrounds, had all been the same, each one preparing for their future duties. Here, the difference between her and the other women was as stark as the line of dust dividing where the maids had cleaned the floor and where they had not. Joanna wasn't like them in any way as they made clear by frowning at her for allowing the children to run wild and interrupt their folly. If they knew she harboured any kind of affinity for Major Preston, and he for her, their disapproving looks would turn into hate of the nastiest kind.

With some difficulty, Joanna wrested the swords from the twins and ushered them to the door, eager to be free of the silent rebukes and the source of her warring feelings. Catherine argued against leaving until a curt insult from Frances sent her all but running away in tears. With an exhausted sigh, Joanna led the twins, who giggled at their elder sister's embarrassment, out of the room, determined to find Catherine and ease her hurt. With the girls demanding her full attention, there was no time to think of herself or what had passed between her and Major Preston. She was glad. She was tired of being reminded of everything she didn't and couldn't have.

Luke stepped off the stage, watching Miss Radcliff as she led her wayward charges out of the room, unable to spare even one last glance at him. He felt more than heard Edward come up beside him.

'You and the governess had a great deal to talk about while you were on stage.'

Luke turned to face his brother, trying to remain civil. 'She helped me in the woods after you nearly ran her down yesterday. I was thanking her for her kindness.'

'I didn't try to run her down. She stepped in front of me, but of course you'd accuse me of being heartless.'

The reminder to not feed their constant conflict showed itself in Edward's stricken expression. It hadn't always been like this. They'd liked one another well enough as boys playing in the woods behind Pensum Manor. Then Edward had gone off to school, the scion of the family, and everything had changed. 'Of course that's not what I meant.'

Edward shifted on his feet, the argument stunned out of him by Luke's near apology. It was the first small victory Luke had enjoyed in his campaign to end the conflict with his brother and even he wasn't sure how to react.

'These came for you,' the butler interrupted,

tossing two letters at Luke before shuffling out of the room as quietly as he'd shuffled in.

Luke examined them. One was from Reginald, the other from Helmsworth Manor. He opened up the one with the Marquis's seal. It was succinct and disheartening. 'Damn.'

'News from the Army?' Edward asked with, if Luke wasn't mistaken, concern. It didn't seem possible and yet it did. His civility with Edward had garnered him the same consideration from his brother. Perhaps the conflict between them could at last be set aside.

'No. Lord Helmsworth. He's denied my request for a meeting.' He stuffed the letters in his pocket. 'I can't discuss the issue with him if he won't even see me.'

'Good, maybe you'll finally stop this fool's errand and take finding a wife seriously.'

Luke levelled a finger at Edward, their truce short-lived. 'I did what you and Father wanted. I gave up all my accomplishments to come home. It doesn't mean I have to strut about like some prized bull every moment I'm here.'

'Bull-headed is more like it. It's hard to find a wife when the only woman you're talking to is the governess. Don't get distracted, Luke, by either a pretty face or Lord Helmsworth.'

Luke stiffened. He detested being reminded of his mission like some new recruit, especially since Edward was right. Miss Radcliff was distracting him like the seized winery with a cellar full of Madeira had once distracted his battalion. If he hadn't rallied them, they would've lost the offensive. If he didn't free himself of this infatuation, he and his family would lose the battle they'd been fighting since his grandfather's time, the one he'd been excluded from when he was younger because he wasn't the heir. 'I won't be made inconsequential again because I'm not you.'

'You think I'm so privileged, but I'm not.' Edward shifted closer and dropped his voice, the tone of it hard. 'Once you find a wife and produce an heir, you'll be free to do whatever you wish. It's an opportunity I've never had.'

Edward marched to where Alma sat looking wan in the deep chair next to the sputtering fire. Edward paced in front of her, railing about Luke.

Luke exited the room, disgusted with Edward, the situation and himself. He'd vowed not to fight with Edward and he'd broken it. He'd also vowed to end the dispute with Lord Helmsworth and by heaven he would. He left the house and followed the long path to the stables. Lord Helmsworth couldn't avoid Luke if Luke appeared on his doorstep.

He reached the stables and called to the groom to prepare his horse. He paced over the packed dirt of the paddock as the groom, as slow as every other Huntford servant, saddled Duke. His determination to ride to Helmsworth Manor faded with each dusty step. Luke's unwelcome appearance would irritate the man further and Luke couldn't hope to speak rationally to him while his insides were twisted like the blown-out end of a cannon. He'd ride instead, and think about the matter, plan and strategise like he used to in Spain instead of rushing in foolhardily and hoping he didn't get hit with a musket ball.

At last the groom finished and Luke stepped into the saddle and kicked Duke into a gallop. He should go home and send a servant back for his things, leave this waste of a party and turn his focus to dealing with Lord Helmsworth until the London Season saw him back in the middle of the marriage mart. There was no point staying on, there wasn't one woman here worth her salt except Miss Radcliff. The thought of leaving her hit him as squarely in the chest as having given up his commission.

The memory of Miss Radcliff heavy across his thighs, her curving ear close to his lips as they'd raced through the woods, was as stinging as the cold air against his face. Duke's stride was lighter, quicker without her, but Luke wanted her here as much as he wanted to be back in Spain. He bent over Duke's neck and urged him into a run, trying to outrace both desires.

He rode for some time, working to clear his mind until the iron gate marking the road to Pensum Manor came into view. Luke tugged on the reins, slowing Duke into a trot. As they passed beneath the metal arch, fields of wheat spread out on the rolling hills on either side of him. The wind whipped across them, bending each stalk in unison like a contingent of men dropping into firing formation. For all its beauty, the wide swathes of desolate earth along the edges of the harvest and the patches of barren ground where the seeds had refused to grow were evident. This harvest would be no more successful than the last one, compounding their problems, the ones they were looking to Luke to solve.

Pensum Manor and the heavy responsibility of it pressed on him. Growing up, he'd never had to worry about it while it had dominated and dictated the lives of his father, grandfather and his brother. Now, it had ensnared him, commanding who he could and could not speak with or court.

He didn't want to admit it, not even to himself, but Edward was right. If he allowed the single woman he couldn't have to distract him from his duty and hers, his family would suffer and she might, too. He was being reckless in his choices simply to be near her and it was wrong and it must stop. It would help neither of them to continue on.

He turned Duke back towards Huntford Place. He despised allowing the manor, the lineage from which he'd once been excluded, to command him like this, but he couldn't walk away. Like sending men under his command into battle and possibly death to achieve an objective, he must sacrifice his friendship with Miss Radcliff, as well as his own wants for his family. She wasn't here to flirt with him, but to make her school proud and he was stopping her from achieving her goal as much as she was interfering with his. He was a heel to withdraw his friendship after she'd accepted it and it burned to imagine the pain it might cause her, but he must. There could be nothing between them. He would do his duty by his family, marry and produce an heir. Afterwards, he'd be his own man, one way or another.

Joanna pushed open the door to the Huntford Place library and peered inside. She wanted to make sure Frances and Mr Winborn weren't completing what Frances had failed to finish with Lieutenant Foreman. Seeing no one, Joanna crossed the dark room to the bookcase on the far wall to peruse the offerings. The twins were with their nurse and Catherine had joined the other ladies for a lesson with the dancing master, leaving Joanna with a free hour to find a book on Huria.

She frowned as she examined the available selection. There was no rhyme or reason to their placement with geography next to poetry and history. Joanna sighed. It would take her the better part of her free time to find anything in this mess.

She finished examining the books on the bottom shelves and climbed the narrow rail ladder to view those on the higher ones. She was at the top, shaking her head at the jumble of subjects, when the door behind her opened. She tensed, expecting Sir Rodger to appear and claim her free time with another errand. It wasn't him, but Major Preston.

A smile split the tense line of his lips at the sight of her, then it hardened around the corners. 'I'm sorry, I didn't mean to disturb you.'

'Please, come in, I have no special claim to this room.' She climbed down off the ladder, trying her best to be prim and proper, but her weak knees and fluttering stomach made it difficult. All she could imagine was him pushing her up against the panelling, lifting her skirt and doing to her the things Lieutenant Foreman had done to Frances.

Her daydream ended when she faced him. He stood like an officer, aloof and formal in a way she hadn't seen in him before. It reminded her of when Madame had summoned her to her private sitting room to say she'd found Joanna a position. She'd been kind about it, but it had been clear the subtle separating of Joanna from her school life had begun. Perhaps Major Preston had proposed to a lady and he was now going to end their brief friendship. She should be glad, for it removed the threat of his presence to her good sense, but she wasn't.

'I'm trying to find a book on Huria,' she rushed, attempting to chase away her encroaching fear and recapture some of the rapport they'd enjoyed during their previous encounters.

'I'm surprised Sir Rodger allows you in here. When I asked if I could borrow a book, he almost made me give him a deposit in case I should damage one.' The flash of humour eased the lines at the corners of his eyes, heartening her.

'Oh, he was quite adamant I read. He said it would improve upon the limited education I must have received at Madame Dubois's.' She rolled her eyes at the memory of Sir Rodger's insulting directive. 'I should have told him how superior my education truly was, but he wouldn't have believed me any more than he would his role in his daughters' behaviour.'

'He sounds like some of the commanding officers I served under. No matter how much it was to their benefit, they didn't want to hear the truth.'

'Who does?'

'No one. Not even me.' He clasped his hands

behind his back and faced her with a seriousness to make her heart race, not with anticipation, but with fear. 'My family has never asked anything of me except one thing, to come home and produce an heir. It seems so simple and yet every day I fight it, especially when I read about the battles in Spain in the papers coming up from London. If I were to be killed over there, my family line would die out and everything they've held dear for centuries would be lost.' He spoke with the rigidity of a teacher explaining a misunderstood lesson, except regret made his words halting and softened the intensity of his eyes. Madame Dubois had fixed on her the same way the morning when Joanna had turned five and the headmistress had felt she was old enough to understand the circumstances of her arrival at the school. Despite Madame's attempt to make Joanna see how wanted she was by her and the teachers, there'd been no concealing how unwanted she'd been by her parents. Major Preston was about to make it clear to her how far apart they were and how they should remain so. 'I must find a wife, surrender my wants for my family's, which is why...'

'Our friendship is a mistake,' she finished for

him, flinching from listening to him say the words aloud. He was being practical and realistic and she must do the same. She brushed a spiderweb from the corner of one ladder step. She didn't want to be practical, but hold on to the hope his friendship had offered, the brief belief someone might come to love her, even while he was pulling it away.

'Not a mistake, only inappropriate.' He cleared his throat as if reluctant to continue. She prayed he would stop and recant his painful declaration, but he didn't. 'You were correct the other night. The difference in our positions makes almost anything, even the most innocent relationship, between us impossible.'

She wrapped one hand around the ladder frame and gripped it tightly. Each of his words pelted her like the rain had during the ride from Sandhills. Except this time there were no friends to brave the onslaught with her or to bolster her flagging confidence in herself and her value to anyone.

'I apologise for pressing you on the matter. I should have known better,' he added. At least he had the decency to recognise and admit his mistake.

She squared her shoulders and faced him with

all the calm required of their situation. She might not be a titled woman, but she could conduct herself with all the poise and dignity of a duchess, even while she was crumbling inside. 'We were silly to be so open with one another, but I appreciate your honesty in this and everything else.'

He bowed, then turned and cracked open the door and checked the hall to ensure it was clear. It was and he slipped out, pausing beyond the threshold for one last look at her. It was more than misgiving or apology colouring his eyes, but a longing which called to her from across the quiet room. He didn't want this parting any more than she did and he was waiting for her to summon him back, to fight for him to change his mind. She felt it as keenly as she did his remorse. It would only take a word or two to keep him and whatever had been building between them here. She opened her mouth to speak and he leaned forward, ready to return, but she said nothing. She couldn't. Everything he'd stated was true and nothing could change it, not his wants or hers. He must leave and she must let him go.

With no reply to his silent enquiry, he backed into the hall and drew the door closed behind him. When the latch clicked shut, Joanna sank down to the floor at the foot of the ladder. The cold wood cut through her thin dress, but it was nothing compared to the loneliness swathing her. A short time ago, she'd believed two people here were concerned about her, but she'd been wrong. She appreciated Major Preston's honesty, and his safeguarding her reputation by being cautious when he'd left, but it didn't matter. He could check a thousand hallways and it wouldn't change the reason why he'd walked away and why she'd let him go. She was nobody.

Not to my friends. But they were hundreds of miles away. Feminine laughter echoed through the room from somewhere outside, the joyful kind she, Rachel, Grace and Isabel had shared so many times in the quiet world of Madame Dubois's. Never again would Joanna enjoy the acceptance of people who didn't judge her because of who she was, or, more importantly, who she wasn't thanks to her parents.

The selfish fools. She pressed her fists against her temples as anger filled her. How could they have done it? How could they have given her up?

If they hadn't, things between her and Major Preston might be different.

She lowered her hands and took a deep breath, willing herself to calm. It wasn't fair to blame them. She had no idea what situation had driven them to leave her at the school. Maybe her mother had been like Grace, too impetuous for her own good and forced to surrender Joanna to keep them both from being cast into the streets to starve to death or worse. She could no more blame Grace for the choice she'd made in giving up her daughter than she could Major Preston for ending their burgeoning friendship. There was little she could offer him which would ease the burdens and responsibilities he now bore.

Out in the hallway, the large clock rang with the quarter-hour. In a short while, her responsibilities would once again consume her. She should get up and prepare to face them, but she couldn't rise. She wanted to avoid reality for a touch longer.

'You're not enjoying the play?' Miss Selton asked, her thin fichu doing little to hide the too-high curve of her breast. She was beautiful, and rich, but neither were enough for Luke to over-look her lack of character.

'I received a letter with some news about my regiment being involved in an offensive. It's dif-ficult to concentrate on this when I'm worried about them.' And the damage he'd done to Miss Radcliff. She'd been brave in the face of his rejec-tion, struggling to conceal the pain he'd caused, but she hadn't. He'd caught it in her white knuck-les as she'd gripped the ladder and in the stiffness of her bearing as she'd faced him.

I had no choice. Everything he'd said about dying in Spain and the end of his family line was true.

'You needn't worry about your men. I'm sure they're fine.' Miss Selton flicked her hand in dismissal as if he'd complained about the over-cooked pheasant at last night's dinner. Miss Rad-cliff wouldn't have been so unfeeling, yet he'd pushed her away because she wasn't the same rank as Miss Selton. He despised himself for what he'd done. He was no better than the command-ers who allowed men to die under incapable of-ficers instead of promoting a more worthy and humble candidate. 'Shall we practise your scene together? I can read the part of the nymph since Miss Radcliff isn't here.'

She leaned forward, peering up at him like a simpleton as she batted her eyelashes at him.

'No, I've had enough for today.' He left her, done trying to be anything more than annoyed at this empty-headed chit. Edward rose, hurrying to intercept him, but Luke levelled a halting hand at him. 'Don't.'

He'd allowed Edward to pressure him into giving up his friendship with Miss Radcliff, he wouldn't allow him to force him to stay in this room. He paused in the hallway outside the ballroom, at a loss for what to do and hating this indecision. He'd never been like this in the Army. Everything there had been clear and concise. He'd make his decisions and not second-guess them no matter what the outcome. Here, he was confounded at every turn by duty, family and rank. No wonder some of the seasoned officers turned to drinking and gambling when they came home. At times, it seemed like no other way to relieve the boredom and frustration. Give him a gruelling march any day over this endless irrelevance.

'You've offered him your favours. Why not

share them with me?' Mr Selton's low voice slid down the long hallway from near the library.

Luke paused, the hairs on the back of his neck rising the way they used to whenever the forest in Spain grew too still, signalling the enemy was near. Miss Huntford and Mr Selton hadn't been in the ballroom rehearsing. What was the chit up to now? The answering female voice made his blood boil.

'I've given no one my favours and I certainly won't give them to you, now let me pass.'

Miss Radcliff.

Luke marched down the hall and turned the corner. Mr Selton stood with his back to Luke, blocking Miss Radcliff's way.

'Let me by.' She tried to step around him but he shot out his arm and slapped his hand against the wall to stop her from leaving.

'There's no reason for you to be rude to me.'

'If a lady asks you to leave her be, then I suggest you do it,' Luke thundered as he came up hard on the man.

Miss Radcliff sagged against the panelling in relief.

'She's not a lady,' Mr Selton snorted, less enamoured by Luke's appearance. 'And a little fun is what governesses, especially ones as pretty as Miss Radcliff, are practically made for.'

Luke pulled back his arm and slammed his fist into Mr Selton's lecherous face. The man staggered back, hitting the wall before he dropped to his knees.

'You hit me,' Mr Selton wailed, clutching his mouth. 'Over a governess.'

'I hit you because you aren't a gentleman.' Luke stood over him, hands clenched, hoping Mr Selton gave him another reason to strike him. The slime deserved it.

Mr Selton pierced him with a slicing look. 'How dare you! I'm a baron's son, and I'll be a baron some day. You're nothing more than a dirty soldier. Who are you to strike me or tell me what to do?'

Luke's foot twitched with the urge to kick him, but he didn't want to scuff his boots. Mr Selton was everything he hated about the aristocracy, the type of man who'd lorded his supposed superiority over him at Eton while unable to take one prize or win one sporting match against him. He was the worthless officer who'd sneered down his aquiline nose at soldiers as he sent them off to die in a futile offensive meant to impress his commanders.

Luke bent down, hands on his knees, bringing his face so close to Mr Selton's he could see the small veins along the sides of his nose. 'If you're insulted, then call me out, show me how superior you think you are. Remember, I've had a lot of practice shooting at men trying to kill me. I doubt I'll miss your big head.'

Mr Selton's bravado slackened as Luke straightened.

Mr Selton picked himself off the floor, staggering against the wall before he steadied himself on his feet. He wiped his mouth with the back of his hand and winced at the streak of blood left there by his split lip. 'There's no need for it.'

Luke stared down at him, a good head taller than the future Baron. 'Then I suggest you depart at once. I wouldn't want your superior rank and honour impugned by having to explain to everyone how you received your bruise from a dirty soldier so obviously beneath you.'

Mr Selton tugged a handkerchief from his pocket and pressed it to his broken lip. He hesitated and Luke wondered if he'd change his mind and meet Luke's challenge, but he doubted it. The man was a coward and he proved it by rushing off down the hall, calling for Gruger and announcing his immediate departure.

Luke turned to Miss Radcliff. She stood, one hand on her chest, confusion as much as surprise swirling in her eyes. He shifted close to her, aching to take her in his arms and run his hand along the arch of her back to smooth her shock. 'Are you all right?'

'Yes.' The whispered word brushed his neck above his cravat. He opened and closed his fingers, wanting to draw her into his arms and let her quick breaths subside against his chest as she leaned against him in comfort. Neither of them closed the small distance separating them. 'Once again you've saved me. Soon I'll owe you so much for your help, I'll have to singlehandedly extinguish a house fire to return the favour.'

Her limp smile punctuated her attempt at humour and Luke felt less like a hero and more like a heel.

'About our discussion earlier,' he stammered, warring with the urge to hold her close and the one to push her away. He could almost hear Captain Crowther's advice to forget everyone and do what he damn well pleased.

She laid a silencing finger on his lips and he almost groaned as her warm skin met his. It hurt to hold back from taking her hand and pressing his lips to her palm, but her gentle touch was a warning, not an invitation. 'There's no need to explain. I understand.'

'You don't.' He shifted closer, his fingertips brushing her skirt as she withdrew her hand.

She stared up at him, head back, lips parted, her desire as strong as his. The conflict ripping at him tore at her, too. It was in the hitch in her breathing, the stiffness of her shoulders and the delicate craving for him in her eyes. If there wasn't so much standing between them, he would claim her lips, and her, but he wouldn't cross the line he'd just pulled Mr Selton away from. 'If things were different...'

'But they aren't.' She darted around him, her skirt whispering against her legs as she fled down the hall, back to her life, leaving him to his.

The faint scent of dust and damp quickly overcame the fresh lavender scent of her. Luke leaned against the wall and tilted his head against the unpolished panelling. This wasn't the first time he'd stepped in to protect a woman from a man's unwanted advances, but it was the most personal. Miss Radcliff was alone in the world, made more so by his rejection of her friendship. It made her vulnerable to men like Mr Selton. Luke might have been here to protect her this time, but he wouldn't be in the future. She wasn't his to protect and she couldn't be. Neither his father nor his brother would sanction a match with a penniless girl of questionable birth. It didn't mean he had to like it. For the first time ever he cursed his honour and sense of duty. It was strangling him, but he wouldn't set it aside. Without the accomplishment of his Army career, honour and duty were all he had left.

Chapter Seven

The yapping and howling of the hunting dogs and the calls of the trainers outside on the drive filled the schoolroom. The guests were gathered downstairs in the entrance hall to escape the misty day, drinking brandy and preparing to ride out. The ladies would accompany them, enjoying the fresh autumn air as they galloped with the men over the rolling hills of the Huntford estate.

Joanna hadn't been downstairs since the incident in the hallway yesterday afternoon. It wasn't Mr Selton she feared. He'd departed soon after leaving them, causing his sister to bitterly complain about it ruining her play. It was Major Preston Joanna didn't want to see.

When she'd laid her finger on his lips, the passion which had sparked between them had stolen the air from the hallway and nearly carried off her resolve to keep her distance. She shouldn't have touched him, but she didn't want to hear his words, not when they contradicted everything in his eyes. She craved him as much as he did her and she could have rested her hands on his shoulders, risen up on her toes and kissed him, but she'd held back. His words in the library had been too fresh, the truth of his situation and hers too raw to allow either of them to weaken. His family's hopes for a future rested on him and she wouldn't be the one to wreck their expectations. If she did, they'd accuse her of ruining him in a quest to raise herself and their criticism would drive a wedge between him and them. He'd been willing to put aside their friendship for his family. He would deny his heart for them, too, and it was to her peril to ignore this.

'I don't want to study French. I want to go downstairs and see the guests getting ready for the hunt,' Catherine whined. The twins joined in the chorus of complaints about being kept upstairs while everyone gathered below.

Joanna was about to change the subject, when she remembered Vicar Carlson's words. If the girls wanted a reward, then she'd make sure they got it, but only if they did their work. 'If you complete your lessons, we might have time to sneak down to the landing and watch the riders before they leave.'

Instead of fighting her as they usually did, they set to work. Joanna might not want to venture down from the third floor, but it wasn't fair to keep the girls locked up here because of her fears. Besides, with so many people about, she and Major Preston weren't likely to be alone together. She'd make sure they weren't.

In a few minutes, the girls' work was complete and they followed Joanna down the stairs to the first-floor landing overlooking the entrance hall. Joanna held tight to the banister as she watched the women in their dark riding habits stand with the men in their breeches and coats. They didn't interest her as much as the possibility of seeing Major Preston, but he wasn't here. Perhaps he hadn't come down yet. Every sense became aware of the hallway behind her as she wondered if he would appear there before continuing down. She hoped he didn't. She couldn't trust herself to be so close to him.

With a surly sneer, Gruger oversaw the footmen

moving among the mingling guests carrying silver trays of hot brandy to fortify the riders against the bracing weather. Sir Rodger's black hunting dog sat beside his master, who chatted with the men in their tweeds and boots. The ladies in their long habits were spattered among the men, their voices filled with their anticipation for the coming ride. The clouds which had hung over Huntford Place all morning began to clear and thick shafts of sunlight dropped in through the windows over the front doors, much to everyone's delight.

'I want to go all the way down,' Catherine whispered, shifting from foot to foot at the excitement just out of her reach.

'Your father said you're not allowed to, but if you're good here, I'll talk to your mother about joining in charades after dinner.' She hoped she refused the request. It would keep Joanna out of the sitting room and away from Major Preston.

Catherine considered the choice and decided going along was better than fighting Joanna and risking her father's reprimand. Even the twins were behaving as they knelt at the balustrade to watch the guests. Whether or not their new obedience would last, or be enough to secure Joanna's position here, she wasn't certain, but she was happy for the change, no matter how small. It restored the confidence shaken out of her by Sir Rodger's warning and Major Preston's rejection.

Minutes passed and Major Preston still didn't appear among the guests. His family wasn't present either and she wondered if the incident with Mr Selton had driven them from the house. If it had, it was for the best. She wouldn't be at ease until he was gone, then he would fade in potency like the overly spiced biscuits Rachel had once baked.

The tinny notes of the hunter's horn filled the entrance hall. Guests filed out of the house, the barks of Sir Rodger's dog mixing with the yipping of the hunters made louder by a footman holding open the front door. The excited chatter of the guests hurrying to their mounts joined the eagerness of the hounds for the hunt. Joanna wished she could share in the thrill of riding out. It would give her something more to look forward to than the dreary passing of one same day into the next.

As the entrance hall grew quiet, the footmen began to collect the drink glasses. More than one of them finished the contents before they carried them out on their trays. Gruger trailed behind them, mumbling his usual abuses. Behind her, the girls rushed to the landing window overlooking the front drive to watch the riders preparing to set off.

Not seeing Major Preston, and not wanting to keep torturing herself with what she couldn't have, Joanna moved to gather up the girls. Then Major Preston's voice caught her notice and made her halt.

'It amazes me how much you want me to stay now that I'm of some use to you. You were all too eager to pack me off when you purchased my commission,' Major Preston accused, following his father who stormed out of the sitting room. 'I'm surprised you spent what you did to make me a lieutenant.'

Lord Ingham whirled on his son, ready to snap back before he seemed to think better of it. He settled his shoulders, his words measured and calm. 'I didn't buy you a posting as a lieutenant to get rid of you! I did it because I wanted you to make something of yourself and you did. I'm proud of you for doing it.'

The tightness along Major Preston's jaw eased

at his father's response, but it didn't settle the tension in each of his arms as he dug his fists into his hips. 'Then you asked me to give it all up.'

'I asked no more of you than my father asked of me when my elder brother died.' His father laid a steadying hand on his son's shoulder. 'I realise the sacrifices you've made on behalf of the family.'

Major Preston glanced past his father, up the stairs to where Joanna stood. 'I'm not sure you do.'

She held her breath, afraid to move and make Lord Ingham aware of her. Like every other guest except Major Preston, he'd failed to notice her.

'I do because I made the same one when I became the heir and had to sell my commission. Trust me, a year from now when you're settled with a wife and, God willing, a son, you'll feel very differently than you do now. However, I can see it won't happen with any of the ladies here, which is fine.' Lord Ingham let go of his son and tugged on his gloves. 'There are more lucrative women in London anyway.'

Lord Ingham strolled out the door, unaware of his son's lingering frustration as he stood in the centre of the entrance hall staring at Joanna. The conflict hardening the lines at the corners of his eyes matched the one in her heart. He lowered his hands to his sides and she dropped down a stair, ready to go to him and ease the pain torturing them both. Despite having silenced him yesterday, if he summoned her to him now, she would answer it. The sound of the barking dogs and chatting guests from outside faded as they continued to regard one another. She shouldn't want this, but she did. In the smoothing of his face as he viewed her, she knew he did, too.

Then, with a small frown, he nodded and strode out the door to join the others.

Joanna grasped the rough handrail, bracing herself against the weakness and relief filling her. Thank goodness he hadn't motioned to her and she hadn't been foolish enough to fly down to him and throw everything away on the promise of a mere conversation. It wasn't her place to be his confidante, especially not with the girls chatting at the window behind her. Anna and Ava would've run through the house yelling about Joanna and Luke at the top of their lungs if Joanna had been so rash.

'Miss Radcliff.' Mrs Winston, the nurse, came

up behind Joanna and the girls. The nurse's crisp voice brought Joanna back to her duties and responsibilities. They did not lie with Major Preston. 'It's time for the twins' walk.'

'Of course, and, Miss Catherine, you have lessons with the drawing master,' Joanna reminded her.

'I hate drawing lessons,' Catherine mumbled as she tromped off down the stairs.

'Miss Radcliff, I almost forgot, this arrived for you.' Mrs Winston removed a letter from her apron and handed it to her.

Joanna took it, thrilled to recognise Isabel's small, neat handwriting decorating the front. Mrs Winston took the twins by the hands and led them to the nursery to collect their coats and sturdy shoes. With the girls occupied, Joanna had two hours to herself.

She ran upstairs to fetch her pelisse from her room, then made for the back garden. She hurried across the weedy gravel path and up the back rise to the Greek temple perched on top. After seeing so many people gathered together, laughing and talking, she needed some words from her friend to remind her she wasn't so alone and to stop her from thinking about Major Preston.

Luke tugged on Duke's reins, forcing the animal to fall behind as the other riders surged forward, fast on the heels of the hounds. This wasn't so much a fox hunt as it was a husband hunt, with the most eligible young ladies circling him like a regiment of Hessians. More than one skilled female rider had tried to isolate him from the herd. He'd outwitted them all, having dodged too many enemy soldiers in battle to let a few Amazons in search of a mate outflank him. After an hour of evasive manoeuvres, he craved the peace of a solitary ride and time to ponder the conversation with his father, and his silent encounter with Miss Radcliff.

He turned Duke around and guided him into the woods to keep from being noticed by any eagle-eyed ladies. The sun warming the moist earth and the tart smell of old leaves and moss reminded him of his time with Miss Radcliff here the other day. When he'd seen her at the top of the stairs this morning, his vow to remain on course and not be distracted by the arch of her hips, the alluring brush of her curls against her ears had almost deserted him. He'd wanted to go to her and not give a damn about anything or anyone else, but his father's words had grounded him, even while he'd struggled to accept them.

He slowed Duke to an amble and the fall of the horse's hooves was muffled by the soft forest ground. His father suggesting he'd adjust to being home was like telling a prisoner he would come to love gaol, yet his father had said something similar the day he'd seen him off to the Army. He'd been right then, as he'd been right about Luke working his way up the ranks. For the first time, Luke wasn't mad at his father for being stingy with money to purchase his commission. He'd had a reason for it, not to foist Luke off on the world with the least amount of expense, but to give him a chance to make something of himself. And he had. The bitter sense of rejection Luke had carried since the day he'd been told of the commission faded. His father had been proud of his accomplishments. He would make him proud again.

If only it didn't mean turning away from Miss Radcliff.

Luke guided Duke out of the forest and back

across the field towards the peaked gables of Huntford Place. The sight of Miss Radcliff this morning had added to the disquiet making every small annoyance from the lack of coal in his bedroom fireplace to the tittering of the ladies grate on him. In the hallway yesterday, with Miss Radcliff's finger on his lips, her pulse flickering faintly against his skin, he'd almost taken back everything he'd told her and every promise he'd made to himself and his family. He couldn't disappoint them or lead Miss Radcliff in a merry dance. She didn't deserve to be trifled with.

He manoeuvred the horses around the house to the stables. In the paddock, he dismounted and left Duke with the groom, who was as slow in coming to fetch him as he was leading him inside. Luke considered going to the sitting room and composing another letter to Lord Helmsworth, or even Reginald, and then changed his mind. He couldn't sit still inside with Miss Radcliff somewhere about. He needed peace, not the constant distraction of listening for her voice.

He followed the winding path leading from the stables through the garden too wild to be considered fashionably unkempt. Heavy ivy covered stone statues and the topiaries had escaped their confines to obscure the original animals. The plants here were a great contrast to those in Spain. They'd been tougher there and more woody, their leaves sparser but green against the dry grass and brown earth of the fields. The air had been warmer, too, except in the mountains in winter.

He started up the small hill at the far end of the garden and the Grecian temple set atop it, all the while imagining returning to Spain when the war was over. He longed to see the country through eyes not looking for an enemy or a tactical advantage. In his musings, he wondered what Miss Radcliff would think of the land of Isabelle and Ferdinand with its mix of Catholic and Moorish influence. He didn't doubt she'd embrace the bright colours and varied flavours of Spain. He would show them to her if he could, help her to break out of the bleak existence trapping her as his duties trapped him, except it wasn't his place to do so.

Luke admired the Grecian temple as he approached it. The stone building with the columned veranda and domed roof appeared out of place so close to a Stuart-era house. In the shadow of the dome, statues filled tall niches set at even intervals. As he grew closer, one of the statues on the far right stepped out of the shadows, revealing itself to be Miss Radcliff.

Instead of waiting for him, she slipped around the back of the building and out of sight.

'Miss Radcliff, wait.' He hurried after her, ignoring the instinct telling him to walk away. He climbed the stairs and rounded the grey stone to see her standing at the far edge, her back to him and a letter dangling in one gloved hand. 'Is everything all right?'

'Yes, I'm quite well.' It was clear the moment she turned that she wasn't. Her pretty lips were drawn thin and her eyes were hard with her troubles. 'I often come here to think when the girls are taking other lessons or with their nurse.'

'But that's not why you're here today, is it?' He dragged his fingers over the rough wall as he approached her, noting how her distress intensified the blue of her eyes.

'Not today.'

'Bad news?' He motioned to the paper.

'No, not at all.' She raised the letter and it fluttered in the breeze. 'It's from my friend, Isabel. She's married Viscount Langford's son.'

Apparently, Luke wasn't the only son of a titled gentleman enamoured with a governess. 'You don't approve of him?'

'I don't even know him. She barely knows him.' She paced back and forth across the unpolished stone. The plain, brown pelisse hanging shapeless over her curves fluttered with each stiff step. 'There's almost nothing in her letter saying why she married him, except that she had to and he hasn't turned out to be the husband she imagined, but she doesn't say how. What if he's a monster?'

'Or better than she expected.' Given what Luke knew of William Balfour and his reputation, Miss Radcliff's worries weren't unfounded, but he said nothing. He didn't want to add to her distress. If Mr Balfour was at last settling down, then maybe he'd changed. He wouldn't be the first wild rake tamed by a gentle hand. He leaned against a pillar, far more philosophical than usual. 'That's the thing about chances, you never know how they'll turn out until you take one.'

She crossed her arms beneath her breasts, pulling the pelisse tight to trace the curve of their fullness. 'Don't tell me you're a romantic.'

'Not at all, but I've taken a chance or two in my time.' He dug the regimental badge from his pocket and held it out to her. She opened her palm and he dropped it on the soft cotton of her glove. 'Back in May, at Fuentes de Oñoro, there was a break in the line. My men, alongside the Light Division, were sent to reinforce the right flank. During the fighting, some distance away, I noticed a squad trapped by heavy fire and on the verge of being overrun. I could've wasted time telling my commanding officer, leaving it to him to order men to their aid. Instead, I took a chance and led my squad to cover them. We were outnumbered, but we held the French off until the men and their wounded could retreat, then we crushed the French, helping to secure the line. It earned me a promotion to major.'

She fingered the badge, then handed it back to him. 'Chance seems a very unpredictable way to plan a life.'

'It's a mistake to think you can plan it.' He slipped the badge back in his coat pocket. 'I'd intended to enjoy my major rank for longer than four months. You came here to mould young ladies. I'd say neither of our plans unfolded as we'd expected.'

'No, they didn't.' Her words trailed off with the same disappointment which racked him every time he thought he might never return to his regiment. He raised his hand to take hers, then rested it on a column instead. He couldn't allow his misguided sense of chivalry to make him cross the boundaries which separated them.

'All will be well with your friend.' He hoped so for Miss Radcliff's sake and her friend's.

She folded the letter and shoved it into the pocket of her drab pelisse. 'Isabel is taking a chance and I should wish her the best, and I do, but...'

'You envy her.' They shouldn't be sharing confidences, but he couldn't walk away. She'd helped him in the woods with Edward. It was only right for him to do the same for her.

She nodded, her pale round cheeks colouring with her shame. 'She's going to have everything I've ever wanted, a real family and children. You must think I'm awful for being so petty.'

'No, I don't.' Together, they stood at the edge of the temple and looked out over the woods at the leaves turning brown and orange and red. Her nearness awed him as much as the stunning breadth of the land and the sky above it. He understood the conflict making her sigh with frustration because it was his, too. 'Yesterday, I received a letter from my friend, Captain Crowther, telling me of their victory in a skirmish. I should've written at once to congratulate him, but I didn't. I'm jealous because he's there and I'm not. We wouldn't be human if we weren't petty sometimes.'

'Maybe it's not even her I'm jealous of, but her position. It gave her opportunity.' A flock of crows took off out of the trees. The wind supporting their flight whipped past Joanna and Luke, making the bonnet ribbons beneath her pert chin flutter over her neck and chest. The satin slid across her fine skin as he longed to do with his fingers while his lips smoothed the small furrow between her brows. 'Here, there isn't even a chance for me to take in order to change things.'

'There will be.'

'When?' She turned to him, the demand for an answer sharp in the cool depths of her eyes.

Chance. It was here in front of him, eclipsing

everything he might lose with what he stood to gain. He should walk away, stay true to his vow to resist the allure of her rich curls beneath her plain bonnet and dismiss the faint scent of lavender distracting him. He should ignore her wit and intelligence and the craving for her understanding that tugged at him, but he couldn't. She held something more precious and necessary to him than money, status or even security. It was peace. 'Now.'

He took her in his arms and pressed his lips to hers.

Joanna fell into his comforting embrace and the temptation in his kiss. Her heart pounded with the risk and the thrill of his body as solid as the temple against hers. She rested her hands on his chest and his strong pulse beneath her fingertips reminded her she was young and alive and all her dreams might still come true. A shiver coursed through her as he traced her lips with his tongue, his breath one with hers as he held her close. He tasted like the drink of strong port she'd sneaked once at a soirée for the school patrons, rich, sharp and forbidden. She savoured him as she had the liquor, each illicit taste making her crave more.

She slid her hands up over the sturdy curve of his chest, past the white cravat and collar surrounding his neck. With small circles she traced the smoothness of the skin before raising her fingers to slide them into his hair. His grip tightened around her and his arms crossed behind her back as he rested his hands on her hips and enveloped her in his embrace. In the circle of his arms was a belonging she'd never experienced before, not even at Madame Dubois's. Despite being hidden away and ignored, he'd seen her for who she was and he wanted her. It almost made every risk she was taking with him worth it.

A faint darkness crept in beneath her bliss, like a mist along the ground at dusk. He had little to lose with this liaison while she might sacrifice everything for a fleeting bit of happiness. She clung to it like she did his biceps, his muscles hard beneath her grip, trying to forget reality, duty and consequences. Beyond the strength of his kiss, the tightness of his fingers against her back, nothing else had changed, not his situation or hers.

She withdrew her fingers from his hair and

broke from his lips, but not his embrace. He eased his arms from around her waist, but left his hands to linger on the narrowness of it. Every argument against their being together nearly died on her tongue as she held his fierce gaze. The dreams of being with him that she'd entertained in the middle of the night felt more real than anything she'd experienced at Huntford Place. Her heart urged her to embrace whatever was happening between them and perhaps gain everything she'd ever desired.

'Miss Radcliff, are you out here?' Mrs Winston's voice carried over the temple, piercing Joanna's bliss. 'I need your help.'

The twins yelled like devils as they tore through the garden, silencing the birds twittering overhead.

Joanna stared up at Luke, reluctant to let him go and step back into the awfulness of her life, but she had to. She wasn't ready to lose what little she had over a single kiss no matter how marvellous.

'Miss Radcliff?' Mrs Winston's voice grew closer and needier.

Major Preston opened his arms. Joanna slowly backed away and eased around the curve of the temple, reluctant to look away from him until she was forced to turn and face the house. Mrs Winston waddled up the rise, through the high grass, her round face red with the exertion of her walk and having to deal with the Ava and Anne.

'Here I am.' Joanna rushed down the stone steps to meet her.

'Oh, thank heavens.' Mrs Winston sighed, laying a hand on her generous bosom. 'I can't control the twins and you have such a way with them.'

Joanna struggled not to roll her eyes at the unconvincing flattery. The nurse was as useless as the rest of the Huntford servants and Joanna was sure Mrs Winston wanted to gossip with the other maids instead of minding the hellish imps, but she held her tongue. She was afraid to speak too much and reveal in her wavering words the fear settling over her. She'd nearly been caught in an intimate situation with Major Preston and her secret was still in danger of being discovered.

Joanna glanced back at the temple as she wrested a stick from Anne before she could pummel Ava. There was no sign of Luke and she was confident he would remain hidden until it was safe for him to leave. It didn't meant she should dawdle here and risk the twins racing up to the temple and finding him. She took Mrs Winston by the arm and led her back towards the house while urging the twins to come along. Thankfully, the promise of a sweet if they listened resulted in the girls following her and the nurse like obedient ducklings.

With the shadows of Huntford Place coming over her, she was more confused now than when she'd left it to read Isabel's letter. It wasn't her friend's rashness which stunned and concerned her, but her own. She'd taken a chance. Time would tell what it would gain her.

Luke stayed at the temple until the sun touched the top of the trees. He watched it drop behind the forest and listened as the songs of the birds gave way to quiet. In the distance, the windows of Huntford Place lit up, but still he didn't return. Inside, ladies who considered the house party the highlight of autumn would be wondering where he was. They would sit down to supper, puzzled the prized catch hadn't joined them. He couldn't, because Miss Radcliff wouldn't be with them and he could no longer pretend it didn't matter.

An owl screeched, and a chill wind whipped across the stone. Luke drew his coat tighter about his neck as he rose at last and left the circle of the temple dome. If he stayed out here much longer, Gruger might be roused to arrange a search party and Luke didn't want the whole house out looking for him. If he found a way to pursue Miss Radcliff, it would cause enough of a stir, especially among his family.

He rounded the curve and descended the steps, thinking of Miss Radcliff as he parted the long grass with each stride. To have her at last in his arms, her curves easy and sweet against his hard planes, proved more tempting than seizing a poorly guarded outpost. Yet the tenderness of her lips, the eagerness with which she'd folded in to him, didn't erase the obstacles facing them.

Luke crossed the garden and entered the house through the music room at the back. He slipped past the sitting room unnoticed, the draw of charades distracting everyone. Inside, Mr Chilton danced around like an Italian opera performer as he tried to mimic who knew what. Luke should announce his presence, but he couldn't, not to these empty-headed twits.

He climbed the stairs to the first floor and instead of making for the bachelor rooms, he turned left and went to his mother's room. Light flickered beneath her door and he knocked. 'It's Luke.'

Her apple-cheeked lady's maid pulled open the door and his mother heaved a sigh of relief from where she sat by the fire. 'Oh, thank heavens. Miss Chilton said she saw you ride back to the house and the groom said Duke was in the stable, but it's been hours. Where have you been?'

'Out walking.' He hugged his mother, wondering how she'd react if he told here where and with whom he'd really been. 'I'm sorry I worried you.'

'Don't do it again.' She swatted his arm, then motioned for the maid to leave them. 'I know your father has given up on you finding a wife here, but I had a chance to speak with Miss Winborn at dinner. She's a very charming lady with a three-thousand-pound dowry, and is quite overlooked by everyone. It must be the red hair, such an unfortunate family trait. I believe she's worth another look.'

He ground his teeth at the frank mention of the lady's true value. 'What if I choose a lady of greater character than Miss Winborn, but with no money?'

His mother fingered the tassels at the end of her shawl. 'Luke, you know the situation we're in and how much a wife with a healthy dowry will help us.'

'And what about my happiness? Does it mean nothing to you?'

'Of course, but marriage is difficult enough without the added burden of bills.' She jerked the shawl across her shoulders, making it clear there were indeed limits for her to his happiness.

'If I resolve the issue with Lord Helmsworth, I wouldn't need a wife with a dowry.'

'It's a very uncertain outcome to base all our futures on.' She laid one finger on her chin. 'Who are you considering? Is it Miss Bell? I understand her family's means are as strained as ours. Imagine Edward's reaction if you chose her. That alone should put you off her.'

'I have no interest in Miss Bell.'

'Then who are you speaking of?'

'No one. It's simply a hypothetical question.'

He wasn't about to reveal the truth because he had yet to determine exactly what it was. Joanna cared for him as much as he did for her, but nothing was settled between them. Until it was, and they could stand proudly together before everyone, there was no point in risking her reputation—no matter how much he wanted to be with her.

Chapter Eight

Joanna hurried down the path in the woods. In the distance, through a break in the trees, she noticed the large grey clouds gathering on the horizon. The faint scent of rain hung in the air. For the moment, the afternoon was warm and the echoes of guns sounded over the trees as the men took advantage of the fine weather to hunt. The ladies were once again rehearsing the play, while the twins were with their nurse and Catherine with her music teacher. It gave Joanna time to visit Vicar Carlson, to escape the house and the agitation of being confined with every possibility of encountering Major Preston.

After yesterday, and a restless night of trying not to think about him, she wasn't ready to face him or the lingering questions left by his kiss. If Rachel, Grace or Isabel were here, she could chat endlessly about Major Preston the way Grace used to gush about her young man, until the enthusiasm had died and her real troubles had begun. Joanna didn't need Grace's kind of problems.

She stopped on the bank of the brook and opened and closed her hands. The press of his fingers against hers was as immediate as the water flowing by. He wanted her, not in Mr Selton's licentious way, but as something more, but what she couldn't say. Caring for him meant defying everyone, including Madame's expectations, and it wasn't like her to flaunt convention for a fling.

But is it more than a fling? She didn't know, and with only one way to find out she wasn't about to try. He was distracting her from her duties enough already. All morning, she'd barely been able to concentrate and her lax supervision had made her charges even more wild than usual. If she didn't focus on her position, and not on a fantasy, she'd soon find herself returned to Salisbury and separated from Major Preston for good. Would he follow her if she left? She wasn't sure and the uncertainty troubled her as much as the memory of his kiss.

She reached the brook and, holding out her arms

to better balance herself, hopped across the rocks. She stepped over the loose one, for there was no Major Preston here to catch her if she stumbled, then finished her crossing and walked up the opposite bank. Isabel might rush headlong into a relationship and Grace might lose her head on a whim, but not Joanna. She was too sensible and practical, or so she'd believed until yesterday afternoon.

At last the vicarage came into view and she hurried towards it. She needed someone to talk to who could distract her, even if the one subject she most wanted to discuss couldn't be broached. Vicar Carlson might understand her situation at Huntford Place, but she imagined he wouldn't approve of a governess dallying with a gentlemen. Few people did.

The gate at the end of the walk hung open and she slowed as she passed it. The tangy scent of chimney smoke didn't greet her, nor did the gentle neigh of the vicar's horse. Her excitement waned at the sight of the front door standing slightly ajar. She pushed it open and her heart dropped. There was nothing in the room except a suite of old furniture in front of a cold fireplace and a few papers scattered across the dusty floor.

'Vicar Carlson,' Joanna called out as she stepped inside, hoping the absence of clutter was he or his maid having cleaned. She moved deeper into the house, past the faded chintz of the armchair and a matching *chaise* to where the bookshelf stood empty except for the dust outlining where the books used to be. She clasped her arms across her chest and rubbed them to warm herself. 'Where did he go?'

'To London.' A male voice sounded from behind her. 'He received a more lucrative living there.'

Joanna whirled around to find Major Preston in the doorway. He wore his tweed hunting clothes and the faint acrid scent of gunpowder clung to him. During every moment when the twins had focused on their work and allowed her to dream, she'd pictured him in the Greek temple, the low afternoon light softening the angle of his chin and the slight scar along his hairline. The memories of his curved and strong lips beneath a regally arching nose were nothing compared to him in person. She glanced at a round water stain on the table beside the chair, already missing the kind old man, especially with Luke standing mere feet away. If he were here, she wouldn't be so worried about being weak with Major Preston. 'He said nothing to me about leaving when he invited me to come see him.'

'You must have made quite an impression on him. He wasn't an inviting vicar. Must be why the Marquis liked him so much.' Major Preston laughed and the low sound moved through her like the tide in Sandhills had. He stepped deeper into the room and set his hat on the bench beside the door.

'I seem to have made an impression on a number of gentlemen here, wouldn't you say, Major Preston?' She didn't have time to be coy or the stomach for sneaking around. She needed to know where they stood, what he hoped might come of yesterday, assuming it was anything at all.

'Yes, you have,' he admitted without hesitation, driving more pressing questions from her mind. 'And, please, call me Luke.'

She should resist this informality, especially after their prior breech of etiquette, but she couldn't. Even without the books and personal items, with Luke here the vicarage was more inviting than the cosiest room in Huntford Place. 'And you may call me Joanna, in private of course.'

'Of course.'

'What are you doing here?' she asked, eager to pull back from the craving for intimacy drawing her deeper into this forbidden friendship.

'I was on my way to Helmsworth Manor when I saw you come in here.'

He followed me.

All night she'd imagined him taking her in his arms and claiming her once again. In the sunlight, the dream faded and reality took its place. Major Preston came here to find a rich wife with a nobler lineage than hers. If she didn't end things between them, they might do something they'd regret. Joanna already mourned the many things she wouldn't have in life. She didn't want to make it worse by losing her heart to a man she couldn't have.

'You shouldn't have followed me. It isn't right for us to be alone together.'

She tried to pass him but he caught her hand.

'Don't leave. Not yet.'

She whirled to face him, and didn't pull away as his fingers tightened around hers.

'I can no longer ignore my feelings or my concern for you. I admire you, and care for you more deeply than I should.'

Her heart began to race with both fear and excitement as he made small circles on the back of her hand with his thumb. She knew she should go, but the tenderness in his eyes was making her insides burn and it wouldn't allow her to leave. Instead, she shifted closer and tilted her face up to his, craving what he offered despite the risks. It went against every rational thought she'd ever possessed about right and wrong, possible and impossible, but his chest against hers and his heavy arms drawing her close were the only things that mattered.

Then their lips met and the fluttering rising in the pit of her stomach filled her entire being. She could think of nothing but his mouth on hers, his hand on the small of her back. She rose up on her toes, eager for his hand to slide lower as she pressed further into his kiss. Against her stomach she felt the intensity of his need and it made her wobble on her toes before his firm embrace steadied her. His breathing matched hers as he at last gripped her buttocks and bent her deeper into the curve of his body. The gentle flick of his tongue against her lips drew hers out to caress his and the salty taste of him made her forget all of her misgivings.

The bliss was broken by the distant peal of the village church bells. They rang out over the forest while the church beside the vicarage remained silent. The sound ended the kiss which had held them together for so many glorious moments. There was no wresting apart, but a slow coming down as she settled onto her heels. She ran her fingers along his temples and across the planes of his cheeks to rest on his shoulders.

Then the clop of a horse's hooves and the low 'whoa' from a rider outside made her stiffen in his arms.

'Who's here?' an angry voice called out from the front gate.

'It's Lord Helmsworth.' Luke pulled her to an open door of a large, empty cupboard and waited for her to climb inside. 'Stay here. He can't see you.'

He closed the door. Light fell through a crack in the top, but there was no way for her to see through the wood. The stomp of boots on the vicarage floor announced Lord Helmsworth's ill-timed arrival. She cringed away from the door and struggled to keep her breathing even and quiet, afraid of being detected and ruined.

'Major Preston, what are you doing here?' Lord Helmsworth demanded. She'd never met the man, but his voice sounded familiar.

'I came to see Vicar Carlson,' Luke answered as if giving him the time. She envied his steady nerves. Hers were running wild.

'Liar. You knew he was leaving, everyone did. You're here with a woman. Where is she?' Lord Helmsworth stomped past the cupboard and Joanna froze as she heard the door to another room creak open on its hinges. 'I thought I saw someone with you through the window.'

'There's no one here but the two of us.' Luke's voice revealed nothing while Joanna swallowed hard against a dry throat.

'Typical military man. This isn't a place for your secret trysts.'

Lord Helmsworth thundered past the cupboard, making the door rattle before another door creaked open, this one too close to where Joanna hid. One more door and he'd find her. Her laughter with

Luke and their easy conversation seemed so much more perilous than before. Even with her heart pounding in her ears, she didn't regret it. He was no Lieutenant Foreman, escaping from a woman in order to save himself the moment they were discovered. He'd find a way to keep her safe, just as he had the night of the ball. He wouldn't abandon her.

'I didn't come here for a tryst,' Luke answered, still polite and calm. 'Given your friendship with Vicar Carlson, I'd hoped he could help us to resolve the land dispute.'

Lord Helmsworth finally gave up his frenzied search. 'There is no dispute. The last land survey—'

'The one you paid to have conducted and then refused to allow my family to observe?' Luke challenged.

'It doesn't matter who paid. The surveyor took the measurements and he said the land along with the river is mine—and it will remain so.'

Luke wasn't so easily dissuaded. Lord Helmsworth's arrival was both annoying and fortuitous. An agreement with him would smooth the way to a more pleasurable one with Joanna. 'Then allow us to lease it from you, or to negotiate the use of the river for our fields. We don't need to own the land to have access to it.'

'You won't trick me into parting with it or anything on it.' Lord Helmsworth crossed his arms as if to say the discussion was over. With his blue eyes narrowed, their colour strikingly similar to Joanna's, it was clear there'd be no rational conversation. 'A captain cost me my daughter, I won't let a puffed-up major cost me my land.'

Luke opened and closed his fist by his side, determined to keep hold of his temper. He'd seen what Lord Helmsworth's grief for his only child had done to the laughing gentleman he remembered from the Christmas party and he pitied him.

'Were it in my power to punish the man who ruined your daughter I would, but I can't. Nor can I answer for his crimes as they aren't mine,' Luke replied with more ease than he normally would have granted a man disparaging him and his hard work for his country.

The anger in Lord Helmsworth's eyes settled down to a more subtle roar. Luke waited, wondering if a touch of sympathy was enough to bring the man around to seeing reason. It wasn't.

'Get out of here and don't bother me again.' He stormed past him and out of the vicarage.

Luke watched him through the window, disappointed but not deterred as the Marquis mounted his horse and rode off. Given the stubbornness of all parties involved, it was no wonder the boundary dispute had continued for so long. It would end with Luke, one way or another. Until then, there was another, more vexing matter dominating him.

He tugged open the cupboard door and guilt racked him as the sunlight illuminated Joanna's wide, nervous eyes. He'd never compromised a woman before, yet he'd almost done so today.

'He's gone.'

She stepped out and peered around, as though still in danger. 'What if he comes back?'

'He won't. Not given the speed with which he left. I'm sorry for jeopardising your reputation. It was wrong of me to do so.'

'And it was wrong for me to go along. I must return to the house.'

She rushed out the door and down the path.

He stared through the half-open door at the dead and sagging heads of the flowers in the garden beyond. He could follow her, mount Duke and ride to catch up with her, pull her into the saddle and savour the sweet curve of her buttocks rocking against him with each pounding thud of Duke's hooves, but he didn't move.

He'd followed her to the vicarage to tease out more of her true feelings for him. In the softness of her lips and the way she'd clung to him, he had. It hadn't clarified anything, but had only made everything much more complicated.

He snatched up his hat and settled it over his hair. Instead of strengthening the growing connection between them, their indiscretion had almost ruined her and had probably driven her away. He shouldn't have been so foolhardy, but when they were alone together his desire for her was stronger than the need for caution. That was dangerous, especially for Joanna.

He strode outside to where Duke stood tied to a tree. He grabbed the edge of the saddle, ready to mount, when the pounding of hooves echoing off the trees made him pause. Down the road, Edward rode fast up on him. His brother pulled the reins of his horse to a stop, his face grave as he stared down at Luke.

'You must return to the house at once.'

'Found another excuse to keep me from visiting Lord Helmsworth, have you?' Luke hauled himself into the saddle. He shouldn't be curt with Edward and risk another fight, but the setbacks in the vicarage had shortened his patience. 'You needn't bother, I've already spoke to him.'

'This has nothing to do with him. Lord Beckwith has arrived to speak with you.'

Luke's heels halted over Duke's flanks. There was no reason for anyone from the Army to come all this way to see him, except one.

Chapter Nine

Joanna stood against the wall across the sitting room, watching Luke speak with the newest addition to the house party. Lord Beckwith had created quite a stir with his unexpected arrival, throwing both Gruger and Lady Huntford into a tizzy. Thankfully, Mr Selton's departure had freed a bedroom, settling the matter of Lord Beckwith's accommodations but not his reason for needing it. If either he or Luke had enlightened anyone as to why he was here, it hadn't reached Joanna. Lady Selton and Lady Chilton hadn't heard the reason either judging from their conversation on the sofa in front of her.

She was as curious as they were, but prudent enough not to approach Luke in search of an answer. Without one, her mind created plenty and none of them were good. The faint darkness beneath his eyes, the hard set of his features as he stood in deep conversation with Lord Beckwith told her something bad had happened since she'd left him. She wished she could cross the room to him and speak as freely with him as she did during their time alone together, but she couldn't. She'd already caught Lady Pensum examining her and Luke on more than one occasion, as though she suspected something between them. Whether she disapproved or not Joanna couldn't discern, but her mere suspicion made Joanna's skin clammy.

It wasn't Lady Pensum eyeing her now, but Lady Huntford. Joanna dropped her focus to the woven swirls in the green rug beneath her feet. If the woman realised her efforts to land Luke for her daughter were being threatened by a mere governess, she'd throw Joanna out of the house tonight. After a short while, she dared to look up, relieved to find Lady Huntford distracted by Frances telling her something before quitting the room, but not Luke. He examined her, his need for her evident in his dark eyes. It tore at her to deny him comfort, but she must, especially with Lady Huntford approaching her in a flutter of purple and red.

'Frances doesn't feel well and is retiring for

the evening. You may go to bed.' Lady Huntford barely paused on her way to the game table to deliver the news.

Joanna walked slowly along the edge of the room towards the door, aware of Luke watching her, but she didn't return his questioning glance. Whatever was troubling him, there was no chance of finding out about it tonight. She meandered down the dimly lit hallway, unwilling to rush. She needed the activity to calm her agitation.

As she reached the stairs, the quick fall of boots on the stone floor behind her made her turn. Luke was hurrying to catch up to her.

'What are you doing?' The question was barely out of her mouth before he caught her by the arm and pulled her into the shadows on the far side of the stairs.

'I need to speak with you. It's important.'

'We can't. What if somebody sees us?' It was one thing to dally with him at the vicarage. It was entirely different in the main hall of Huntford Place. She tried to peer around him, but the staircase jutting out from the wall above kept them in the shadows. They were out of view of guests leaving the sitting room, but in plain sight of anyone coming down from the first floor. She wouldn't put it past the twins, or Catherine, to be up there right now trying to catch a glimpse of what was happening downstairs. If they saw anything it would be the end of her time here. She must think of her employment and her future.

'No one followed me. I told them I didn't feel well and was going to bed.'

'Then you'd better go to your room and allow me to go to mine.' She tried to step around him, but he slid in front of her, blocking the way. It didn't send a chill of fear through her as it had with Mr Selton. Luke's determination to be near her and the bracing scent of his cologne overwhelmed her. She wanted to fall into his arms, press her lips to his and enjoy the weight of his hands on her back. It was a powerful and dangerous urge.

'Please, we must speak,' he implored.

He should be turning to his family or someone else, not her, but the anguish in his voice pierced her and she couldn't leave him to suffer. 'Meet me at the vicarage in an hour.'

'Thank you.' He laid a lingering kiss on her forehead and she sighed, wanting to be with him now, to not even wait until they were safe. Let Catherine or Frances see them, it would be a relief to stop this sneaking around and admit to everyone how much she wanted him.

Then he fled from the shadows and up the stairs.

Joanna leaned back against the wall and pressed her fingertips against the smooth panelling. What was she thinking to suggest a private meeting? To do so meant risking being caught sneaking in and out of the house, or not in bed should some emergency arise with the girls. Lady Pensum's earlier scrutiny in the sitting room had been a warning, and if Joanna was wise, she'd put an end to this little affair. She couldn't, not before she found out what was wrong with Luke. If Lord Beckwith was here, it must have something to do with Luke's commission. Perhaps he was going back to the Spain. If she didn't meet him tonight, she might never see him again, unless he decided to take her with him. In Spain, they could escape the demands of his family and society, but she doubted it. He was too honourable to leave his parents to deal with their troubles, or to run away from duty. He needed her and she would go to him, but it didn't mean she'd be foolish enough to compound her mistakes with the greatest one an unmarried woman could make. She was too sensible to forget herself, or so she hoped.

Joanna followed the path through the woods to the vicarage. Overhead, thick clouds filled the sky. The gaps between them allowed the moonlight and a few stars to peek through, but with the stiff wind pushing them together, the faint light would soon be gone. The smell of rain which had punctuated the air all evening was heavier now and seemed to dampen the forest sounds. Joanna pulled her pelisse tighter around her neck as the vicarage came into sight. She hoped the rain held off until this meeting with Luke was over. It would be difficult enough to sneak back into Huntford Place and up to her room without leaving a trail of wet footprints behind her.

The first flash of lightning lit up the darkness as she slipped inside the vicarage and closed the door. Luke knelt in front of the fireplace, blowing the embers beneath a log to life. The curve of his back as he bent over the fire entranced her. She gripped the smooth door handle tight. Alone with him, it was only her own determination keeping them apart and it was already wavering.

'Aren't you afraid someone will see the smoke?' she asked, worried, keeping the danger in mind despite her eagerness to warm her frigid hands.

'No.' He stood to face her as the rising flame sent its light out into the room to illuminate the chairs, the walls and him. His face was ashen, and his mouth tightly drawn.

'What's wrong?' Joanna hurried to him, stopping before she reached him. She was here to listen and comfort him, not to tempt him with her touch.

'Captain Crowther and the rest of my squad are missing. They were surprised by the French in a narrow pass. There was no escape.'

'Are they alive?'

'I don't know.' He raked his hand through his hair, causing a few strands to fall over his forehead. 'The commander hasn't received a request to exchange prisoners or officers.'

'Then they might have survived.'

'Or no one has found their bodies yet.' He paced the small room, his heels striking the floor. 'I've seen it happen before, men slaughtered and left for the birds to pick at until another regiment finds them.'

'You can't give up hope until you hear more,' she encouraged. His losing his friend would be like her losing Isabel, Grace and Rachel and she could imagine his despair.

'I should've been with them. I know those passes and the local men, informants and sympathisers, all of them. I might have learned of the ambush, or found another way out of the pass before it was too late.' He stared out the window into the darkness. Rain began to plink against the roof, lightly at first before falling hard and steady. 'I could've helped them.'

She slipped up behind him and stroked his back. In the face of his pain, she couldn't remain aloof. 'Or been captured or killed. Think what your death would do to your parents.' *To me.* Her heart almost stopped at the thought.

'Yes, they'd have been crushed along with all their hope for their precious heir.' His muscles tightened beneath her palm. 'I shouldn't have left my men.'

Joanna wrapped her arms around Luke and laid her cheek on his back, hoping to soothe the bitterness marring his words. She shouldn't touch him like this, it was too intimate and enticing, but he was hurting and he needed her comfort. 'Don't give up on them. They may still be alive.'

'And if they aren't?' He turned in her embrace and rested his chin on her head, his chest rising and falling beneath her cheek. She closed her eyes and inhaled his scent of smoke mixed with the faint heat of his skin. He held her as if she alone could provide the strength to hope for his friends. She would give it to him, as he'd given it to her.

'Then make sure they, and the families who need them, aren't forgotten. Speak with Lord Beckwith, the War Office, anyone who can make a difference to your men and their loved ones.'

He leaned back to look down at her, the wild grief in his eyes settling. 'It seems a paltry reason to be spared from sharing their fate.'

'Not to those they left behind.'

He brushed a strand of hair off her face before his hand came to rest on the nape of her neck, heavy against the faint exposed skin. 'What if it isn't enough?'

She didn't want him to doubt himself, but to be the determined man she'd come to adore, the one who'd stand beside her the way he did his men. It was the real reason she was here, risking everything to be near him. She wanted him, despite all her efforts to convince herself and him otherwise. In his embrace, so many things she'd yearned for at last seemed possible. 'You won't give up. It isn't who you are. You'll keep fighting until it is enough and then you'll do more.'

He rubbed his thumb against the fluttering pulse on her neck. Hesitation marred the smoothness of his touch and it made her breath catch in her throat. Like her he was wavering between holding back and pressing forward. Then, the frustration and desperation which had filled his eyes was gone and she knew he'd made his decision, and so had she.

'I used to think duty and honour were the only things worth coming home for, the only things keeping me here, even at Huntford Place.' He lowered his face so close to hers each word whispered across her cheeks. 'I was wrong. It's you.'

The roar of the rain on the roof overhead faded as he claimed her mouth, his need for her deeper than lust. She didn't dare call it love. It couldn't exist in so short an amount of time no matter what the old fairy tales said. This was a bond between the two of them which eased her aching loneliness. It might not last beyond the sunrise, but she didn't care. Only Luke and the thrill of being in his arms mattered. She hadn't wanted to be a governess any more than he'd wanted to leave the Army, but she'd done what was expected of her. Tomorrow she would do the same, but tonight was for her, and him.

Lightning flashed as he lowered her onto the *chaise* behind them, covering her body with his. The weight of him on top of her, his lips teasing and tickling her neck, were exquisite. Fire swept through her as he raised the hem of her skirt and traced the smooth skin of her calves, his hand hot against the cool air of the house. The faint voice of reason urged her to end this, but she ignored it as she sank deeper into the desire pulling them together.

As he stroked the line of her thigh, she freed his cravat from the confines of the knot holding it closed. She drew it out from around his neck and dropped it to the floor. With hesitant flicks of her tongue, she tasted the sweet flesh of his neck, as curious as she was tempted by the play of his fingers over her hips. In this moment, she wasn't the governess, prim, proper, mute and ignored, but shameless and free with a man who'd made her glow like one of the embers.

Luke drank in Joanna as she lay beneath him. He shouldn't compromise her or surrender to this fervour, but he couldn't pull himself away. He'd never been carried off by emotions like he was with her and tonight he didn't fight it. He wanted her in his life, to make her happy and no consequences or anyone's opinions could separate them.

Rising up, he slid his hands along her slender waist and over her flat stomach to undo the small buttons holding together the front of her pelisse. Her eyes were alight with her desire as she watched him remove the layers of clothing separating her flesh from his. The cold of the room faded as he slipped the chemise off her shoulders and past the curve of her hips. She was gorgeous in the soft firelight, her unpinned hair falling over her full breasts which rose with each breath. He sat up on his heels and took off his coat, waistcoat and shirt, making himself as vulnerable and open to her as she was to him.

She shivered, her breasts drawing tight with the chill. He knelt before her and raised one of her curving legs. Her calf was supple against his palm as he removed the plain stocking covering her skin. He dropped the simple garments still warm with her heat onto the floor, then lowered her foot to the *chaise*. He guided her down against the rumpled pillows and lowered himself to cover her. She didn't question him, but followed his lead, believing in him as his men had done. He wouldn't betray her any more than he had them, but lead them on to a victory neither of them could've imagined before they'd entered this cottage.

He stood and removed his breeches, revealing his full need. Far from shrinking away, she embraced him as he continued to explore her body. Her soft moans when he found her centre were more precious to him than even the cries of triumph over a battlefield. She was not an enemy to conquer or to avoid like the other ladies in the house, but a joy to savour and celebrate and he would.

He slipped between her legs and claimed her mouth as he sought entrance. She granted it, drawing him into her body as she had her heart. As they moved together, he lost himself in her. He didn't want it to end, but as her breath quickened in his ear and her moans gave ways to cries of pleasure, a wave of release carried them both beyond everything except each other.

The fire crackled in the grate while the storm outside continued to rage. Joanna lay entwined with Luke on the *chaise*, more at ease than she'd ever been before. Sweat glistened on their bodies and the cold nipped at her back as they hugged one another close. A gust of wind drove the rain against the window and another bolt of lightning lit up the room. Regret seemed as far away as Huntford Place while she lay in his arms, this peace worth every chance she'd taken tonight to be with him.

'I'll be right back.' Luke made for the bedroom down the short hall past the cupboard where she'd hidden the other day. The firelight caressed the curve of his buttocks as he walked, emphasising every taut ripple of his muscles. Joanna bit her lip at the temptation in his stride as he returned with a blanket and nothing else.

'Quite the devilish smile.' He grinned as he flicked the blanket over her.

'You bring out the hellion in me.' She threw her leg over his hips as he joined her beneath the thick quilt.

'I like this wanton Joanna, it's quite a surprise.' His heavy arm pressed against her back, keeping her close beside him.

'You'll have her all night. I won't be able to cross the stream, not in this rain.' It was as if Mother Nature was granting them this special time together.

'Good, because even if you could, I wouldn't let you go.' He pressed her against the *chaise*, claiming her once more. She surrendered, eager to be one with him. In a few hours, the sun would rise and she'd be forced to face the consequences of her decision, but not now. Despite everything trying to keep them apart, tonight they were together and she would accept him for however long this lasted.

Chapter Ten

The sun, tempered by the fading storm clouds, poured in through the vicarage window. The fire had burned down to a smouldering red glow, leaving a stern chill in the room. Joanna snuggled deeper under the heavy quilt and against Luke, craving his heat and the languid pleasure of him. She closed her eyes, about to fall back asleep when the distant church bells rang across the forest.

Joanna jerked upright, all the peace of last night shattered by the stark morning light. Their time together was over and with it the fantasy of an illegitimate governess being with the second son of an earl. Despite what she'd done with him, she hadn't been raised to be a mistress, nor would she become one and bring shame on Madame Dubois, the school or herself.

'Good morning.' Luke ran his wide hand down the curve of her exposed back.

She twisted around to see him propped against the faded chintz pillows, one arm behind his head, the quilt draped across his hips to conceal the tempting part of him. He smiled at her and she wanted to press her bare chest to his, bring their mouths together and forget all the reality waiting for them at the edge of the forest. She tugged her side of the quilt up to cover her breasts. 'We should be getting back. If they discover we're both gone, they'll think the worst.'

'Let them. They'll dismiss you anyway once they learn we're to be wed.' He slipped his hand in her hair and drew her into a kiss of promise.

She allowed the quilt to fall away, her breasts taught against his bare chest, the desire which had consumed her last night flaring once again. He craved more than her body, but her life and future. It was everything she'd ever wanted and all impossible. His family wouldn't accept her and she'd always be an outcast, despised for stealing their son and their one chance at a much-needed dowry. She wouldn't be hated in the very family he wanted to make her a part of, it would be like spending the rest of her life in the employment of the Huntfords.

She pressed her hands against his bare chest and pushed herself away from him. 'We can't. It's impossible.'

It hurt to utter the words.

His chest stilled beneath her palms. 'I've been outnumbered in battle more than once and seized victory. Don't tell me our wedding isn't possible.'

His determination made her sit back. Here was a man who always strove to achieve what he wanted and it was clear he wanted her. Despite the answering challenge in her heart, she remained steadfast against it and him.

'Yes, you've faced down armies, but you know as well as I do how difficult it is to face down society.' She rose, gathered up her discarded clothes and began to dress. 'The Huntfords have treated me poorly because they think I'm below them. Imagine the scorn they and their friends will heap on me for marrying before Frances and above my station?'

'I've faced too many real perils to be intimidated by imaginary ones.' The languid brown of his eyes hardened.

'Is your family an imaginary one? I'm illegiti-mate, Luke. What will happen when your parents or your brother learn of it? I've heard the things he's said to you, I doubt he'll shrink from voicing his disapproval of me.' She slipped her chemise over her head and took up her discarded stays.

'You'd rather remain in drudgery than take a chance on defying others to claim your own life?' He flung back the coverlet and stood. Joanna did her best not to stare at everything he revealed, afraid it would pull her back into the sweet mem-ories of last night and distract her from being rea-sonable and realistic.

'Of course not, but I'm not foolish enough to be-lieve in fairy tales.' She tugged tight the laces of her stays, then snatched up her dress. Everything seemed clearer in the bright morning light, includ-ing the mistake they'd made in forgetting them-selves last night. 'You've been wrestling with your responsibilities ever since you've come home, not happy about the requests your family has made of you, or the sacrifices you've made for them. A relationship with me, a nameless governess, is a way of granting their wishes while also showing your rebellion.'

He snatched his breeches off the floor. 'You think my concern for you so slight?'

'No, but I won't have you break your pledge to help your family, to compromise your honour because of me.' She was convinced he cared, very much, but she knew it wasn't enough. Perhaps her mother had loved her, but it hadn't stopped her from giving Joanna up. Madame Dubois had been like a mother to her, but it hadn't prevented her from sending her to the Huntfords. Luke might prize her company this morning, but it didn't mean he could defy everyone to be with her, no matter what he said. 'But constant criticism and rebukes will erode your regard for me, and even if you can win your family to our cause, what about Lord Beckwith? What will he think of this arrangement?'

'It doesn't matter. I allowed him to pressure me to leave the Army. I won't let him decide who should be my wife. He no longer commands me.'

'But he commands those who can help your men and those influential men have wives who'll gossip and turn their husbands against you. You won't be able to help your soldiers if you become an outcast because of me and I won't allow people to suffer so that I can be happy.'

He pulled up his breeches then halted, his bare chest rising and falling as he breathed. 'Aren't you tired of others dictating your life? Of not fighting for what you want?'

She pulled on her pelisse and with shaking fingers fumbled to button it. 'It's easy for you to say when you have choices for earning a living. Not all of us are so fortunate.'

'I say it because I've done it, not because it's easy. I clawed my way up from lowly lieutenant to a major in command of men. I didn't do it by making the best of things, but by exceeding all expectations, taking risks, challenging people and proving my mettle and my worth to my commanders and myself.' He strode up to her and cupped her face with his hands, his words powerful despite the softness of his voice. 'You're a brave woman, Joanna. Don't allow your fears to make you throw away everything you've ever wanted.'

His tender hands on her face made her hesitate and consider sharing in his conviction, but everyone would despise her if she did. Eventually he would too. She stepped out of his grip, struggling to reclaim the calm and steady countenance which had served her so well for so many years. It warred with the part of her which wanted to believe in his confidence.

'I don't have the same freedoms you do, so don't demand the same things of me.'

She made for the door before his single question stopped her.

'And if there's a child?'

She fingered the cold, brass doorknob. If there was a child, she couldn't do to it what her mother had done to her by denying it a place in society, or the knowledge of its father, but she wouldn't allow the phantom of it to guide her now. She looked over her shoulder at him, her heart aching. 'We'll deal with it if the issue arises.'

She fled out the door, her boots sending up splashes of rainwater from the wet ground as she rushed through the woods. The rising sun cut through the trees and she knew, no matter what she did or said once she arrived back at Huntford Place there'd be no hiding her absence. She struggled through the emotions torturing her to come up with some excuse for her tardiness or a legitimate reason for why she'd been out of the house the morning after a storm, but she could think of nothing except Luke and leaving him behind.

When the roof of Huntford Place at last came into view, a new failing began to trail her. In her selfish desire to be special, to forget everyone and everything for one night, she'd betrayed Madame Dubois and the people who'd raised her. Perhaps she shouldn't have walked away from Luke, but marry him the way Isabel intended to marry Mr Balfour. Luke had offered her the protection of a union, but not even his name or a ceremony could stop people from condemning or insulting her and it was a long way between here and the banns.

Poor Madame La Roche, the French teacher, had once fallen in love with the son of a Salisbury magistrate, a man of title and property. His family had objected so strongly, in the end the young man had cried off a mere week before the wedding. Madame La Roche had returned to the school embarrassed and alone. How much castigation she'd received for her ill-advised engagement, Joanna wasn't sure, but shortly after her return she'd resumed her teaching duties. Joanna hoped Madame Dubois proved as generous with her as she'd been with Madame La Roche if she was forced to return to the school. There was nowhere else for Joanna to go. In the end, even if she went home in disgrace, it was better to leave. It would place distance between her and Luke, make him fade from memory, even as his touch still burned on her skin.

Joanna skirted the front drive, then followed the house around to the back. She tried the library doors, but they were locked. Cursing her luck, she tugged at the music-room door, relieved when it swung open. She slipped into the dark room and stood quietly in the semi-darkness beside the pianoforte and struggled to compose herself. She picked a few leaves off her skirt and swiped at a bead of water clinging to her bodice, unsure how she'd face her charges or her employer.

Lady Huntford's muffled voice, and those of some other ladies, carried in from the adjacent sitting room. It plucked at Joanna's already tense nerves. Joanna couldn't reach the stairs, or anywhere else in the house without moving past it. Unable to stand here all day, or hide behind the pianoforte until everyone dispersed to their chosen amusements, she screwed up her courage and hurried down the hall. She moved on the balls of her feet, trying to slip unnoticed past the sitting room. She was nearly away when Frances cried out, 'There she is!'

Joanna froze, wincing at her failure.

'Miss Radcliff, come in here at once,' Lady Huntford ordered.

With heavy steps Joanna entered the room. From the looks of it, the entire house had been roused in a search for the wayward governess, or, more likely, they'd been gathered to participate in Joanna's total and utter downfall. Everyone sat in silence except for Miss Winborn and Miss Chilton, who whispered together near the back of the room.

Luke's parents stood among the guests, more mortified than amused, while his brother stared at her with the same look of disgust as Lady Huntford. Lady Pensum sat beside him, not looking well and perhaps the one person least interested in the drama playing out before her.

Lady Huntford rose out of her chair and advanced on Joanna, her puce dress fluttering ominously around her legs. Joanna braced herself, hoping this reprimand would involve nothing more than a scolding for disregarding her morning duties with the girls, but the hard line of Lady Huntford's lips, and Frances's smug look of revenge from where she sat beside her father and his dog told Joanna otherwise.

'Where have you been?' Lady Huntford peered at her with eyes made narrower by her overly full cheeks.

'I'm sorry I was late for my duties, but I took a walk...'

'Don't lie to me. We all know where you've really been and who you've been with.'

'Come, Lady Huntford, we don't know for certain if she was indeed with Luke,' Lady Ingham interjected with an edge of exasperation.

'Yes, I'm sure it's only a coincidence he and the governess were both missing this morning,' Lord Pensum huffed. 'Especially since they've been noticed conversing so much.'

Miss Chilton and Miss Winborn gasped at the not-too-subtle accusation. Lady Ingham pressed the heel of her hand to her forehead and Lord Ingham rolled his eyes at Lord Pensum having aired his suspicions about his brother in mixed company. Whatever the Inghams thought of her and Luke's behaviour, it was clear they didn't appreciate his misstep being announced for all to hear. No one seemed concerned with discussing Joanna's failings aloud.

'I was not with Major Preston.' Joanna stared down her accusers, determined to be convincing in an effort to save something of her reputation. It wasn't like her to lie, and guilt over this as much as her rash behaviour last night with Luke needled her, but she was forced to ignore it. With Lord Pensum and Lady Huntford all but accusing her of acting like a tart in front of so many titled people, it wouldn't be long before they wrote to their London friends about it. Joanna's reputation as an employable woman would be destroyed, assuming an illegitimate child didn't wreck it for her. Her one chance at salvation was to convince everyone she was innocent. It was a Herculean feat and one she hated trying to achieve with deceit.

'Don't you dare lie to me, you whoring little wench,' Lady Huntford screeched and her hand twitched at her side as though she wanted to slap Joanna. She probably would have if there hadn't been so many people present. 'You're dismissed. Pack your things at once and go back to that awful school of yours. If this is the kind of governess they're educating, I want nothing more to do with it and will tell all of my friends to avoid it, too.'

Joanna willed her shoulders not to slump in defeat. In her one act of defiance, she'd ruined her whole life and quite possibly the prospects of many other girls at Madame Dubois's school. For the first time, she understood why her mother had given her away. She'd probably stood in a similar position once, with all chance of a respectable life gone and no ability to bring up her child.

Her dignity and reputation in tatters, Joanna moved to curtsy and take her leave when Gruger shuffled into the sitting room.

'Lord Helmsworth has arrived to see you, Lady Huntford,' he mumbled as though inconvenienced.

Vicar Carlson entered as the butler finished his announcement.

'It's an honour to have you grace us with your presence this morning. What can we do for you?' Lady Huntford all but grovelled in front of the distinguished man before rising out of her curtsy and hissing at Joanna, 'Show the proper respect, girl.'

'My apologies, Vicar Carlson.' Joanna curtsied,

confused by the stillness which had enveloped the room.

'Vicar Carlson? He's the Marquis of Helmsworth!' Frances spat out with contempt hot enough to boil wine. Her mother glared her into silence.

Joanna stumbled a bit as she rose, her head spinning at this latest revelation. She'd poured out her heart to a marquis and given her body to a major. The morning was turning out to be more stunning than last night.

'Miss Radcliff needn't kowtow to me.' Lord Helmsworth smiled at her. 'The two of us are already friends.'

Lady Huntford looked as confused as Joanna.

'You said you were the vicar. Why did you lie to me?' Joanna asked, struggling to reconcile his real identity with his false one and the contrast between the kind man in front of her and the one who'd raged against Luke in the vicarage.

'You wouldn't have talked to me so openly if I'd told you who I really was.' He took her hand and patted it. It was warm and soft, not like Luke's, but in the way she imagined a father's might be. 'Since you now know who I really am, I must tell you who you really are.'

'I'm a governess.' In reality she was no longer even this, but she didn't want to see the kindness in his eyes replaced with the same disgust which the Huntfords and their guests had flung at her. It would follow soon enough when Lord Pensum, Frances or Lady Huntford decided to blurt out their very correct assumptions about what she'd been up to last night.

'You're much more than a governess. You're the granddaughter of a marquis.' He laid his hand over his heart, examining her as if she'd brought him the greatest treasure. 'You're my granddaughter.'

The gasp from everyone in the room almost extinguished the fire.

'No, you're mistaken. I'm nobody's granddaughter. I don't even know who my parents are.' This elicited another small squeak of surprise from Lady Huntford as she realised she'd been employing not just a governess with questionable morals, but an illegitimate one.

'Your mother was my dear daughter Jane.' He explained to her about her mother and father, their illicit love, his death, her mother's confinement and leaving Joanna with Mrs White who'd brought her to Madame Dubois. All the guests leaned in to catch every word of the story. Joanna guessed it would be included in their letters to London within the hour. Her mind reeled as she worked to comprehend everything Lord Helmsworth said. The family she'd always wanted, the lineage she'd often wondered about, was being revealed to her at last. It far surpassed even her most childish dreams and the plot of any of the fairy tales she'd ever read. It couldn't be real. 'How can you be sure I'm the child?'

'After my solicitor located Mrs White she told us about the school. She was amazed you knew nothing of your background. She said that she'd not had time to stay and explain, but that she'd pinned a note to your blanket with your name and who you belonged to when she'd left you before departing for Austria. When my solicitor visited Madame Dubois to discuss with her my suspicions about you, she confirmed having found you on her doorstep, but said there'd been nothing but a torn piece of paper with your first name on it. If there'd been more, she would have contacted me at once.'

'Of course.' Madame Dubois was too caring

to have left her an orphan if she could have prevented it.

'I had this miniature of your mother made on her sixteenth birthday.' He held out a gold locket on a chain and opened it. Inside was a painting of a young lady with Joanna and Lord Helmsworth's blue eyes and slender nose.

Joanna took the locket and cradled it in her hands. For years she'd wondered what her mother had looked like, now she knew. Seeing her mother's face was like seeing her own and Lord Helmsworth must have noticed the resemblance at once. It explained his reaction to her when they'd met at the graveyard.

'Jane meant to return for you, but she didn't have the chance.' Sadness deepened the lines at the corners of his eyes. 'Had I known of your existence, I would have claimed you at once.'

Joanna closed the locket and curled her fingers around it, the gold warming beneath her skin. 'What does this mean?'

'You have a good heart, Miss Radcliff. I recognised it the day I met you. You were kind to me when I was hurting and I appreciated it. Not everyone is so understanding of my grief.' He slid an accusatory look at Lord Ingham before focusing back on her.

'You're the one who listened to me,' Joanna countered with a humble smile. 'Your advice made a great deal of difference.'

'I want to make even more of a difference in your life.' He reached out to touch her cheek, then pulled back his hand, as awkward as Joanna about where they stood. 'Will you come with me, allow me to make up for the years of my absence and do for you all I wished I could have done for Jane?'

He was offering her the truth about who she was and where she'd come from. She was the granddaughter of a marquis who wasn't afraid to publicly claim her. It should be the happiest day of her life, but worry tainted her excitement. Lord Helmsworth disliked the Inghams. When Lord Pensum's suspicions about her time with Luke reached Lord Helmsworth's ears, would he still be proud to call her his granddaughter, or would he cast her back where he'd found her?

Luke's words about giving in to her fears echoed through her mind. She'd allowed fear to dictate her actions with Luke and surrendered a chance to marry an honourable man. She wouldn't allow them to stop her from seizing the opportunity to claim a real family and a place in the world. Whatever happened between her and Lord Helmsworth, whatever stories he heard or judgements he made because of them, she would face them and do her best to overcome them. She laid her hand on her grandfather's arm. 'Yes, I will.'

Luke emerged from the woods and stepped onto the main drive. Between him and the front door to Huntford Place stood Lord Helmsworth's carriage with its gold crest on the green-lacquered sides. Luke groaned. Of all the days for their paths to cross, this had to be the worst. Between the news of Captain Crowther and his men, and Joanna's sound rejection of him after a pleasurable night together, he was in no mood to face Lord Helmsworth's vitriol.

He considered going to the stable, fetching Duke and riding home. He was finished with this party and his visit here, but he didn't. Too many times he'd entered a battle mourning friends or dealing with a myriad of other troubles. Today, like then, he wouldn't allow his personal feelings to dissuade him from doing what needed to be done.

He'd resolve this lingering issue between Lord Helmsworth and the Inghams by meeting the Marquis's anger with kindness.

To his astonishment, the front door of Huntford Place opened and the Marquis himself appeared with Joanna at his side. Lord Helmsworth escorted her outside, beaming as if he'd just been made a duke. Joanna glowed as much as he did, her joy a far cry from the parting despair she'd left him with at the vicarage.

Luke gaped at them. There was only one reason Lord Helmsworth could be leaving with Joanna, and for them to appear so ecstatic together. She must have been entertaining him as well as Luke, and Lord Helmsworth intended to make the governess his wife. It didn't seem possible, and went against everything Luke had come to believe about her, but he couldn't deny the evidence.

Her happiness dimmed at the sight of him watching them from the middle of the gravel drive. Lord Helmsworth scowled at him like a badger. As they passed, Joanna paused to say something, but Lord Helmsworth didn't break his stride, drawing her along.

'Come, my dear, we must hurry.' Lord Helmsworth patted her hand in a way which made Luke want to pull her away from him, but he didn't. He was too furious.

Once again he'd been tossed over by a lady in search of a husband with a loftier title and more money. No wonder she'd been so eager to get away from him this morning and so fast to come to him last night after all her prior protestations. She'd probably wanted a taste of a virile man before binding herself to one with more lineage than stamina.

Luke stormed up to the house without sparing the happy couple a second glance. It turned his stomach to think of Lord Helmsworth's gnarled hands on Joanna and her willingness to endure his touch. He ground the bottom of his boots against the iron scraper outside the door, not caring if he tore up the leather. Despite everything he'd done for her, it hadn't been enough to trump his lack of position or wealth. Nothing ever was.

Leaving a small pile of mud beside the door, he marched inside and jerked to a halt in the entrance hall. Everyone stood there and their conversation ceased at the sight of him.

What the hell happened while I was gone?

* * *

'Lord Helmsworth's granddaughter.' Luke groaned. His family had waited until they were alone in his mother's room to tell Luke the news. The one consolation was he hadn't been thrown over for the old man, at least not in the disgusting way he'd imagined. It still didn't ease the sting of Joanna having run from his proposal. When he'd held her last night, he thought he'd won her. He'd been wrong.

'And all you could do was treat her like your whore,' Edward fumed, shaking off Alma's restraining hand. 'Do you know how embarrassing it was to have your peccadilloes announced to everyone by a hysterical Lady Huntford, or was that your intent all along? To court a governess to spite us?'

'Contrary to what you believe, not everything I do, or each decision I make, is done with you in mind,' Luke hissed, struggling to control his temper. 'I pursued Miss Radcliff because she has more intelligence, common sense and regard for me than any other lady I've met.'

'Apparently not enough to avoid bedding you.'

Luke grabbed his brother by the lapels and slammed him against the wall.

'Boys!' their mother shouted, advancing on them as she used to when they fought as children. Luke let go of Edward, his anger checked but not cooled.

'Enough of this. What's done is done.' She scowled in motherly disapproval at them. 'Miss Radcliff has gone with Lord Helmsworth to lead her life with him and we must go on dealing with the challenges of ours.'

'One thing about Miss Radcliff being Lord Helmsworth's granddaughter is she'll probably receive a grand dowry now,' his father mused, as practical as ever. 'If she and Luke have an interest in each other, I see no reason why they shouldn't continue to pursue it.'

'Except Miss Radcliff has already refused my offer of marriage,' Luke clarified for everyone, his pride smarting.'

'That's a pity.' His father shook his head, his optimism fading. 'Perhaps she can still help us resolve the land dispute?'

'Not once Lord Helmsworth hears of her little tryst with Luke—and he will,' Edward spat out.

'Lady Huntford will probably attach a note about it to Miss Radcliff's things when she sends them over. Lord Helmsworth hated us before. Imagine how he'll react once he learns Luke has had his way with his long-lost granddaughter.'

Luke winced at the truth. In his desire to be with Joanna he'd inadvertently driven them apart. If he'd shown more restraint last night, then this morning and perhaps even the future might have unfolded differently. But he hadn't.

He reached into his pocket and clutched the bugle badge. His mistake was as sharp as the thin edge of the metal. Between her having already rejected him and Lord Helmsworth's animosity there was little Luke could do to overcome the consequences of their intimacy. However, if she asked him to, he'd find a way to stand with her against the mounting rumours, and even against her new grandfather's disapproval.

He let go of the badge. Even as he thought it he doubted it would happen. Joanna hadn't been willing to fight with him for their future when their ranks had been so different. As the newly minted granddaughter of a wealthy marquis, she wasn't likely to want anything to do with him now, not after he'd humiliated her in front of the entire countryside.

The idea of giving up pricked at him, but he couldn't chase after a woman who didn't want to be won. He must focus on his lost men and ignore the upsetting of all his plans and the severe blow to his heart.

Chapter Eleven

Joanna shifted in her seat and the silk of her dress rustled as she tried to concentrate on the play. The new blue gown was tasteful and flattered her eyes, or so the expensive French modiste had insisted during her fitting. Or perhaps it was her grandfather, or Mrs Petit, her lady's maid and sometimes chaperon who'd said it. After the whirlwind of the last month, it was difficult to remember.

Joanna adjusted the thick strand of pearls around her neck, their weight too heavy against her exposed décolletage. The Drury Lane theatre was far more dazzling than the one she'd been to in Sandhills, and its production of *Romeo and Juliet* opulent.

Thousands of candles in wide chandeliers illuminated the players and the numerous guests filling the seats. Lord Helmsworth sat beside her in the private box he'd hired for the evening. He'd insisted they come to London, thinking the small Season the perfect time to introduce her to society. She wasn't so certain. While he watched the young lovers, Joanna tried to overlook all the people watching her, as she searched among the curious faces for one. With the House of Lords in session, Lord Ingham might be here and possibly Luke. After all, there was no better place than London for Luke to search for a rich wife.

The realisation that it would not be her made her sides ache more than her new stays. She'd spied Lord and Lady Pensum in a box across the way, but Luke wasn't with them. She hadn't seen Luke or heard anything from him since the morning she'd refused his proposal. She flicked one stick of her fan with her finger. For all his confessed determination to be with her, he hadn't even tried to seek her out, or concocted some reason to come to Helmsworth Manor while she'd been there.

It's for the best, she reminded herself for the hundredth time since leaving him. The spectre of her indiscretion with Luke had haunted her until her courses had arrived. Not being with child had given her some peace, but it hadn't quietened the rumours racing through the countryside or the fear that her grandfather would cast her aside once they reached him. To her amazement, he either hadn't heard the stories or had chosen to ignore them, and Luke had stayed away. She was both disappointed and glad. His presence might have forced her grandfather to face the truth about Joanna's lapse in judgement, and possibly tainted her in his eyes.

Joanna tapped her fan against her palm. *If only Lord Helmsworth had found me sooner, then there might never have been rumours.*

She and Luke could have become properly acquainted at country events and behaved together like a respectable courting couple instead of being so secretive. She let out a long sigh, making the lace along the edge of her bodice quiver. Even if Lord Helmsworth had found her months ago, his prejudice against Army men and the Inghams would have prevented him from considering Luke as Joanna's suitor. It seemed that, no matter what the situation, they weren't meant to be together.

'You're not enjoying the play, my dear?' her grandfather asked.

'I'm distracted by everyone staring at me.' It

was a half-truth. She'd long ago wished to be the centre of attention for one night. This wasn't exactly what she'd had in mind. By now the tales from Huntford Place must have reached London and she could imagine what everyone was saying about her.

'They're merely curious. In time it'll pass,' he assured her, seemingly oblivious to the scrutiny. Her grandfather raised his hand in greeting to someone across the theatre then rose. 'If you'll excuse me, Lord Jarsdel, an old friend of mine, is here and I must see him. I'll return shortly.'

He left, and a few moments later she saw him enter a box across the way to speak with a gentleman she didn't recognise. His absence left her to face the audience alone. She stroked the warm pearls and watched Romeo climb the wall into the Capulet orchard, but then a tingle of awareness made her turn. Her fingers froze on one of the smooth orbs as across the theatre her eyes met Luke's. He stood at the back of the box below where her grandfather was, his black coat austere compared to Lord Beckwith and the other high-ranking officers with their medals, ribbons and blue Horse Guards uniforms. She pulled the long strand through her closed fist to click against her new rings, still able to feel his chest beneath her fingertips, the ecstasy in his arms and the pain of having walked away.

One of the officers said something to Luke, forcing his attention back to them. Then a moment later, Luke made his excuses and left the box. His leaving should have been a relief. She'd already been made enough of a spectacle without him being here in London to make it worse. However, the first sight of him after so long proved as precious as her new family. In spite of everything, she still cared for him but doubted he even thought of her.

She settled against her seat, trying to lose herself in the drama and the way the tale of forbidden love pulled at her heart. She shouldn't ruminate on her troubles but enjoy her advantages. She was very lucky to be here, as all the letters from Rachel, Grace, Isabel and even Madame Dubois and Miss Fanworth had told her. She didn't feel lucky, but alone. This wasn't her world and it was difficult settling in.

She shivered as a light draught played along the

back of her neck, followed by the flutter of the curtain behind her.

'Good evening, Joanna.' Luke's voice slid over her, making her heart still in her chest.

She hazarded a look at him, cautious not to turn too far and alert everyone, especially her grandfather, to his presence. Despite her change in status, they were as unable to converse openly here as in Hertfordshire. He stood in the shadow of the doorway, around the slight bend blocking him from view of the audience. Each of his steady breaths plucked at her like a harp and she clasped the side of the chair. He shouldn't be here and they shouldn't speak but she didn't have the will to send him away.

'Good evening, Luke.'

. The strain that had marked him at the Ingham's ball hardened his expression and spread out to envelope her.

She turned back to the stage, mourning the loss of their easy rapport and what it had meant to her. The spicy scent of his cologne filled the box like incense. She closed her eyes and inhaled, silently willing him to defy everyone to reclaim the intimacy they'd experienced in the country.

She longed to feel his heavy hands on her bare shoulders and she listened over the noise of the play for the fall of his boots behind her, but there was nothing. She opened her eyes and the theatre seemed less magical and even more lonely and isolating than before.

'I'm sorry if my coming here troubles you,' he offered.

'Why did you come?' she asked over her shoulder.

'I wanted to make sure all is well with you.'

The intent of his question was clear and she swallowed hard, ashamed of herself. He'd been considering the consequences of their night together as much as she had. No wonder he'd crossed the theatre to speak to her. She shouldn't have left him wondering. 'There was no child.'

He didn't sigh with relief, and a shared sense of disappointment passed between them. A baby might have forced them together when people and expectations had driven them apart. However, force was a terrible way to enter a marriage.

'How are you adjusting to London?' he asked, his concern as genuine tonight as when he'd protected her from Frances.

It made her heart catch with a spark of hope before she could smother it. His concern was part of who he was, not an indication he still held any regard for her. She could give him a glib answer, ease his worries and be done with this meeting, but she wouldn't. She had trusted him with the truth many times before. There was no reason to lie to him tonight.

'It hasn't been easy dealing with so much in such a short amount of time. I haven't said anything to anyone because I don't want to appear ungrateful. Grandfather has given me so much, not just clothes or jewellery, but stories about my mother and my family, and a place in it. It's everything I've ever wanted.' Almost.

'You aren't ungrateful. A wise young lady once told me, it can be difficult after so long in a situation to leave it. Eventually, you'll settle in.' The intimacy they'd shared during their stolen moments at Huntford Place whispered between them once more. He shifted on his feet before settling himself. 'I should go.'

'No, wait.' She turned to face him, loath to snip the faint bond between them.

His eyebrows rose a touch before the façade of a disciplined officer settled over him again.

'Is there any news about Captain Crowther and your men?'

'No.' He cut the word with his teeth and she crossed her ankles beneath her gown to keep from rushing to soothe him as she had at the vicarage. 'There were rumours they were being held in Ciudad Rodrigo, but nothing solid. I'm doing all I can to make sure the Army continues to search for them and provides for their families until we learn of their fate. Returning to London has made speaking with Lord Beckwith and other influential men in Whitehall much easier.'

'I'm sure your efforts won't be in vain.'

'We'll see.' He looked past her to the stage. 'None of the other goals I've set for myself these last two months have been achieved.'

Her cheeks burned under his none-too-subtle reminder of their last few moments together.

'I'm sorry. I shouldn't chide you for your decision in Hertfordshire.' His low voice was nearly drowned out when Mercutio laughed on stage. 'At the time I didn't agree with your reasons, but I came to see they were sound.'

'No, they weren't.' She opened and closed the fan over her skirt. 'They were made from fear of having to fight your parents had we told them we were engaged.'

'It wasn't fear, but the truth. You should've heard Edward rail at me. You being the granddaughter of a marquis didn't silence him, although my father hasn't given up on us maintaining something of an acquaintance.'

'Have you?' she asked, her heart racing with her daring.

She shouldn't crave any connection with him, either slight or deep, but with her memories of their time together and what it had meant to her as potent as his presence, she couldn't help it.

He didn't answer right away and she held her breath, waiting to see if anything between them could be salvaged. Then he laced his hands behind his back and stood, as he had in the library when he'd tried to end their friendship.

'I don't think Lord Helmsworth would approve.'

'No, he wouldn't.' Her heart dropped, especially when she glanced across the theatre. 'Grandfather has left his friend's box and will return soon.'

He didn't challenge her silent request to go, but

bowed, his eyes never leaving hers as he backed away, allowing the curtain to fall closed between them.

'Where have you been?' Edward asked when Luke entered the box they'd engaged for the evening.

'Speaking with Lord Beckwith.' Edward didn't need to know Luke hadn't been in the Horse Guards box this entire time. His brother had been less irascible since they'd come to London, but it didn't mean there wasn't a fight in him waiting to be unleashed.

Luke took the chair on Alma's other side, as tense as he usually was before a battle. He looked up at Joanna. She sat like an unobtainable princess in the box above the stage, radiant in her silk. The blue brightened her eyes and emphasised the faint blush of her skin. She watched the play while her fingers worried at the creamy pearls caressing the tops of her full breasts. He hadn't expected to see her in London, not with Lord Helmsworth's well-known distaste for town. Her presence brought back everything he'd worked hard to forget in the country: her sweet smile, her wit and the moment she'd spurned him.

In this regard his expectations hadn't been disappointed. She'd gone off with a titled man and forgotten about Luke, not even bothering to write and calm his concerns about her being with child or the impact of the rumours surrounding her. With silence she'd conveyed her wish to have nothing more to do with him.

Then why was she so reluctant to see me leave her box?

The about-turn baffled him, but he knew better than to give it much credence. The request had probably been an attempt to ease the cut of her rejection, but it had failed.

She glanced at him and he looked away, trying to focus on the play. He had no patience for tragic love stories tonight.

He was about to rise and leave when Lord Helmsworth and an older gentleman Luke didn't recognise entered Joanna's box. Luke settled back against his chair and watched as Lord Helmsworth introduced his companion, who bowed over Joanna's hand with a solicitousness to make Luke bristle. Then the man sat down beside her to say whatever he needed to say to a woman half his age. Joanna didn't shift away but smiled and chatted, appearing quite charmed by her new acquaintance. Lord Helmsworth hovered behind them like an eager mother and Luke crossed his arms over his chest at the spectacle. It was more gripping than the one on stage.

'Who's the gentleman speaking with Miss Radcliff?' Luke asked Alma. He shouldn't begrudge Joanna her new life but something about the exchange bothered him.

Alma tuned her spyglass from the stage to the Helmsworth box. 'Lord Jarsdel, a widower with a sizeable estate outside Bath. He has two grown sons, so the woman he marries this time won't be the one to give him an heir.' The mention of a child brought a slight smile to her lips instead of her usual frown.

'She'll be married to a man nearly in his dotage.' Regrettably, Luke couldn't call him old or gouty. Lord Jarsdel was slender and fit, with a full head of dark hair greying at the temples, making him more distinguished than handsome.

'His next wife will be a countess and quite wealthy. It could be Miss Radcliff, unless a more suitable candidate offers for her first.' She lowered her glasses and threw him a wry smile, her humour matched by the new fullness in her cheeks. The return to society had been good for her, adding a little weight to her lithe frame and removing the strained expression she'd worn in the country.

Luke didn't share her amusement 'There isn't much an alternate suitor can offer when a young lady has a marquis for a grandfather and an earl for an admirer.'

'There's a great deal a man can offer a lady which has nothing to do with titles or money.' She reached out and took Edward's hand and raised it to her lips. He smiled at her and squeezed her hand before lowering it to rest on his thigh. She didn't let go of her husband as she faced Luke again.

'And without either, most of it is debt and worries.' Edward might not have given Alma wealth, but he had land and a title. It was more than Luke possessed.

'I remember you once telling me not to despair because you'd seen miracles. It sounds as though you need to start believing in them again. I have.' Her eyes twinkled with the reminder as she turned back to the play.

Around them the theatre quietened while Romeo crept beneath the balcony to listen to Juliet. As the scene played out Luke studied Joanna. She seemed oblivious to him as she watched Romeo embrace Juliet with a tender kiss. Then her attention darted to him, and this time he didn't look away. In her eyes was the same mournful longing which had pulled him away from the Horse Guards box and nearly had him stepping over the audience to reach her now, but he didn't move. She was surrounded by the trappings of her new life and he didn't want to intrude on it. Regardless of the change in her situation, with the softness of her voice and her concern for his men she'd shown she was still the woman he'd fallen for—the one he would have fought to keep if she'd wanted it.

Lord Helmsworth leaned close to say something to her and she turned to him.

Luke rose and left the box. She'd made her choice and it hadn't been him.

'What did you think of Lord Jarsdel,' her grandfather asked from across the dark carriage carrying them home from the theatre.

'He was very nice.' She'd given little thought

to the earl since he'd left them. His company had been pleasant enough, but it had been Luke who'd dominated her attention. Before he'd left her, he'd made it clear that there was nothing more between them. His distant gaze from across the theatre had told her something different. It was as if he still wanted her. It didn't seem possible.

'Your future is my greatest priority. I very much want to see you settled, to have a home and a family of your own in case something happens to me,' her grandfather continued with enough concern to make her stop musing and listen. 'It would mean a great deal to me if you'd consider Lord Jarsdel as a suitor. He's a very kind man and I think the two of you would do well.'

She gaped at him, his announcement as shocking as seeing Luke tonight. 'You wish me to become a countess?'

'You're the granddaughter of a marquis. Why shouldn't you become a countess?' He puffed out his chest with a pride she didn't share.

She could think of a number of good reasons, including her illegitimacy. He might ignore it, or pretend it didn't matter, but no one else would, especially if she gained so lofty a title. 'I barely know him.'

'You needn't decide anything tonight. I simply ask you to become better acquainted with him and see what happens.'

'All right, I will.' Something in this exchange reminded her of the day she'd agreed to Madame Dubois's suggestion to accept the offer of employment at Huntford Place. It had been a disguised demand, one which had determined the course of her life, just like her grandfather's might. She picked at the edge of the leather seat with her finger, irked by the way others kept deciding things for her while she went along. She was growing as tired of it as her turmoil over Luke.

She twisted the pearls around her finger as she leaned back against the squabs. In the country and tonight he'd been willing to let her go, yet in the midst of the play he'd watched her as if in need of her solace. While her eyes had held his there'd been a moment when she'd thought he might climb the box to reach her, as Romeo had done to Juliet, and show everyone his admiration of her until no one—not even her grandfather— could keep them apart.

She'd held her breath, waiting to see if he would. But instead of coming to her he had left.

She let go of the pearls and they clacked together as they dropped over her chest. But the disappointment of the night didn't overwhelm her. In the silent exchange, before he'd stormed out of his box, she'd sensed she could have called him back to her. She wondered if she still could, and if she had the conviction to stand with him if she did? She wasn't sure, and there hadn't been a chance for her to find out. There probably never would be. Even if a future gathering brought them together, she doubted he'd speak with her.

There was little left for them to say.

Chapter Twelve

Luke stepped into Hookham's Lending Library and stopped short. Joanna stood browsing through the selection in one of the aisles. It had been three days since he'd left her at the theatre, but the sight of her struck him like the recoil of a cannon. Besides battling the Army Pay Board on behalf of his men he'd thought of little else except her—much to his chagrin. He didn't want to pine for a woman who didn't want him.

She stood on her tiptoes, the hem of her dark green walking dress rising to reveal slim ankles covered in fine silk stockings tinged cream by the skin beneath. He touched his fingertips to his palm, the memory of cupping her calf at the vicarage teasing him. She must be wearing silk now and he imagined the softness of the material and the suppleness of her skin against his. Then she

raised one lithe arm to reach for a book. It emphasised the swell of her breasts beneath the spencer
covering them and made his cravat tight against
his throat.

Luke might not like the Marquis, but he couldn't
deny the change he'd wrought in Joanna. She'd
been beautiful in her plain clothes in the country.
In fine muslin, tailored to suit every curve, she
was stunning.

She failed to notice him as she stretched towards
a book on the top shelf. Luke cast a quick glance
around the library. He didn't see Lord Helmsworth, but he knew that either the Marquis or a
chaperon must be lurking nearby. He'd be wise
to slip off and leave her to the tranquillity of her
new life while he tried to recapture his, but her
struggle to grasp the book drew him to her.

'Do you need help?'

She dropped down on her heels and faced him,
her mouth forming an O of surprise. 'Y-yes. I can't
reach that book on Huria.'

He plucked the book off the shelf and handed it
to her, avoiding touching her fingers, which were
covered by new kidskin gloves. In the narrow
aisle, with his back to the library, he blocked her

from the view of the other patrons, giving them a touch of privacy.

'Thank you.'

She rewarded his assistance with a smile, but there was no mistaking the tension marring the corners of it. He wondered if she wanted him to go. He should—but he couldn't. Instead, he watched her flip open the tome to a coloured plate of a palace decorated in rich red and gold and a garden filled with exotic birds and plants. A slight crease furrowed her brow, as it had the day in the Huntford Place ballroom when she'd read her friend's letter.

'It's not what you're looking for?' Luke asked, her dismay troubling him.

'It is, but it reminds me of how much I miss Rachel and how far away she is.'

'Since your fortune has changed, surely you could visit her?'

'I suppose I could, if Grandfather allows it.'

He hooked his thumbs in his waistcoat pockets, his indignation rising at the mention of the Marquis. 'He shouldn't object to you leading your life.'

She snapped the book closed and hugged it against her chest, something of the governess coming over her. 'He's very protective of me and I'm grateful for it.'

'Good, you deserve to be cherished.' He shifted closer to her and inhaled her new scent. The simple aroma of soap and lavender which had flavoured her skin in the country had been replaced by the richer fragrance of cherry blossoms and cinnamon. Like the cloth of her walking dress and the fine bonnet covering her luminous hair, the more fashionable attire didn't diminish the simplicity of her beauty or turn it garish, but adorned it like a fine sculpture did a well-tended garden. 'But don't let gratitude make you surrender who you are, or what you want. I know the torment of sacrificing even the most cherished things for family duty.'

Her eyebrows rose in surprise as though he'd discovered a secret. The image of her and Lord Jarsdel together rushed to him but it was blotted out by her unsettling frown. 'At the theatre, you didn't think we could maintain an acquaintance. Now you're concerned with how I conduct my life?'

'I've always been concerned about you. I still am. It's your concern for *me* I question,' he challenged. 'You couldn't even spare me a word in the country.'

'I wanted to, but I feared if I encouraged you it would create problems between me and Grandfather.'

She bit her bottom lip, as nervous as when he'd approached her near the fern stand at Huntford Place. Luke stared at her, stunned out of his ire. She hadn't ignored him because she'd coveted wealth but because she thought she'd had no choice.

Then her spirit flashed, and it was her turn to accuse him. 'Besides, you made no effort to come and see me.'

'I didn't think you wanted me to.'

Their honesty with each other dissolved the tension between them.

'While we were apart it seems we were mistaken about each other's intentions,' he said.

For all the many times he'd been the one to search her out, she was the one approaching him now. In her eyes was the same hesitant anticipation which had been there when he'd first kissed her in Hertfordshire.

'I think we still are.'

Her fingers, clasping the book in front of her, were close to his. If he reached out, he could touch her, but he didn't move.

'Are we?'

'Yes.'

She curled one finger around his and his pessimism about her place in his life faded, along with every reason he'd concocted for trying to forget her. It was as impossible as leaving his men's families to starve. She'd been a tranquil retreat in the midst of the chaos of his worries and family concerns, a unique woman among the many he'd met since returning home. He should have fought against her excuses, remained stubbornly beside her and told anyone who challenged them to go to Hades.

He could do that now. And it was clear in her azure eyes that she wanted him to.

He opened his mouth, ready to speak to all the questions and uncertainties passing between them, when a man's voice shattered the moment.

'Joanna, is this man bothering you?' Lord Helmsworth bore down on them like a constable did a pickpocket while Lord Jarsdel remained politely at the opening to the aisle.

'No, not at all.' Despite his ominous approach, Joanna didn't shrink away or stutter in her response as she held up the book. 'Major Preston retrieved this book about Huria for me. He was quite helpful on the matter in Hertfordshire.'

'Yes, I'm sure he was.' Lord Helmsworth eyed Luke with enough suspicion to tell him he'd heard something about the dust-up concerning Luke and Joanna and the storm.

Joanna noted it, too, for she lowered the tome, more reserve coming over her than at his hasty approach, but she didn't cower in silence. 'He's campaigning on behalf of soldiers now, trying to ensure their families are provided for while their men are missing in Spain.'

'Are you?' Lord Helmsworth eyed Luke as if he was about to snatch his watch and dart out the door.

'I'm working to secure their pay for their families if they're still alive and their pensions if they're not.' Luke paused, refusing to imagine them lying forgotten in some field. He had to believe they'd survived. 'The treatment of our veterans who've given so much for their country is deplorable.'

'I agree, and something should be done to help them.' Her grandfather rubbed his chin. Luke and Joanna exchanged surprised glances at his having agreed with Luke. 'I'm glad someone is fighting for their due, even if it is you.'

Luke kept his expression passive. The man was stubborn in his dislike, except this time Luke was to blame. Luke's behaviour in Hertfordshire had convinced the Marquis that he wasn't worthy of honourable company, or Joanna.

'Lord Jarsdel, would you please escort Miss Radcliff to the carriage?' her grandfather asked.

'It would be my pleasure.'

Luke's irritation flared as the earl offered Joanna his elbow. He eyed her, silently challenging her to stand with him and refuse, but she didn't.

'Good day, Major Preston.' She walked with Lord Jarsdel to the door, but when the earl stepped forward to open it, she turned and threw Luke one last look. He caught it, and the conflict between wanting to stay with Luke and obedience to her grandfather. Lord Helmsworth noticed it, too, before she hurried outside.

'You might fool an innocent girl, but you won't fool a man of my experience,' Lord Helmsworth warned in a low voice. 'I've dealt with a poor military man in search of an easy life with a rich wife before.'

'I'm not trying to fool anyone.' If Lord Helmsworth were a younger man, Luke would strike him for the insult and call him out, but he'd been raised to respect his elders, even when they didn't extend him the same courtesy. 'I have a great regard for your granddaughter, one I developed long before her situation changed.'

'And how convenient for you it has. Now you can hold your head up when you try to seduce her instead of sneaking around.' He slapped Luke on the chest with the back of his hand. 'Chase after all the heiresses in London if you want, but you will not wed Joanna.'

Lord Helmsworth strolled past Luke and out the door, twirling his walking stick as he went.

Luke watched through the large front windows as the Marquis climbed into the curricle where Joanna and Lord Jarsdel sat together. Lord Helmsworth smiled too widely at the couple as the driver took up the reins and snapped the horses into motion.

Determination rose up in Luke as the vehicle

melted into the London traffic. Alma was right. There was more to affection than money or titles, and no obstacle Luke couldn't overcome. In the faint sweep of Joanna's finger against his, and in her potent look from across the library, she'd made it clear she still wanted him as much as he did her.

He wouldn't secure her hand at the expense of her relationship with the only family she had. Winning her and her grandfather's approval would take more tact and subtle manoeuvring than he was accustomed to. But Luke possessed the strength for battle. Hopefully Joanna did, too.

Joanna sat in the window seat of her grandfather's Grosvenor Square town house, the book on Huria resting on her lap. She tried to read about its history, but she couldn't picture the palaces and villages it described. She could only see Luke, standing in front of her in Hookham's. She could feel his finger intertwined with hers and hear his words echoing in the quiet.

I've always been concerned about you. I still am.

She'd spent the last month resigned to letting

him go, but their brief time together today had changed everything. She'd invited him back to her, and with his firm touch he'd answered her call. This—his explanation for staying away and the softness of his touch—had rekindled the possibility of her being with him once more.

Unease undermined her elation and she struggled to sit still on the bench. Luke's warning not to surrender what she wanted to others had resonated deep inside her. However, speaking up had never been her strength, not at school, in Hertfordshire or here. She hadn't even been able to tell Luke of her agreement to entertain Lord Jarsdel's interest. It would have meant admitting he had been right about her inability to govern her own life.

There was also her grandfather to consider. With everything still so new between them she was hesitant to begin demanding her way. After all, her small attempt to make her grandfather see Luke in a different light by telling him about Luke's good works hadn't accomplished anything. She could well imagine how her insisting he see Luke as a rival to Lord Jarsdel would only further harden him against Luke, and possibly her.

'Jane loved to read, it's why there are so many

novels in the library, though I'm afraid they're a little out of fashion,' her grandfather announced as he strolled into the room.

'It doesn't matter, they're all new to me.' She slipped the ribbon in the book on Huria and set it beside her. It was a potent reminder of Luke and everything she stood to lose if she didn't learn to ask for what she wanted, but so was her grandfather smiling down at her.

'This house was going to be hers when she married. It belonged to her mother's family and came with her when we wed.' His gaze slid to the portrait of her mother as a young girl cradling a small, black-and-white spaniel. It hung near the door across the room, opposite the painting of Joanna's grandmother in her wide hoops and powdered hair. A winsome look dulled his expression before he turned back to her. 'It'll be yours when you marry.'

'No. You've already been so good to me, I can't take more.'

He settled down on the window seat beside her, wrinkling the brocade pillows propped against the wall. 'I want you to have it and everything that isn't entitled to the estate to make sure you're secure, no matter what happens to me.'

'I don't know what to say.' She'd worried so much about her future at Huntford Place. Now, she'd never have to worry about it again, except where Luke's place in it was concerned.

Her grandfather sat back, serious in his regard of her. 'My gift makes you quite the wealthy heiress and a very eligible young lady. It means you must be on guard. You don't want to fall prey to a fortune hunter like your mother did.'

Joanna clasped the locket and ran it back and forth along its gold chain, sensing where the conversation was leading. 'I'll be cautious.'

'I'm sure you will be and I'll do my best to guide you through this Season, as I should have done with your mother. I could ask my sister, but a spirited girl like you doesn't want some old bat hovering around and she was too careless with your mother for me to trust her again.' He sneered in displeasure before he settled himself. 'It also means you must not speak with Major Preston again. Army men know how to wheedle their way into a lady's affection.'

Her heart thundered in her chest. She appreciated his looking after her, but not his dictating with whom she could and couldn't consort. If she intended to stand up for what she wanted, then now was the time to begin.

Taking a deep breath, she steeled herself against her fears and with a trembling voice she spoke. 'You've asked a great many things of me and I've happily done them all, but I can't do this. Whatever you may think of Major Preston, he's my friend. He was kind to me at Huntford Place and protected me when my employers would have done me ill.'

He cocked his head, the gesture as close as he'd ever come to chastising her. 'I understand he was a touch too kind to you.'

Joanna's hand stilled the locket on its chain. He had heard the stories of her and Luke and suspected the worst. Fear made her shiver, despite the blazing fire in the grate, and all desire to challenge her grandfather vanished. 'I'm sorry.'

'There's nothing to be sorry about. You aren't experienced enough with gentlemen to realise the lengths they'll go to in order to get what they want. I'm sure Major Preston promised to defy his family and society in order to win your trust, all the while keeping things between you a secret. Then, when it became known, where was he? Not beside you defending you against the Huntfords, but protecting himself.'

'I was the one who left him at the vicarage after I refused his offer of marriage,' she whispered, admitting two sins at once.

'At least he had enough honour to make an offer,' he grudgingly conceded. 'But if he really loved you, he would've followed you and refused to take no for an answer. Instead, he stayed where he was and left you to your fate.'

'It wasn't like that at all.'

'Are you sure?' her grandfather pressed.

No, she wasn't. At the vicarage, Luke had been adamant he could overcome any obstacles to them marrying, but as soon as she'd refused him, he'd dismissed her as fast as Lieutenant Foreman had left Frances. He hadn't tried to visit her at Helmsworth Manor or contrived any other meeting between them. He'd said it was because he thought she didn't want him, and she'd believed him until this moment.

'I imagine you're far more appealing to him now

that your situation has changed,' her grandfather pointed out, further increasing her doubts.

My situation. She rubbed the locket with her thumb. Luke had spoken of his family seeing the advantage in her new position. Perhaps they were the ones who'd changed Luke's mind and that was why he'd been so friendly in the library. Maybe they were encouraging him to use his connection with her to press their case about the river land. Luke was dedicated to his family and he'd do almost anything to help them, including woo her.

No, Luke wouldn't be so deceitful.

Joanna pinched the bridge of her nose, trying to sort out her warring feelings. Everything she'd heard today from Luke and her grandfather swirled in her mind until she couldn't decipher what was the truth and what wasn't. Her exchange with Luke in Hookham's spoke to her heart. What her grandfather said added to all the warnings from Miss Fanworth and the other teachers about gentlemen and minding herself in their presence. She hadn't minded herself today.

'I'm sorry if I upset you.' Her grandfather patted her hands, as loving now as he'd been through the last month. She turned her hand over in his and clasped it tight, grateful for his unfailing faith in the face of her weakness. It soothed her worries of being separated from him, but it didn't settle her confusion about Luke. 'What happened between you and Major Preston no longer matters and, as long as you don't see him again, we'll never speak of it.'

She didn't agree to his demand, but she didn't reject it either. Her grandfather had proved patient with her and she didn't wish to test the limits of his acceptance, especially with so much between her and Luke still unsure. As much as she cringed at having everything dictated by her grandfather or anyone else, she balked at leaving it to Luke's changing whims or her own. She'd be practical and realistic and decide nothing today. Instead, she'd wait for their next meeting and press him enough to discover the truth of his heart and hers.

'Can't you see the importance of making sure my men's families aren't left to suffer?' Luke paced in front of Lord Beckwith's desk, exasperated by this continued foot dragging. He'd spoken to half the superior officers in the Horse Guards and quite a number in the War Office. Each one had promised to help him, then foisted him off on another who'd done the same. Luke had got nowhere in securing funds for Reginald's sister, or his men's families. Despite the government's stalling, he wasn't about to give up.

'I can, but it isn't up to me.' Lord Beckwith twirled his pen between his fingers. He'd been sympathetic and helpful in his assistance, but all too willing to stop when he faced any resistance. 'Regulations state the soldiers must be dead before their families can receive a pension.'

'Then make sure they receive their pay.'

He tossed his pen on the desk. 'They can't be paid if they're missing and not confirmed dead'

Luke dug his fists into his hips and stared down at Lord Beckwith, fighting to remain calm. It seemed it wasn't just Edward who could rouse his emotion, but the dithering of the Army Pay Board. 'This isn't acceptable and it has to change.'

'Lieutenant General Calvert is already working to implement many changes, including treatment of our wounded.'

'It isn't enough.'

'The government is a monolith which cannot be easily moved, if at all.' Lord Beckwith leaned back in his chair and laced his fingers over his wide torso. He was sturdy like an ox, with a square chin with a divot set in the centre and the first hints of fat creeping in beneath the line of it. He'd been out of the field and in Whitehall too long. 'What we need are more men like you.'

'To do what? Rail at the lords who refuse to take action?' It wouldn't win him any allies any more than railing against Lord Helmsworth would win him over. He hadn't seen Joanna since Hookham's two days ago. He'd visited Lord Helmsworth's twice, but had been told both times they were not at home, and his few notes to the Marquis and her had gone unanswered. More than likely, Lord Helmsworth had stopped them from reaching her and no society events had brought them together, further frustrating Luke's attempts to see her. He was trying to be patient and smart in his pursuit but if it didn't produce results soon, he'd change his tactics.

'They'll listen to you before they do other soldiers.' Luke levelled a disbelieving look at Lord Beckwith who held up his hand, motioning for him to hear him out. 'You may not be the earl, but you come from their class, you speak their language, as well as the enlisted man's. We need someone like you who can attest to what conditions are really like and why they must be changed. I could find a commission for you and a position within the Army here in London.'

Luke stared at the sword lying across the top of the mahogany desk, Lord Beckwith's gold regimental insignia engraved on the lancet. Luke hated the wrangling of politics as much as he did the rules of society, but Lord Beckwith's suggestion intrigued him. This was the first time anyone had suggested Luke use his status as an earl's son for more than securing a loan to purchase a higher rank. He'd have to do it again to obtain enough money to pay for a commission. If he did, he could make a difference while he was stuck here in England, but it would take months or years and his soldiers' families needed help now.

'I'll think about it, but at the moment I have the more pressing matter of my men's pay. Who else can I speak with?'

'Lord Craven didn't return for the little Season and Lord Farley is too entrenched in his ways to see reason.' Lord Beckwith held up five fingers and lowered them as he ticked off men until one remained. 'You haven't spoken to Lord Jarsdel yet. If you can make progress with anyone, it's him. He's the most reasonable of the lot and very sympathetic to the plight of enlisted men. He's well acquainted with the Duke of York, too. Appealing directly to the Duke through him could be your best chance of getting what you want.'

Luke bit back a groan of frustration. Lord Jarsdel was the last man Luke wanted to speak with, but the answers he'd received to his enquiries into his men's families, especially Reginald's sister, weren't good. They were struggling. If it was in Luke's power to give them money, he would, but with the funds he'd secured by selling his major's commission tied up in Pensum Manor, there was little to be spared. Time was also working against him. When the special session of Parliament ended, the lords would exit town as fast as they'd returned, making it difficult to rouse them to do anything before the next session opened in the spring. He wasn't sure Miss Crowther or the other families could make it through the winter without assistance. Luke must swallow down his reluctance and speak with Lord Jarsdel.

Chapter Thirteen

Luke entered the hallowed entrance hall of White's, still amazed Lord Jarsdel had agreed to this meeting. After Lord Helmsworth's numerous refusals to see him, Luke was beginning to think the only titled men he might ever speak to were Lord Beckwith and his father.

The butler led him down the hall, past a room where young bucks stood drinking, talking and laughing. They paid no attention to Luke as he passed. He'd come here once before with Edward and found it as tedious as a night watch on an outpost.

The butler stopped at the last door on the left and pushed it open. He announced Luke to Lord Jarsdel and then ushered him inside. It was a small sitting room with dark panelling covered with paintings of terriers and cavaliers in gilded frames hung three high on every wall.

Lord Jarsdel rose to greet Luke.

'Major Preston, it's an honour to meet you. I'm well acquainted with your exploits in Spain.' Lord Jarsdel sat in a chair beside the fire and waved Luke into the matching one across from him. Luke perched on the edge of the fine leather, noting the faint scent of polish mixing with tobacco and coal. 'Miss Radcliff told me about your work on behalf of your men at tea yesterday. Lord Helmsworth mentioned it, too.'

Luke wondered what else Lord Helmsworth had told him and hoped it hadn't damage his cause. It was also galling to hear Lord Jarsdel had seen more of Joanna in the last three days than Luke had, but he wasn't here to press his suit with her, but his soldiers' cause.

'My men have faithfully served the Crown. I ask the Crown to show them the same respect until we discover what's happened to them. Their families need their pay or the pensions to survive.'

Luke described their plight with hunger and housing while they grieved and worried for their missing fathers and brothers. Lord Jarsdel listened, nodding sympathetically every now and again, instead of yawning and fidgeting as Lord Stuart or Lord Hadden had done when Luke had approached them.

'I can't guarantee anything, some of my fellow board members are quite stubborn about rules and regulations, but I assure you I'll do my best to convince the pension board to grant them money. If the Duke of York is at Vauxhall Gardens tonight when I accompany Miss Radcliff and Lord Helmsworth there, I'll speak to him on your behalf. If not, I'll arrange to visit him tomorrow,' Lord Jarsdel offered when Luke finished.

As much as Luke wanted to despise Lord Jarsdel for his interest in Joanna, his willingness to consider the case for Luke's men impressed him. 'I greatly appreciate anything you can do.'

Luke rose to bow and take his leave, but Lord Jarsdel waved him back into his seat. 'A moment more of your time, if you don't mind?'

'Not at all.' Luke sat down, wondering what the man wanted.

'I understand from Lord Helmsworth you're well acquainted with Miss Radcliff from your time in the country.'

'I am.' Luke regarded the languid earl, wondered if he was going to take him to task for the rumours swirling about the two of them.

'She's a rare lady among many in London, quick witted, sensible and caring. She reminds me of my late wife when she was young.' He took up a drink from the table beside him and swirled it over the edge of the chair arm as he spoke. 'Do you know my wife and I were married over the anvil at Gretna Green?'

'I didn't.' He knew very little about Lord Jarsdel except what Alma and Lord Beckwith had told him.

'My family didn't approve of her. She was a baronet's daughter with a modest dowry, too humble for a man destined to be an earl, and I was one year away from my majority.'

'So you defied your family.' His admiration for the man was growing even while he anxiously waited for him to make his point. Luke was certain he wasn't going to like it.

'Not until the night she told me if I didn't claim her she would marry another.' His eyes wandered to the ceiling and a smile of delight made the years fade from his face. Then he turned serious as he studied Luke. 'I had a decision to make, Major Preston, and I suspect you do, too. If you fail to offer for Miss Radcliff, I will. My wife may still hold my heart, but it doesn't mean I can't care for another or wish to remain alone for the remainder of my years.'

It wasn't a threat, but a polite warning. 'I intend to propose to Miss Radcliff once certain impediments are removed.'

'And if they can't be removed?' Apparently, Lord Helmsworth had offered Lord Jarsdel his opinion of Luke.

'I don't court defeat.' *Not from the Army Pay Board or a stubborn marquis.*

'Nor should you.' Lord Jarsdel rose and extended his hand to Luke. 'Good day to you, Major Preston.'

As Luke took his leave Lord Jarsdel's warning added a new urgency to his pursuit of Joanna. The very things Luke admired about Joanna—her understanding of hard work and sacrifice, her desire to place duty and responsibility to family above her own whims and wants—might now be the very things which would end any chance of them being together. If Lord Jarsdel proposed before

Luke could secure Lord Helmsworth's approval the Marquis might pressure her into accepting the Earl and he'd lose her.

No, he would not. If Joanna was going to be at Vauxhall tonight, then he would be, too. It was time to stop being patient and become more aggressive in his campaign.

Fireworks exploded above the lake, sending sparkling tendrils of red to cascade down over Vauxhall Gardens. Joanna clapped along with the other guests filling the private box.

'Quite a spectacle,' Lord Jarsdel commented to Joanna as another burst lit up the sky.

'It's amazing.' Almost as much as her sitting here. Every one of her grandfather's friends who'd joined them tonight for a light supper and the opening of the garden had been kind to her. It was the various people passing outside the box who hadn't been as considerate. They'd stare at her, then duck behind their fans to whisper together, less curious than contemptuous of her sudden rise in prominence. Like her grandfather and Lord Jarsdel, she did her best to ignore them, but it was difficult, especially when Lady Huntford, Frances and Catherine came strolling by.

'Lord Helmsworth, what a pleasure to see you return to London at last,' Lady Huntford sang out. She approached the edge of the box from the path, staring down her nose at Joanna even as she all but grovelled before her grandfather. Frances trailed behind her, as peevish as ever while Catherine gawked at everything as Joanna had done when she'd first entered the pleasure garden.

'I didn't have a good reason until now.' He motioned to Joanna, making it clear his neighbour must acknowledge her.

Tugging her wrap up higher on her shoulders, Lady Huntford dipped a grudging curtsy. 'Miss Radcliff.'

Frances wasn't as polite, staring everywhere but at Joanna, determined to cut her until Lady Huntford snatched her daughter by the arm and pulled her up to the box. 'Frances, you must greet Miss Radcliff.'

'It's a pleasure to see you again.' The sarcastic sneer already dampening her natural good looks became more pronounced as she curtsied, then rose and called out in a loud voice to her sister, 'Catherine, come greet your former governess.'

The conversation in the box quietened at the not-too-polite reference to Joanna's previous position. Joanna wondered if the chit would climb the Chinese pavilion to announce it to the entire garden. Joanna shouldn't be ashamed of her background, and her grandfather's title staved off a great deal of open criticism about it, but it was clear by the whispers behind her not everyone wanted to be reminded of her humble origins.

'Good evening, Miss Radcliff,' Catherine greeted, with a genuine smile. She wore a new gown of yellow muslin trimmed in blue, but it didn't match her sister's elegant attire.

'I see your father allowed you to come out at last,' Joanna remarked, encouraged by Catherine's pleasant attitude. It appeared Catherine had taken Joanna's advice to be kind and it heartened Joanna to think she'd made something of a difference to the girl.

'Yes, he thought the small Season the perfect opportunity for it, especially now Frances is engaged to Mr Winborn.'

Joanna was as amazed by the announcement

as the thought of a gentleman willingly yoking himself to Frances, but it was far from her place to question the better sort, even if she was now, strangely, one of them.

'He only did it to spare the expense,' Frances scoffed and Catherine's shoulders slumped.

Joanna caught her eyes and raised her chin, reminding the young lady to do the same.

Catherine, bolstered by the silent encouragement, set back her shoulders and Joanna winked at her in approval of her confidence. With any luck, the girl would find a husband and a life of her own where she could blossom away from the cruel remarks and painful indifference of her family.

'Come along, girls, we're expected at our box,' Lady Huntford announced, drawing away her daughters with unnecessary alacrity. She was probably eager to escape from Joanna and any taint she might visit on their family.

'Don't allow them to trouble you,' Lord Jarsdel encouraged from beside her.

'I'm worried they're saying what a number of people are already thinking.' She didn't belong here and it was true.

'People in society will always find a reason

to judge everyone else. It's something you must harden yourself against.'

'I hope I don't become so hard I turn to stone, as or sharp with my tongue as Miss Huntford.' Or as alone as Madame Dubois and without a husband or children. She'd never thought of Madame Dubois as lonely, but one time she'd seen her from an upstairs window in the garden reading an old letter with a melancholy expression to make Joanna's heart hurt. Whatever Madame's regrets, and she'd never shared them with Joanna, Joanna didn't wish to carry any of her own into her maturity, although it seemed unavoidable. Already she was burdened with too many about Luke. It had been three days since Hookham's and she'd had no word from him, nor had she seen him, leaving her to be tortured by her doubts about him.

'A woman as generous in spirit as you could never be so petty,' Lord Jarsdel complimented, but it didn't reach into her heart the way Luke's did. Lord Jarsdel was kind and caring, but with him there was no passion or eagerness to defy everything to be near him. Perhaps she should be glad. She'd seen what passion had done to Grace, what it had nearly done to Frances, and how it had ruined her mother. It was something to be avoided.

'Let's take a walk. I'm tired of cold ham and I want to see the bonfires down by the lake,' her grandfather called out to the delight of his guests.

Soon they were making their way along the wide, winding walk leading to the lake. Overhead, the fireworks continued hissing, whining and popping as they launched, then exploded. Lord Jarsdel strolled beside Joanna, explaining to her his work with the Army Pay Board. She could barely concentrate on what he said as she studied every passing male face in the flickering light of the torches, hoping to see Luke.

Surely he'd take advantage of this opportunity to try and see her? However, he hadn't done so at any of the art showings or fashionable hours in Rotten Row over the past few days. Maybe her grandfather was correct and he didn't really want her. No, that couldn't be right.

Then why isn't Luke here? A moment with him might settle everything.

Then, in the white burst of a firework, she spied him standing near the water's edge with his parents and Lord and Lady Pensum. While the others oohed over the bright explosions, Joanna stared at Luke. She wanted to hurry down to him, slip her hand around his arm and breathe in his cedar scent. Her grandfather's warning to be cautious and avoid him kept her at Lord Jarsdel's side. She couldn't risk her already fragile reputation, or reward her grandfather's kindness and patience by spitting in his eye in front of everyone. It was a good thing she chose to be prudent.

Luke hailed a young woman who stood nearby with a few older people. The strange young lady was petite with dark hair and round eyes. She left her party to meet Luke, admiring him as though he were as bright as one of the sparklers on the floating pavilion. He was generous with his smiles as he spoke to her and overly friendly with her in a way which made Joanna's heart drop.

Grandfather was right. Her desire to be loved had kept her from seeing the truth. Joanna had been good enough for Luke in dark corners and isolated houses, but not in front of others.

As if sensing someone watching him, Luke turned and noticed her as the white light faded overhead. She clasped her locket to steady herself against the pain eating at her, refusing to allow him to see her hurt. His glance flicked to Lord Jarsdel and he pressed his lips together in disapproval, then turned back to his companion, making it clear he was finished with her.

'Lord Jarsdel, come and explain how they make fireworks,' one lady implored, drawing him away from Joanna's side and closer to the front of the group.

Joanna fell behind the others, the distance between them widening as they approached the lake. If she could slip off back to the carriage and home, she would. The sparkle of the garden had lost its appeal.

The quick fall of boots on the path behind her made her step out of the way of whoever was coming. She was stunned when a hand took her by the arm and pulled her into the shadow of a large oak tree beside the path.

She whirled around, ready to strike her attacker when she came face to face with Luke. He stood over her, his chest so close to hers she could see the flourishes on the buttons of his coat in the faint lantern light. 'What are you doing?'

'This.' He leaned down to kiss her but she

pushed against his chest and twisted to one side, avoiding his lips.

The hardness of his body beneath her palms shocked her as much as all the questions and anxieties surrounding them. Her stiff elbows weakened under the urge to revel in his embrace, but she remained strong. She was a sensible, controlled woman, not some senseless flirt. 'No. I won't sneak around with you any longer, not when you're courting another woman in plain sight.'

He kept his arms tight around her. The pressure of them weakened her resolve as much as the earnestness in his eyes. 'I'm courting no one except you.'

'Because I'm rich now and I can convince my grandfather to give you and your family the river land?' She winced at the harshness in her voice and the way it made him pull back in disbelief, but he still didn't let go of her.

'You think so little of me?'

'My grandfather does and I don't know what to think.' In his embrace it was easy to believe in his affection for her, but difficult to calm her fears and concerns. 'First you want me, then you don't, then you do again but in secret while you cavort in the open with another woman down by the lake.'

'The woman by the lake is Captain Crowther's sister and recently betrothed to a vicar in Hampstead Heath,' he answered gently, not flinging the truth at her in the same harsh manner she'd delivered her accusation. 'It's why she and her friends are here tonight. She needs a bit of joy since her brother has gone missing.'

Joanna stumbled in her anger, but not her determination to continue on until she had the truth, all of it. 'And my ability to help you and your family?'

'It has nothing to do with my desire for you. Despite your relationship to Lord Helmsworth, you're still the woman I came to adore in the country, the one who cares about me and others, who understands duty and honour and loyalty to those you love.' He brushed a strand of hair off her forehead and tucked it behind her ear. His hand lingered near her cheek as the shimmering light of another rocket lit up his face. 'I still want you for my wife, I would even if you weren't a marquis's granddaughter.'

She held tight to his arms and stared into his

eyes, made brighter by the intensity of his regard for her. He admired her as much tonight as he had the day she'd stumbled in the stream and he'd caught her, when he'd protected her from Mr Selton and when he'd asked her to marry him in the vicarage.

He pulled her closer and she didn't resist, but fell against him, clinging to him as she had the night they'd been intimate. Beneath her fingertips, she felt his heart beat with the same power as the exploding fireworks. 'I love you, Joanna.'

She clutched his lapels, steadying herself as the truth of what he said and what it meant struck her. Not even Madame Dubois or Miss Fanworth had ever uttered the sentiment. In their own way, they'd given her love, but the words had never reached her ears until this moment. Beneath the flickering torches, with the fireworks flashing, all the chances she'd taken with him, the risk and losses, insults and censures no longer mattered.

'Tell me you love me,' he urged, bringing his face close to hers.

'I do.' She raised her lips to his, all fear of rejection and her grandfather's demands disappearing in his passionate kiss. Despite the difficulties separating them, he'd remained true to her, never giving up and neither would she. She wanted to be his wife and she would struggle with him to achieve it.

'Joanna?' her grandfather's worried voice carried over the topiaries. 'Where are you?'

She broke from Luke's kiss to peer through the bushes. Her grandfather stood in the centre of the walk, searching for her. 'What about him? I can't break his heart the way my mother did.'

He clasped her shoulders and turned her to face him, his eyes piercing hers. 'I promise I'll never make you choose between duty to your grandfather and your heart. We'll find a way to win him to our cause.'

She rested her hands on his trim waist, elated by his promise. He would fight for her as he did his men and their families and love her as she'd always longed to be loved.

'Now go, before he worries.' He swept Joanna's lips with a parting kiss, then nudged her back towards the walk.

She stumbled out from behind the tree, struggling to settle herself as her grandfather rushed up to her.

'My dear, where have you been?'

'I'm sorry, I didn't mean to wander off, but the garden is so confusing.' She prayed the dim paper lanterns hanging overhead hid her moist lips and her too-red cheeks from his notice. It was difficult to tell from his expression if they did.

'Don't do it again or you'll be mistaken for a woman of easy virtue.'

He'd raised his voice, saying it more in the direction of the tree where Luke hid than to her. Joanna fingered the gold chain and locket, now heavy on her skin. He'd guessed where she'd been and with whom.

'Come, the others are waiting.'

She followed him back to their party and Lord Jarsdel's side. Thankfully, a dazzling display of sparklers and candles from a pavilion situated in the centre of the lake kept everyone focused on it and not her. She couldn't see how this mess would end, but Luke loved her and she loved him and somehow all would be well.

Luke watched from the shadows as Lord Helmsworth guided Joanna back to the party and directly to Lord Jarsdel. The earl was as solicitous in his attention to Joanna as a besotted suitor. Luke wanted to march down the walk, take her in his arms and make it clear to everyone she was his, but he didn't move. Making a scene wouldn't help them. Instead, he returned to where his family stood a short distance away by the lake, ignoring the hard stares being flung at them by the Marquis.

Miss Crowther approached him before he reached his parents.

'I want to thank you again, Major Preston, before my party and I leave, for all you're doing on Reginald's behalf and mine.' She had her brother's dark hair and pale brown eyes, but she was much shorter and more slender in build. Luke suspected it had more to do with meagre meals than natural inclination. 'He always said you were too honourable for your own good and his.'

'I did my best to influence him, but he always resisted, especially where frequenting tavern gaming rooms was concerned. At least he has a knack for winning.'

'He's probably gambling with French soldiers right now, assuming he survived.' Her smile faded at the very real possibility they might never see Reginald again.

'He'll come back. He's too charming to perish,' Luke encouraged for her sake and his.

'You're right. We must continue to have faith. Goodnight, Major Preston.'

She left him to rejoin her party, her steps a little slower than before.

'Luke, come here quickly.' His father waved him over. 'Your brother has the most exciting news.'

Edward stood beside Alma, the hard planes of his face softer than Luke had seen them at any time since coming home. Even Alma seemed different. The glow which had surrounded her in London was brighter and Luke wondered what had brought such a change over them.

'Well, go on, tell them,' his father insisted, nearly hopping back and forth on his feet in excitement. Edward took Alma's hand and opened his mouth to speak when their father cut him off. 'Alma is expecting a child in the new year.'

A rocket exploded overhead, making Edward and Alma's smiles dazzle beneath its silvery light. Luke's mother's burst into tears. She rushed to Alma and embraced her, blubbing out words of congratulations. Luke's father shook Edward's hand, his eyes red with his tears of excitement.

Luke stared at them, amazed. A child. He looked to Alma, who winked at him over his mother's shoulder. So this was what she'd meant by still believing in miracles and it was one. Alma and Edward would be parents at last and he would be an uncle, and with luck a husband soon, too. It was an exhilarating night.

Their father let go of Edward and Luke stepped forward to clasp his brother's hand and give it a hearty shake. 'Well done.'

'Alma said you believed it would happen and helped her to do the same.' Edward pulled him off to one side, away from their parents, who were gushing over Alma. A rare humility came over him as he let go of Luke. 'Thank you for not giving up on us and your willingness to make sacrifices. I'm sorry if I haven't been kind to you. It's been difficult these last few years. You were right, I was jealous of your accomplishments because I'd failed in the one most expected of me. I shouldn't have taken out my frustrations on you. Siring a child might not seem like much to a man of your achievements, but for me it means not seeing all of my hard work and Father's come to an end. We've fought so long for Pensum Manor. To have someone to pass it on to and to give a child the security we've always lacked, means a great deal to me.'

The strain between them evaporated like a horse's breath in the cold. Joanna had been right about his brother and, for the first time, he saw how alike he and Edward were. Like Luke, Edward had been struggling with his failures, but in the end he'd triumphed. Luke hoped to emulate him in this regard. 'I admire what you've done for Pensum Manor and the line. I haven't always given you enough credit for it. You're a good man, Edward, and you deserve your success and all the happiness of a family of your own. I can't wait to welcome the new Ingham.'

He grabbed his brother and gave him a hearty embrace before stepping back.

'If all goes well, you could return to the Army,' Edward said, sobering Luke.

'I could.' He looked to where Joanna stood with her group at the lake's edge. The joy he'd longed to see in her face in Hertfordshire decorated it now, filling him with as much happiness as her.

The rush to return to Spain, which had once been so powerful, had lost its grip. Lord Beckwith said he could serve his men in a new way. It wasn't the same as standing beside them in a hail of musket fire, but it would make a difference and he could do it here in England near Joanna. Once they were married, she could help him. For the first time since coming home, he had a purpose, more than one, and both important enough to make him stay.

The carriage wheels against the cobblestone mimicked the steady rhythm of Joanna's heart as the vehicle carried her and her grandfather home. Outside, the streets were still and dark except for the swinging lanterns of the young boys lighting groups of men home. Their breath rose about their heads in the autumn chill. Inside the carriage it was as warm as Luke's lips had been against hers.

He loves me.

His words were as precious to her as his commitment to see them together. After years of everyone letting her go, her mother, Madame Dubois, here was someone at last striving to keep her close. She pressed her lips together, savouring the taste of Luke lingering there. He wanted her, not out of guilt for seducing her or to help his family, but as his wife and nothing could ruin her elation.

'I have a surprise for you. I've arranged to hold a ball in your honour next week.' her grandfather announced.

Except this.

'Why didn't you discuss it with me before you decided?' She sat up, rocking to one side as the carriage made a turn, trying not to be scolding. She should thank him and be grateful. This was something any young lady might wish for, but she was as annoyed by the news as the constant squeak of the carriage wheel behind her seat. She didn't want to be the centre of so much attention, most of it unpleasant as Lady Huntford had made clear tonight.

'I'm sorry, but I've wanted to do this since the moment we met.' He shifted across the carriage to sit beside her. 'I have something to show you.'

He produced a letter from inside his coat pocket and handed it to her. The paper, despite the fine quality, was yellow with age and the edges were wrinkled. She turned it over to reveal the one line indicating who it was meant for.

To My Daughter

'What is this?' Joanna asked.

'A letter to you, from Jane. She wrote it the day before she died and gave it to Mr Browning in the hopes he'd find you. He gave it to me once you were found. I'd thought of showing it to you sooner, but I decided to wait until you were more settled.'

Joanna swallowed hard, afraid to hold the paper too tight for fear it would crumble and she'd lose the only words she'd ever had from her mother.

'Go ahead, open it,' her grandfather urged.

Joanna turned the letter over and gently unfolded it to reveal her mother's cramped and shaky handwriting.

My dearest daughter,

There is so much I wish to say to you, but in my weakness I struggle to write the words. Last year I followed my heart and it has brought me both great joy and crushing sorrow. Your father is gone, died in battle, and I fear I will leave you, too.

I wish I could be there when you take your first steps, to teach you to ride like my father taught me. Perhaps some day your grandfather can give you the coming-out ball I used to dream of when I was carrying you. I cry to think I will not be there to see it.

There isn't enough time for me to tell you everything you will ever need to deal with the world, so I'll write the most important. I loved you from the first moment I felt you move inside me, and I love you still. Never doubt this, or how much you were wanted, and never be afraid to follow your heart, but do it wisely. It is a lesson I fear I learned too late.
Your loving mother

Joanna's chest tightened, but there were no tears. There was too much regret for everything she and her mother had lost for her to cry. The childhood she might have had if her mother had lived teased her in the darkness, but she refused to entertain the sense of loss for too long. Joanna rested her head on her grandfather's shoulder and he put his arm around her. She was grateful for the gift of the letter. For so many years she thought she hadn't been wanted by her parents, but she'd been wrong.

'Do you see now why I arranged the ball?' her grandfather asked, his voice thick with tears.

'I do.' She stared down at the yellowed edges

of the parchment resting on her lap and read the last line over and over.

Follow your heart, but do it wisely.

Her mother hadn't regretted her time with her father, but the damage it had wrought. This, more than her desire for a coming-out ball, spoke to Joanna. In her mother's words was the permission to pursue a life with Luke and how she might accomplish it. If she was smart in her choices, less impetuous in her decisions, and more willing to work to earn the approval of her grandfather than her mother had been, she might succeed in love where her mother had failed.

'I think the ball will be lovely, but there is one thing I'd like to request.' She sat back from her grandfather. Her fingers shook as she folded the letter and guilt gnawed at her over the stipulation she was about to place on her concession, but she must do it. If Luke was willing to fight for her, she must do the same for him instead of being afraid to act because of her worries. She would follow her heart, but in a way her mother had failed to do. 'I should like you to invite the Inghams.'

Her grandfather started in surprise, and then his

eyes began to narrow with his old hate. 'I won't have them here.'

Joanna braced herself and continued on. 'You speak of making things right for your daughter and me. Now there's one more thing that must be righted. This disagreement between the two families must end.'

'I asked you not to see that man,' he reprimanded, but she didn't allow it to stop her this time.

'I know.' She took his hand and squeezed it gently. 'But you've been so kind and generous to me over this past month and I want everyone, including the Inghams, to see what a loving and wonderful man you are.'

Her grandfather didn't answer, but stared for a long moment at their intertwined fingers. In the silence, punctuated by the clack of the carriage over the cobblestones, she struggled to beat back her worry. She'd asserted herself and it remained to be seen how he would react.

At last he raised his face to hers. There was something stiff about his expression, a reluctance of sorts, but it clashed with his words, giving her hope. 'You sound like your mother tonight. She used to be the peacemaker in the family when her mother was alive, until nothing could bring peace between us. You're right, this feud has gone on too long. I will invite the Inghams and do what I can to put this rift behind us.'

'Thank you, Grandfather.' She kissed him on the forehead, her heart filled with a love and confidence she hadn't experienced in a long time. She'd spoken up and the world hadn't come crashing down on her. Instead, her courage had brought her grandfather and the Inghams closer to reconciling and opened the way for her happiness with Luke.

Chapter Fourteen

'Lord Helmsworth to see Major Preston,' the Inghams' butler announced.

Everyone set down their silverware and forgot the roast as they turned down the dinner table to stare at Luke.

'It looks like you've finally succeeded with the old man. Well done,' his father congratulated, lifting his wine goblet to Luke. 'This is turning out to be quite a week.'

'I wouldn't be so quick to celebrate.' Luke pushed back his chair and rose, wondering what had brought Lord Helmsworth here. Perhaps Joanna had worked her subtle charm on the old man, but he doubted it. Like a too-quiet morning before a battle, this unannounced guest made Luke wary.

'Major Preston, what a pleasure it is to see you

this morning,' Lord Helmsworth offered with an overly wide smile as Luke entered the sitting room.

'To what do I owe the pleasure of your visit?'

'I wish to speak with you about Miss Radcliff.'

The two of them remained standing, eyeing each other like a couple of cocks in a pit. Lord Helmsworth had lost some of the wildness of his appearance from the country. It was as if the Savile Row tailors had finally had a crack at him instead of the local ones from the village. It wasn't so much his fine suit which made Luke pause, but the cat-who-ate-the-canary gleam in his eyes. 'You see, I'm holding a ball in her honour in a few days and I'd be delighted if you and your family could attend.'

'Delighted?' He didn't believe it.

'Very much so because I think it's time we finally put our differences aside. I'm prepared to deed to your family the disputed land on one condition.'

'Which is?'

'You must never see Joanna again after the ball.'

His offer nearly knocked Luke across the room with the same force as the cannonball that had once exploded too close to him. 'You think my regard for her so slight I can be bought off?'

'I know it was you she was dallying with at Vauxhall. You weren't content to ruin her in the country, but wanted to compromise her here so that no man will have her. I'll not have it and I will see to it she doesn't make the same mistake her mother did.'

'The only mistake she'll make is walking away from what she wants because of someone else's demands. I won't let her do it, not for land or money or anything else you wish to throw at me.'

'Then let me to appeal to your sense of honour and responsibility. If you continue in your pursuit of Joanna, I will not only withdraw the very generous dowry and inheritance I've settled on her, but my protection. I will return her to the school where she was raised and leave her to make her way in the world without me.'

Luke levelled a hard look at Lord Helmsworth. 'How can you be so heartless?'

'Because I had my heart ripped out once before and lost my only child and nineteen years with my granddaughter because of a scheming man like you. I can't bear it again,' he shouted, his eyes wild with hurt and his hands shaking at his sides.

His pain pierced Luke's fury and he took a deep breath. He'd seen so many men wounded without scars or physical injuries, their ability to endure hardship and horrors weakened by their experiences. The same suffering drove Lord Helmsworth to make this awful proposal and he pitied him. Luke addressed him as he would one of his soldiers afflicted by the mental anguish of war. 'Joanna has a very generous heart with enough love for both of us. There's no need to make her choose.'

Lord Helmsworth's frenzied grief eased with Luke's reassurance, and a long minute passed, filled by the laugh of a servant from somewhere in the house. It was clear the Marquis loved Joanna, but the past was blinding him so much he could no longer discern between events from twenty years ago and now. Luke hoped his compassion could convince the good man he remembered from the long-ago Christmas party to assert himself over the wounded one standing before him.

Then Lord Helmsworth jerked at his lapels, the stony façade of the titled man he'd always worn with Luke descending over him again. His pain had won in the struggle against his goodness. 'I will if you force me to and it might not end the way you wish. She may choose me over you and then where will you be? Without the river. I know about your family's debts. A few more bad harvests and they'll overwhelm you until you're forced to sell Pensum Manor. If that happens, it'll be your fault.' Lord Helmsworth removed a paper from his pocket and held it out to Luke. 'Here's the deed to the land. If you promise to walk away from her, I'll give it to you today so your family may do with it as they please.'

Luke stared at the deed folded in on itself and tied with a slender red ribbon, struggling to find some way out of this ultimatum, but he couldn't. He didn't doubt Lord Helmsworth's resolve to make good on his threat and place Joanna in a heartrending situation. Luke couldn't be the means of her suffering or see the glow which had surrounded her at Vauxhall Gardens extinguished because of him. With Lord Helmsworth, she would have a comfortable life, all worries of money and a home vanquished. As a second son, Luke could offer her little except debts, or the hard life of an officer's wife. Instead of managing a grand estate, she'd be trudging through the mud behind troops, exposed to disease or advancing armies, always worried he might not come back from the front and then she'd be left destitute, or reliant on the charity of his family who could barely afford to keep Pensum Manor. He couldn't see Joanna in peril because of his own selfish wants. He'd regret what he was about to do, but he had no choice. He'd sworn to not make Joanna choose between him and her grandfather. He must keep his promise.

'I will end our relationship, but not for the deed or for you, but for her. I love her enough to give her up to ensure that she has a better life than I can give her. The kind of life she deserves.'

To his credit, Lord Helmsworth appeared more surprised than gloating at Luke's announcement, as if at a loss for what to do because he hadn't expected his plan to work. Then he tugged at his waistcoat and recovered his usual crotchety stance. 'Good. You'll come to the ball and tell her yourself that there can be nothing further between the two of you.'

Luke nodded, his own heart clenching at the thought of having to break hers.

'And, since you've proved yourself a man of honour, you may have the land.'

'I don't want it.'

'Take it anyway. After today I want nothing more to do with you or your family.' Lord Helmsworth flung down the deed on the table beside him, then turned and strode out of the room, head held high in triumph.

Luke watched him go and for the second time since coming home cursed his honour. It had cost him his heart.

Joanna stood in the receiving line in the ballroom of her grandfather's London house, trying not to shift and fuss like the little girls at school used to do before they became accustomed to Madame Dubois's discipline. The last two hours had been an endless round of people, titles and introductions. Everyone had been too eager to openly scrutinise the new granddaughter of the Marquis of Helmsworth to avoid the receiving line, except for Luke. He had yet to arrive.

She'd nearly skipped with delight when, during

a walk in Rotten Row a few days ago, her grand-father had told her he'd sent the invitation to the Inghams and they'd accepted. He said he'd paid them a visit, too, and settled the dispute between the two families, although he hadn't told her how. It didn't seem possible and it had made all her preparations for tonight more thrilling.

'I think we've had enough standing about. Any-one else who wants to greet us can find us in the crush,' her grandfather announced to the hoarse butler.

He escorted Joanna to the dance floor. Mrs Petit, Joanna's chaperon, followed close behind, less awed by their surroundings than Joanna had been at the Pensum Manor ball. Luke had been the brightest point of that night as he would be again tonight.

If he arrived. *No, he'll come, he must.*

They passed beneath the evergreen garlands hanging between the pillars of the room. The fin-est musicians played on a raised platform at the far end while disciplined and liveried footmen offered the best wine to an overflowing room of guests. Joanna searched the crowd for Luke, at last un-derstanding Frances's obsession with finding her lieutenant. Nothing else mattered except seeing him, not her new dress, the dancers, the guests, or even the strange looks she received from more than one matron. Luke's acceptance of the invitation, the fact her grandfather had sent it at all, created possibilities she hadn't allowed herself to imagine a few days ago. It made his having not arrived yet even more troubling.

They reached the edge of the dance floor and worry continued to undermine her excitement. Luke wasn't among the many gentlemen who came forward to claim a dance. She had no choice but to accept one short young man's hand, the son of a peer whose name she couldn't recall. A month ago, men like him wouldn't have acknowledged her, tonight they clamoured to dance with her, a possible connection to a marquis and a fine dowry enough to make them overlook her less-than-sterling past. It amused her to turn their heads, but not enough to make her forget Luke, or to stop fretting about why he wasn't here.

Then the dance began and she was forced to concentrate on the steps the dancing master had taught her over the last few days. The other young ladies surrounding her moved with effortless elegance while she focused on not stumbling. Her partner was patient when she missed more than one turn, but it was clear a few women lined up along the side of the floor weren't so charitable. Her inability to dance properly reinforced their view of her unsuitability to be in society. She wasn't sure she disagreed with them, but accepting her grandfather meant accepting her place with him. She must learn to adjust to this as she had to being at the Huntfords'.

She held her head high and moved with her partner through the promenade. That cold lonely life seemed like so long ago, never to return again. There were people here hoping she'd fail and she wouldn't allow them to lower her as Lady Huntford and Frances had tried to do at Vauxhall Gardens. This was who she was and she would at last embrace it instead of shying away. It would be a greater triumph if Luke were at her side.

Her partner stopped and raised her hand as she circled him. Awareness rippled across her bare shoulders and slid beneath the gold chain holding her mother's locket encircling her neck. She glanced at the crowd. Luke stood at the edge of the dance floor, ignoring the ladies on either side of him turning to and fro in an effort to catch his eye and secure a partner. His black coat increased the sharpness of his chin and the dark brown of his hair. She opened her fingers, ready to rush to him before she remembered herself. Instead, she rewarded his arrival with a coy smile.

His only response was a slight twitch in a muscle along his hard jaw. Her joy dropped to the floor to be trod on by the other dancers. Something was wrong, terribly so. She made a turn, getting another look at him. He appeared as he had the night he'd told her of his men's disappearance, his expression dark with trouble. She trussed up her resolve, refusing to allow his stern appearance to drag her down. He was here, and whatever was bothering him, they would make it right together as they had every other challenge they'd endured since the night they'd first met.

At last the dance ended, and Joanna forced herself to walk slowly next to her companion as he escorted her back to her grandfather. Tonight, Lord Helmsworth played the role of chaperon more than Mrs Petit. He was about to offer her to another partner when Luke shifted forward, blocking the man.

'May I?'

She glanced at her grandfather, expecting him to object since the next dance was a waltz, but he waved Luke forward to Joanna. A strange smile split her grandfather's pale lips, not of irritation or amusement, but something more unnerving. Whatever it was, her concern vanished the moment Luke's fingers curled over hers.

While they walked side by side to the dance floor, the memory of him covering her in the vicarage and the sense of peace she'd experienced in his arms teased her. The peace wasn't here. There was no amusement in his stride, no interest when he rested his hand on the small of her back, then took her other one to bring her into the circles of his arms and prepare for the dance. All around them people whispered and practically pointed, their presence together reinforcing all the rumours they must have heard. Joanna ignored them, too concerned with Luke and what was wrong to worry about what others said or thought.

'You're so late I thought maybe you'd changed your mind.' Joanna eyed him from beneath her lashes, prodding as much as tempting him. She'd dared to doubt him before Vauxhall Gardens and been proven wrong. She wanted him to counter her qualms again.

'How could I stay away?' It might as well have been Mr Selton saying it for all the feeling in his words.

Her stomach rolled as the music began and it grew tighter with each turn as her feet moved in rote steps to match of his. They danced with as much passion as the wooden figures on her grandfather's German cuckoo clock.

'What's wrong?' Joanna demanded, unable to keep the note of panic out of her voice.

Luke stared over her head as if it hurt him to acknowledge her. 'I must speak with you alone at some point this evening.'

'Tell me what you need to now, I don't want to wait.'

'Not here in front of your guests.'

Her hand stiffened in his, his need for secrecy as potent as Grace's when she'd first told Joanna she was expecting a baby. 'Then escort me off the dance floor.'

'People will talk.'

'Then tell them I'm ill.' She was sick with worry.

He stopped them in their whirling, making more

than one couple break stride to stare before better sense swept them back into the dance. Luke escorted her away from her grandfather who was too deep in conversation with Lord Jarsdel to notice. The watching crowd parted to let them through, casting a parcel of whispers at them as they left the dance floor. What should have been the dance of the evening, the one she'd looked forward to for days, became a long, painful march.

In a moment, Mrs Petit was behind them, giving their spectacle a modicum of respect.

They passed through a door at the far end and cut through the empty and silent music room separating the ballroom from the rest of the house.

'Miss Radcliff, where are we going?' Mrs Petit asked, her slippers fluttering over the wood floor in time to Joanna and Luke's decided stride.

'Major Preston and I have something to discuss.'

'Alone? You can't.' She rushed to place herself between Joanna and the door to the sitting room on the far side of the music room. There was no one in this part of the house, the ball having been relegated to the more spacious rooms at the front.

'I must, now stay out here,' she snapped, as irritable as Frances had been. Shame engulfed her and she reached out to rest one hand on the thin woman's arm. 'I'm sorry, I don't mean to be cross, but I must be alone with Major Preston for a few short minutes.'

'But, Miss Radcliff...' she began to protest.

'Please,' Joanna begged. 'It's important.'

Mrs Petit glanced between her and Luke. He stood with arms stiff at his side and back straight. It was clear whatever she and Luke were about to discuss didn't involve lovemaking.

At last Mrs Petit relented. 'All right, you may be alone, but only for a bit and I'll be right here outside this door.'

'I wouldn't expect you to be anywhere else.' She gave Mrs Petit's arm an appreciative squeeze, then pushed open the sitting room door and led Luke inside.

'You haven't come to propose, have you?' she demanded before the door was even closed. The silent portraits of her mother and grandmother watched them as they faced one another.

'No, I've come to end things.'

Joanna grasped the back of a chair as the entire house shifted around her. She stared at him, trying to convince herself she'd heard him wrong, but it was clear in the set of his jaw she hadn't. All the eagerness to see him, the expectation they might be free to be with each other shattered, leaving nothing but a hollow sensation in the centre of her chest. He'd chased her through Hertfordshire and then London, slowly undermining her refusals and protestations while capturing her heart. After all his effort, his words, the risks they'd taken, her grandfather had been right. He didn't love her. No, it wasn't possible. This wasn't the Luke she'd come to know, the one who struggled and fought against any difficulty in his determination to succeed. 'Why?'

'In the last week, I've realised the obstacles between us are too great to overcome.'

'You're giving up? I don't believe it.' There must be some reason why he'd suddenly changed his mind. Over his shoulder, the portrait of her mother stood out against the green-papered wall. At once, she knew what had happened. 'My grandfather made you break with me in return for the land, didn't he?'

Luke silently cursed Lord Helmsworth and his wicked demand. He couldn't tell her the truth.

It would make her hate her grandfather and he'd vowed not to come between the two of them, no matter how much it pained both him and Joanna. She wanted a family and she would have one, but not with him. 'No.'

'Then what's going on? Please, tell me the truth.' Her sweet fragrance embraced him as she came forward. He wanted to kiss away the pain clipping her words, but he couldn't. He could only stand and retain a measure of dignity while he tore himself down in her eyes. 'You said you loved me.'

She might as well have shot him for the hole it left in his gut.

'I do and I always will, but it was wrong of me to court you, especially since it was always my plan to return to Spain. I can now since my brother's wife is with child.'

'You mean it was wrong of you to finally admit in front of everyone there was a connection between an earl's son and an illegitimate governess whose reputation you ruined.' Hate turned her sapphire eyes stormy and she balled her hands at her sides. He braced himself, ready to feel her blows on his chest but she stood still. 'Grandfather was right. You got what you wanted from me in the country, in secret, but when it came time to make it known you were too ashamed to be seen with me. No wonder you arrived late. I'm surprised you came at all or had the courage to dance with me since it might compromise your ability to find a woman with a purer past and lineage than me.'

He ground his teeth at the insult, but he let it stand. If hate eased her pain she could hate him for ever. 'You're wrong about yourself. You're worth more than any other woman in the ballroom and you deserve a man who can give you everything you've ever dreamed of. I'm not him. It was never possible for me to be him and I'm sorry.'

'You're only sorry your lies have at last been exposed. Get out.' She jabbed one slender finger towards the door, her stiff arm shaking with rage. 'I'm through with you.'

He nodded, and placing one foot behind him, turned as if taking leave of an officer. Outside in the music room, the chaperon grasped her fan in worry as Luke passed. He said nothing as he forced himself across the marble floor, away from

Joanna and everything he'd fought in his attempt to win her.

The doors to the ballroom opened and the music washed over him along with a hundred curious stares. He only saw Lord Helmsworth observing him from his place beside Lord Jarsdel. Luke stopped and, from across the room, bowed to the Marquis in surrender. If he'd had his sword he would have broken it across his knee and chucked it at the man's feet. He straightened and strode out of the entrance, leaving the candlelit room. Each step hurt as much as if he'd marched a hundred miles barefoot, but he kept going. His reputation and honour were all he'd possessed when he'd returned to England. It was all he had now. He'd left his heart behind with Joanna.

Joanna paced until the muscles of her legs protested and still she continued on, eyes dry, too furious to cry. The grating of metal against metal met the fall of each of her feet as she tugged the locket back and forth on its chain. It wasn't Luke's rejection feeding her fury, but her gullible stupidity. She'd been so desperate to be loved, she'd believed in his lies and continued to entertain his secret advances even in the face of her grandfather's evidence.

'How could I have been such a fool?' If she'd kept away from Luke as her grandfather had warned her to, guarded her heart instead of throwing it at him, she'd be dancing and having a wonderful time in the ballroom, not hiding here in humiliation.

She stopped and stared out the window at the carriages filling the street outside. The drivers stood together laughing at jokes Joanna couldn't hear. She envied their good humour, hers was at an end.

The door squeaked open behind her, but Joanna didn't turn to see who it was.

'Miss Radcliff, are you all right?' Mrs Petit asked.

'Yes, I need some time alone. I'll be out soon.'

The door clicked shut and Joanna sighed. She couldn't stay in here all night. She'd have to return to the ball soon and smile and pretend everything was all right. She wasn't sure she could. Raising her hand, she touched the cold window, tempted to throw the sash up, slip outside and command one of the drivers to carry her away. Except there was nowhere for her to go. The school was no longer her home, this was. Even if she could go back to Salisbury and Madame, it would mean running from her troubles instead of facing them with the comportment and dignity Madame had instilled in her. She wanted to prove to her headmistress she was the strong, capable woman she'd raised her to be, not a senseless goose, despite having acted like one with Luke.

Joanna turned and caught the silent eyes of her mother watching her from the portrait. Regret as powerful as that over never having met her mother smothered her. She let go of the locket, wondering if she'd avoided sharing a similar fate with her. If she'd continued with Luke, they might have met again in a dark room in defiance of everyone and she could have found herself with child. She'd wanted to make a decision about her life, but Luke had proven she wasn't capable of doing so, or trusting her own heart. When he'd held her in Vauxhall Gardens, she'd been as convinced of his love as of Grace's, Rachel's and Isabel's friendships. When he'd told her he still loved her tonight, she'd wanted to believe him, despite the anger driving her to deny it. It was difficult, even now, to accept she'd been so misled, but she had been. She'd craved him and had imagined their future. In the end, he'd disappointed her and her expectations as much as the position with the Huntfords' had.

'I wish you were here,' she said to her mother, craving another letter, and more words to help her deal with the pain crushing her heart. She would have understood Joanna's torment and wouldn't have judged her for her mistakes, but she wasn't here. No one was. There was nothing except silence. Once again Joanna was left to forge ahead alone.

The door opened. This time it wasn't Mrs Petit, but Lord Jarsdel who entered.

'Is everything all right, Miss Radcliff? You've been gone from the ballroom for a long time.'

'Yes, only I haven't had a moment to myself all night.' Despite his kindness, she couldn't admit her mistake with Luke and have him think less of her than she already thought of herself.

'I saw Major Preston leave. Is everything all right between the two of you?'

'There's nothing between us any more.' Her voice cracked and she closed her mouth, afraid to say too much for fear the dam inside her would break. Once she began to cry, for herself, her mother and everything she'd lost and would never have, she feared it wouldn't stop.

Lord Jarsdel nodded sagely, not gloating over his rival's departure. Her anger lost some of its edge under his calming presence. He didn't press her to speak, or ask her awkward questions, but remained with her so she wasn't alone. She appreciated the gesture. She needed friends now. Grace, Rachel and Isabel were too far away.

The clock on the mantel chimed eleven times.

'We should be getting back.' She wasn't sure how she would maintain her composure in a room full of strangers determined to stare at her. In the past they'd ignored her, she wished they would again, but they wouldn't. It would be like facing down Lady Huntford the day after she and Luke had made love. She must endure it, like everything else in her life, and not speak out or complain. Frustration chipped at her as hard as disappointment. She'd spoken up about Luke and it had won her nothing except a broken heart.

'Before we go, I'd like to ask you something,'

Lord Jarsdel began, his usual steadfastness ruffling around the edges.

Joanna clasped her hands in front of her, having an inkling of what he might say. She would have stopped him a few hours ago but so much had changed since then. 'Yes?'

'I'm sure you're aware, your grandfather is very interested in us marrying.'

She remained silent and the part of her which had come alive under Luke's touch settled back to sleep. She let it. It was no longer of any use to her.

Lord Jarsdel approached, his confidence tempered by humility. 'I may not be as dashing or young as Major Preston, but I'll be a kind and respectful husband. With me you'll have a home of your own and children. We can be happy together. Miss Radcliff, will you marry me?'

He held out his hand, silently urging her to take it.

She studied the lines of his white glove crossing his palm. Here was an earl willing to raise a former governess to a countess, to openly share his life and wealth with her despite the rumours. It spoke to his good character, yet all she could think was, *he's not Luke.* In the end, Luke had abandoned her, too ashamed of her to resist whatever influence her grandfather had exercised over him. Lord Jarsdel wanted her for better or worse. She didn't have to accept him. She could take her grandfather's money and remain single, but it seemed a very lonely life.

She glanced past him to the silent portrait of her mother. Her mother hadn't found lasting contentment with the man she'd loved and neither had Joanna, but it didn't mean Joanna must remain alone. In Lord Jarsdel's offer was the chance to be a wife and to give future children security and a place in society. It wasn't a grand passion, but the safe and sensible arrangement her grandfather wanted for her. Joanna had followed her mother's advice, and her heart, and it had resulted in rejection and sorrow. It was time to follow her head and sensible guidance.

She laid her hand in his, unable to meet his eyes as she answered, 'Yes. I will marry you.'

Chapter Fifteen

'Let's raise another glass to Major Preston. In two weeks he'll be back kicking Napoleon across Spain.' Captain Arnold toasted and the gathered officers lifted their tankards and shouted.

'Huzzah!'

Their cheers echoed through the walls of the Army Service Club in St James's Street, a rollicking London refuge for officers on leave between campaigns or on half-pay. The white-plastered walls were lined with portraits of battles, rearing horses and solemn officers in full dress.

Luke raised his tankard, too, but set it aside while his mates drained theirs. The red coat felt heavy on his shoulders and the tinkling of his medals as he moved irritated him today. He'd borrowed a tidy sum to buy back his major's epaulets, to get away from London and Joanna. Even with the money already spent, he wondered if he'd made a mistake.

Lord Beckwith, who stood out in the sea of red uniforms in his Horse Guard blues, slapped Luke on the back. 'Not having a change of heart, are you?'

'No.' Although he should.

His parents had tried to talk him out of re-enlisting, for the first time allowing their anguish over his safety to show. In it he'd seen that it wasn't the family line they feared dying, but their son. Luke had no intention of getting himself killed, even if, at the moment, a bullet through the chest seemed preferable to the ache lodged there since his last meeting with Joanna.

'Too bad. I still believe you'd better serve the military here than risking becoming cannon fodder in Spain.' Lord Beckwith took a sip of his port, preferring the genteel and more potent spirit to the common one being consumed *en masse* around them. 'I can still find you a place at Whitehall. It isn't too late.'

Yes, it is. He'd read the announcement in the papers about Joanna's engagement to Lord Jarsdel and their wedding date. Remaining in London where he would see the new Lady Jarsdel at every social event of the Season wasn't his idea of a good time. 'No, I'm going back to Spain.'

Another cheer went up from the gathered men, this one louder and more enthusiastic than before. Officers crowded around someone Luke couldn't see near the door. They'd already saluted Wellington's health, the ladies of Drury Lane and Luke. There wasn't much left to give them a reason to drink, although they hardly needed one. They'd toast any old sod for a sip.

'Captain Mercer must have smuggled in a few actresses again?' Lord Beckwith mumbled. Women without reputations were the only ones who could enter a club in St James's without being ruined and even they had a difficult go of it.

Luke tried to peer through the mass of drunk and celebrating men, but it was difficult to tell one red coat from another. 'I don't think they're cheering for a woman.'

Then the group parted and Luke almost dropped his tankard.

'Having a party without me, are you?' Reginald threw open his arms as he approached Luke. He was leaner, his hair longer and touching the dirty collar of his coat. The circles beneath his eyes were thicker, too, but his smile was as wide as ever.

'You're alive.' Luke shoved the tankard at Lord Beckwith and rushed to grab his friend in a hearty embrace.

'I've been gone for ages and you don't even offer me a drink.' Reginald laughed as Luke stepped back.

'I'll buy you a whole bottle.' The heavy mood which had crushed Luke for the last two weeks began to lift as he sat down with Reginald. A bottle was procured and with it cold meat and cheese. Reginald ate and drank while regaling everyone with the harrowing account of how he and the squad had barely escaped being caught in a narrow pass and had ended up trapped behind enemy lines. They'd avoided capture for weeks by dodging patrols, collecting intelligence and being sheltered by sympathetic Spaniards.

'One Spanish family hid us in their barn for a week. Seeing them made me realise I'd like one of my own and a more settled life.' Reginald threw his worn boots up on the table. After rounds and rounds of good cheer, the two of them had been left alone near the corner to speak. 'I'm grateful for the help you gave my sister. All the men were thankful to come home and find their families not starving.'

'It was the least I could do.'

'Now, let me help you. How come, at your hail and farewell, you look like a man about to be hanged? What's been going on since I left you at the Bull?' Reginald took an ivory toothpick out of his coat pocket and slipped it between his lips.

Luke rapped his knuckles against the top of the table. 'The woman I love is at the church today, about to marry another man.'

The bells rang, one after another, their deep toll reverberating through the old church. Joanna sat in the still of the vestry room, waiting for her grandfather to collect her for the service. The white-silk wedding dress covering her was soft against her skin and she worried a small section of lace on the cuff between her thumb and forefinger. The last two weeks had been a flurry of activity to prepare for today. The dress had been rushed to be sewn, the special licence secured, the wedding breakfast arranged and a bevy of invitations sorted and sent. She'd been thankful for the activity. During the day it had kept her distracted, but at night, when it was quiet, her conscience tortured her. It still did.

I shouldn't marry Lord Jarsdel, I don't love him. She rose and crossed the marble floor, her veil whispering against her dress with each step. He didn't love her, but his caring way was reminiscent of Miss Fanworth's. There were worse men she could wed, someone like Lieutenant Foreman who might abandon a lady when she needed him most, or someone like Luke who'd never cared at all.

I should have listened to Grandfather.

She made a turn, flipping the veil behind her so as not to step on it. Her grandfather had tried to guide her with Luke but she'd resisted. Yet she'd followed his counsel in this instance, and instead of being a radiant bride she was fretting.

She crossed the room again, her feet falling faster and faster on the stone. She wished Grace, Isabel and Rachel were here to make her see how marrying Lord Jarsdel, like Isabel marrying Mr Balfour, was the best decision she could make. Despite Joanna sending them invitations, none of them had been able to come for the hastily arranged affair, not even Madame Dubois. She and Miss Fanworth had pleaded the expense for sending their regrets. It meant all the guests in the pews were friends of her grandfather or her fiancé and there were few in the church for her. She was almost as alone as the day in Hertfordshire when she'd stumbled upon her grandfather in the graveyard. It made what was supposed to be a happy day even more dreary.

The church bells ceased their ringing and the deep tones of the organ began to fill the room. Joanna stopped in panic to listen. The time for the ceremony was quickly approaching.

'My dear, you look gorgeous.' Her grandfather entered, regal in his new dark green coat and gold waistcoat. He'd been near fluttering with elation for the last three days. 'I have a surprise for you.'

'What is it?' She tried to meet his announcement with the appropriate pleasure and gratitude. It was growing more difficult with each organ note to stand still, much less appear excited.

He pulled open the door and waved to someone outside. 'I couldn't let the day pass without doing this for you.'

Madame Dubois stepped into the room. She was in her Sunday best, a dark blue velvet dress with a high collar rimmed in white lace. Her hair was done up in her usual tight twist, but the smile gracing her lips and lighting her grey eyes softened the severity of her appearance. She appeared to Joanna as she imagined a mother would on the day of her daughter's wedding, proud, thrilled and with the mist of tears in her eyes.

Instead of squealing in delight at her arrival, Joanna burst into tears.

For the first time ever, Madame Dubois came to her and enveloped her in a tender hug. Joanna held her tight while sobs shook her entire body.

'Perhaps you should leave us alone for a while,' Madame suggested to her grandfather, who stared at them, stunned by Joanna's response.

'I think you're right.' He backed out of the room, drawing the door closed behind him.

Madame held Joanna tight until the sobs began to subside.

'What's wrong, Miss Radcliff?' Her pointed question, delivered with the same authority as when she used to speak at the school, snapped Joanna out of her crying.

Joanna rubbed her wet cheeks with the back of her hands. 'I don't want to marry Lord Jarsdel.'

'Sit down, we must talk.' She guided Joanna to the sofa beneath the window, then laced her hands together in front of her and raised one sharp eyebrow. 'Tell me why, despite standing in your wedding dress, you don't want to marry him.'

The words began to pour out of Joanna while they sat in the warm sunlight falling through the window. Joanna told Madame everything about her relationship with Luke, their meeting at the ball, in the woods, even their night at the vicarage and his saying he loved her. She described his having left her, and how it had led to her accepting Lord Jarsdel.

'You must think I'm foolish to not want to marry an earl.' Joanna sniffed, too wrung out to fear Madame's disappointment in her being so misguided about so many things. 'Or for being so weak with Major Preston.'

'You're not foolish for having followed your heart. I wish I had.'

'You?' This silenced Joanna's sniffles.

Madame rested her hands on her lap and a remorse Joanna had only seen the time she'd spied her in the garden with the letter came over her. 'When I was young, I fell in love with the oldest son of a titled man. It wasn't a girlish passion or a backstairs liaison, but real and true love. He wanted to marry me, but I was in no position to claim a place as his wife. Not wanting to stop him from fulfilling his role as the heir, I refused him. He married a woman he didn't love because of it and I lost him. I've regretted it every day of my life since.'

'Oh, Madame.' Joanna grasped her hands in sympathy. 'I didn't realise.'

'Because I never told you.' Madame covered Joanna's hand with her other one, clasping it in her tender grip. 'I haven't always been the most mothering of guardians to you, but I believed if I didn't coddle you, you'd grow up strong and prepared to face the difficulties and challenges of life. I was right. Already you've dealt with so much and so well. You've made me as proud as any mother can be of her daughter.'

Joanna's heart stilled and tears threatened to overcome her again. She'd been so wrong about Madame and everything. 'All my life I prayed for a real family, but I shouldn't have, not when I already had one in you and Miss Fanworth and my friends. Instead of appreciating them, I kept looking for something else. I shouldn't have.'

'We're all capable of not seeing what's in front of us while reaching for something else. It takes great courage to admit it and to reject other people's plans in favour of your own.' She settled back and looked down at Joanna just as she used to whenever she wished to impart something important to her. 'It is time for you to be courageous, Miss Radcliff, and to tell everyone exactly what you want.'

'Yes, you're right.'

A knock at the door interrupted them.

'Is everything well in there?' Her grandfather's anxious voice followed.

Madame Dubois rose with her usual elegance and crossed the room to open the door.

'Lord Helmsworth, Miss Radcliff has something she wishes to discuss with you.'

She didn't remain, but slipped outside, leaving Joanna and her grandfather alone. He rushed up to her, concern clouding his aged blue eyes.

'What's the matter?'

Joanna took a bracing breath. Once the words

were out there'd be no taking them back, but she must be brave and trust in his love. 'I can't go through with the wedding.'

She explained to him everything she and Madame Dubois had discussed. Her grandfather stared at the floor beneath her feet while she spoke, rubbing his chin in contemplation. She wasn't sure what he thought, but she kept speaking, revealing everything in her heart, especially his place in it.

'I appreciate all you've done for me. It's the whole reason I agreed to this marriage.'

His hands stilled on his chin and at last he looked up at her, not angry or disappointed but accepting. 'I suspected as much. Many times over the last two weeks I have thought I was imagining your distress. I told myself that once you married Lord Jarsdel everything would be well. I was mistaken. You were suffering in an effort to make me happy. I was wrong to allow it to continue and to do what I did with Major Preston.'

Shock rippled through Joanna. 'What do you mean?'

Her grandfather took in a deep breath before

he continued. 'I offered him the river land in exchange for his promise to end things with you.'

'And he accepted it?'

'No.' He took her hands, more serious than he had been when he'd warned her not to speak with Luke. 'But I deeded it to him anyway, because when I asked him not to take you away from me he behaved more honourably than I did.'

She stared at her grandfather, an elation she hadn't experienced since Vauxhall rising inside her. 'Then he wasn't lying or ashamed of me. He really did love me.'

'Enough to leave you because he thought you would have a better life without him rather than with him.'

'Not at all.'

'I see that now.' Tears filled his eyes and his hands trembled in hers. 'Please don't hate me for what I did. I'm not cruel. I simply wanted to protect you.'

'I know.' She threw her arms around him, unable to withhold her forgiveness. His confession had raised her hopes. It was more than she'd allowed herself to believe in the country, or during these last two weeks. Luke loved her and she loved him, and there was still a chance that they could at last be together.

He hugged her tight with relief and then held her at arm's length. 'All these years I've been bitter and angry over what I had lost. Then, when I gained you, instead of letting it go, I allowed it to guide me. You aren't Jane and Major Preston isn't Captain Handler, I see that now, and I want grandchildren, little ones to liven up Helmsworth Manor and that draughty London house.' He winked at her, the caring humorous man with her once more.

Joanna smiled sheepishly at him. 'I'm sorry I didn't say something sooner, before all this expense and effort. I should have told you how much Luke meant to me instead of allowing things to go on for so long.'

'And I should have listened instead of trying to make you do things my way. Don't worry about the expense, I can afford it.' He chuckled before turning serious. 'But you have no time to waste if you want to claim your young man.'

'What do you mean?'

'Lord Jarsdel told me Major Preston purchased

a commission and is leaving to rejoin his regiment tomorrow.'

'Then I must see him, at once.' She didn't know if she could win him back, or if he still wanted her. With her grandfather's blessing secured, she had to try before he was beyond her reach.

'Take the carriage and go to his parents' house in Kensington. They can summon him from the Army Service Club to speak with you.'

Assuming he would. No, she had to believe she'd succeed. She gathered up the veil, about to rush to the door, then stopped. 'What about Lord Jarsdel, shouldn't I tell him?'

'I'll talk to him and don't worry too much about it. He's a man with a great deal of experience who can deal with a little disappointment. If nothing else, his sons will be relieved to not have to share their inheritance with any new half siblings.' He laid a tender kiss on her forehead, then examined her with the same pride Madame Dubois had shown. 'For all my pig-headedness in regards to Major Preston, I do believe he will make you happy. You haven't glowed this much in all the time you've been with me.'

'Thank you, Grandfather.' Joanna grabbed the

hem of her dress and rushed out of the church. She hurried down the steps and into her grandfather's open-topped landau. The driver turned around, stunned.

'Shouldn't you be inside, Miss Radcliff?'

'No, drive on at once.'

'Where to?'

Joanna considered his question. If they went to Kensington it would waste valuable time. Luke might leave for Greenwich or Portsmouth and she would miss him. There was only one place she could go. 'The Army Service Club on St James's Street.'

The driver shook his head. 'No respectable woman can be seen riding alone there, much less going into a gentlemen's club. What would Lord Helmsworth say?'

'He's the one sending me there.' It was a white lie, but a necessary one. She wouldn't be stopped by a coachman. 'Now hurry, we must reach Major Preston before he leaves. It's urgent.'

'If Lord Helmsworth wants it.' The driver shrugged, then took up the reins and flicked them over the backs of the horses, setting them off in the direction of St James's.

Joanna unpinned the long veil from her hair and laid it on the seat beside her. She'd walked away from one suitor and was about to toss aside her already questionable reputation for another. If Luke refused to see her, she'd never recover from the scandal. It didn't matter, she had to try. She loved him and it was time to fight for his heart.

'Sir, there's a young lady here insisting to see you.' Tibbs, the club butler, announced to Luke. 'She's in her wedding dress.'

Silence settled over the party which seconds before had been quite rowdy.

'A lady in her wedding dress?' Luke questioned. He hadn't drunk enough to have his brain so fuddled he couldn't understand the butler. 'What's her name?'

'Miss Radcliff. I tried to tell her women aren't allowed in here, but she won't listen.'

'It seems your lady has had a change of heart and at the altar of all places.' Reginald threw back his head and laughed.

Luke could only stare at his friend, stunned. Joanna hadn't married Lord Jarsdel. She'd walked away from him and come here of all places. Excitement as much as curiosity pulled Luke out of his chair. He should stay where he was and not debase himself any further with her, but he couldn't.

'Show her in, Tibbs, I'm dying to meet the woman who's captured Luke's heart,' Reginald ordered before Luke could answer.

'No, I'll go to her.' Luke pushed past the butler and into the hallway.

He elbowed his way through the huddle of soldiers gawking at Joanna from along the balustrade at the top of the entrance-hall stairs. Luke jerked to a stop at the sight of her. She stood beneath the high ceiling of the columned room, a feminine contrast to the arms and weapons, men and battlefield paintings surrounding her. Her smooth skin was radiant against the white silk of her dress. Her light hair was done up in little ringlets woven with small, white flowers which shivered each time she took a breath. The sight of her was more glorious and beautiful than the first sunrise after the close cannonball blast had knocked him unconscious. He'd awakened that morning thankful to be alive, like he was at this moment in the presence of her beauty.

The confidence of her arrival was betrayed by

the twisting of her gloved hands in front of her and the nervous dart of her eyes to the sniggering men staring at her. Luke couldn't leave her to suffer their curiosity and marched down the stairs towards her.

'Luke,' she exclaimed at the sight of him, her smile increasing her radiance. The intensity of it almost made him halt, but he continued on, taking her by the arm and drawing her into a small room off the entrance hall. There was no door here and nothing to stop the officers from shuffling by as they gathered outside, not too close, but close enough to hear, as curious as a bunch of cats.

'What are you doing here?' Luke demanded, aware of each subtle move of her lovely arm beneath his fingers. He let go, not wanting to be so affected by her presence, or her cherry blossom-scented skin. He'd left her to protect her relationship with her grandfather. He didn't want his weakness or hers to make him renege on his promise. 'You're supposed to be at the church getting married.'

'I'm not going to marry Lord Jarsdel. I love you too much to pledge myself to him.'

It was as if Luke had been concussed by the cannonball all over again. For two weeks he'd thought her lost to him, now she was proclaiming her love to him and everyone listening outside the door.

'Please, don't tell me it's too late.' Her eyes shone like the ocean at sunset as she studied him. 'Grandfather isn't against us any more. He told me about the promise he extracted from you and he won't hold you to it.'

Luke didn't believe what he was hearing and he forced himself not to march back to the sitting room and drain his tankard. Luke had been relieved from his obligation to his family. Now he'd been released from his promise to Lord Helmsworth and Joanna was here before him, as free to be with him as he'd dreamed of in the country. It was everything he'd wanted since the ball at Pensum Manor and yet he still couldn't have her. 'I leave for Spain tomorrow to rejoin the regiment.'

'Then take me with you.'

'I can't.' He traced her cheek with the back of his fingers, her smooth skin increasing the ache of desire building inside him. He couldn't place her in danger, no matter how much he wanted her by his side. 'There are very real threats to the wives of Army officers—the enemy, hunger, disease. If you were to die, think of what it would do to your grandfather, how he would blame me for your loss. I'd blame myself if anything happened to you.'

She laid her gloved hand over his and pressed her cheek into his palm. 'Then don't go. Stay here with me.'

'I can't turn my back on my commission now I've pledged myself to it.' His honour wouldn't allow it.

'Then it's over, isn't it, us and our future?' Her hope dimmed, as did his.

He glanced past her and out the arched doorway to where Lord Beckwith and Reginald leaned against a high table, trying to pretend they weren't watching, and it came to him. He didn't have to leave and he didn't have to surrender his commission. 'No, it isn't over.'

He took her by the hand and pulled her with him out of the room.

'Lord Beckwith,' Luke called out to the Lieutenant Colonel.

'Yes, Major Preston.' He and Reginald jerked

up, looking at everything but Joanna and Luke in an effort to pretend they hadn't been listening. Let them eavesdrop, it made no difference now.

'You said if I wanted it, there was a position for me at Whitehall, a way to work here in England towards Army reform.'

Lord Beckwith's mouth dropped open before he pulled it shut. 'Yes, of course. You have only to ask for it.'

'Then I want it. You're right, I can make a difference to the soldiers in Europe.'

Lord Beckwith extended his hand to Luke. 'I'm glad to hear it. I'll tell Whitehall at once.'

'And Captain Crowther, he must have a place, too,' Luke insisted before facing his friend. 'What do you say? Do you want to fight a different battle with me here?'

'If it means seeing you accompany this beautiful woman down the aisle, then I do.'

Luke turned to Joanna. 'We'll visit the vicar at once and prepare the banns.'

'Banns nothing, you'll have a special licence,' Reginald proposed. 'What do you say, Lord Beckwith, do you think it can be arranged?'

'Him being the son of an earl, and with my connections to the Archbishop's office, I'm sure it can be done.'

'I can't pay for it,' Luke protested. He was in debt enough for his commission and refused to become a husband on the verge of penury.

'You won't have to.' Reginald snatched a shako from the line of them on the bench beside the front door. He turned it over and hustled to the gathered officers snorting and chortling at the spectacle. 'Pass the hat, men, Major Preston is getting married and needs a licence.'

While they dug in their pockets for coins, Luke turned to Joanna. 'What do you say? Are you ready to be my wife?'

With a bright laugh, she waved her hand over her dress. 'Were I any more prepared we'd already be in a church.'

'We soon will be and together for good.'

He took her by the waist and pulled her to him, the silk and her curves soft beneath his grip. He ignored the whistles and hoots from the men in the hall as he lost himself in her cobalt eyes.

'Imagine what society will say when they hear about this?' A grin drew up one side of her mouth, her question more amused speculation than worry.

'They'll say I caught the most beautiful woman in London.'

He pressed his lips to hers, the taste of her the sweetest victory he'd ever known.

* * * * *

If you enjoyed Joanna's story, you won't
want to miss the other three books in
THE GOVERNESS TALES *series:*

GOVERNESS TO THE SHEIKH
by Laura Martin

THE RUNAWAY GOVERNESS
by Liz Tyner

THE GOVERNESS'S SECRET BABY
by Janice Preston